Reading
BOROUGH COUNCIL

Reading Borough Libraries

Email: info@readinglibraries.org
Website: www.readinglibraries.org.uk   Whitley 0118 9015115

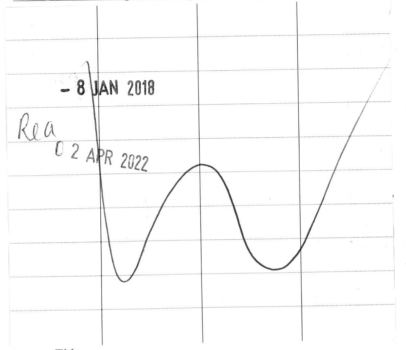

- 8 JAN 2018

Rea
0 2 APR 2022

Title:

Class no.

To avoid overdue charges please return this book to a
Reading library on or before the last date stamped above.
If not required by another reader, it may be renewed by
personal visit, telephone, post, email, or via our website.

DEATH in AUGUST

About the author

Marco Vichi was born in Florence in 1957. The author of eleven novels and two collections of short stories, he has also edited crime anthologies, written screenplays, music lyrics and for radio, and collaborated on and directed various projects for humanitarian causes.

There are four novels in the Inspector Bordelli series. The latest, *Death in Florence* (*Morte a Firenze*), won the Scerbanenco, Rieti and Camaiore prizes in Italy.

Marco Vichi lives in the Chianti region of Tuscany.

You can find out more at www.marcovichi.it.

About the translator

Stephen Sartarelli is an award-winning translator. He is also the author of three books of poetry, most recently *The Open Vault*. He lives in France.

MARCO VICHI

DEATH in AUGUST

THE FIRST
INSPECTOR BORDELLI
MYSTERY

Originally published in Italian as *Il Commissario Bordelli*
Translated by Stephen Sartarelli

**HODDER &
STOUGHTON**

First published in Great Britain in 2011 by Hodder & Stoughton
An Hachette UK company

I

Copyright © Ugo Guanda Editore, S.p.A., Parma 2002
Translation copyright © Stephen Sartarelli 2011

The right of Marco Vichi to be identified as the Author
of the Work has been asserted by him in accordance with
the Copyright, Designs and Patents Act 1988.

A CIP catalogue record for this title is available
from the British Library

Hardback ISBN 978 1 444 71220 9
Trade Paperback ISBN 978 1 444 71361 9

Typeset in Plantin Light by Palimpsest Book Production Limited,
Falkirk, Stirlingshire
Printed and bound by Clays Ltd, St Ives plc

Hodder & Stoughton policy is to use papers that are natural, renewable and
recyclable products and made from wood grown in sustainable forests. The
logging and manufacturing processes are expected to conform to the
environmental regulations of the country of origin.

Hodder & Stoughton Ltd
338 Euston Road
London NW1 3BH

www.hodder.co.uk

To Véronique

For crickets, it's enough to have won on earth.

Florence, Summer 1963

Inspector Bordelli entered his office at eight o'clock in the morning after an almost sleepless night, spent tossing and turning between sweat-soaked sheets. These were the first days of August, hot and muggy, without a breath of wind. And the nights were even more humid and unhealthy. But at least the city was deserted, the cars few and far between, the silence almost total. The beaches, on the other hand, were noisy and full of peeling bodies. Every umbrella had its transistor radio, every child a little bucket.

Before even sitting down, Bordelli spotted a typewritten sheet of paper on his desk and craned his neck to see what it was about. He noticed that it was typed very neatly, clean and precise, the lines nice and even, with nothing crossed out. He was astonished to see that it was a routine report. There was nobody he knew at police headquarters capable of drafting a report like that. Just as he started reading it, somebody knocked at the door. Mugnai's round head appeared.

'Dr Inzipone wants you, Inspector,' he said.

'Oh, shit . . .' said Bordelli, squirming. Inzipone was Commissioner of Police. He always sent for Bordelli at the worst moments. It was a good thing the commissioner was about to go on holiday too. The inspector stood up from his chair with a wheeze and went and knocked at the commissioner's door. Inzipone greeted him with an odd smile.

'Sit down, Bordelli, I've got something to tell you.' The inspector sat down listlessly and made himself comfortable. The commissioner himself stood up and started walking about, hands clasped behind his back.

'I wanted to have a chat about last Friday's dragnet,' he said.

'I had the report drawn up yesterday.'

'Yes, I know, I've already read it. I just wanted to tell you a couple of things.'

'All right.'

'I'll be clear about this, Bordelli. As I've always said, you are an excellent policeman, but your concept of justice is, well, a bit peculiar.'

'What do you mean?'

Inzipone paused for a moment, to find the right words, and looked out of the window, turning his back to the inspector.

'I mean . . . there are laws, my dear Bordelli, and we are paid by our citizens to make sure they are respected. We can't take matters into our own hands; we can't decide when to enforce the law and when not to.'

'I know,' Bordelli said calmly. He couldn't stand all this beating about the bush, this false way of saying things. Inzipone turned round and looked at him.

'During Friday's dragnet, you let a number of offenders get away,' he said drily.

'Nobody's perfect.'

'No, no, Bordelli, you haven't understood what I said – or rather, you've understood all too well. They didn't escape from you; you deliberately set them free, after you'd arrested them.'

'I must be getting old . . .'

Inzipone sighed and resumed pacing about the room.

'A thief is always a thief, Bordelli. The courts will decide on the punishment. Don't you think Robin Hood is a little out of date?'

Bordelli started feeling a strange tingling in his hands.

'Dr Inzipone, we're here to enforce the law, that much is clear. But so far I've come across no law that ensures everyone's survival.'

'This has nothing to with politics.'

'Politics? A man who needs to eat wipes his arse with politics.'

'Must you always be so vulgar, Bordelli?'

'Oh, I'm sorry. I thought vulgarity was something else.'

'This is a simple matter of either doing or not doing your duty.'

'I have a duty to myself, too.'

'I realise that. But it's not yours to decide whether thieves go free!'

'I didn't let any thieves go free. I simply released a few poor bastards.'

'That is precisely what I'm trying to say. It is not your decision to—'

'Let me tell you something, Dr Inzipone. When I returned from the war, I hoped I had done my small part to liberate Italy from the shit we were in; but now all I see is mountains of shit, everywhere . . .'

'We all know about your great valour during the war, Bordelli.'

'Cut the crap. You know as well as I do that we're worse off now.'

'That's a bit of an exaggeration . . .'

'I hate dragnets, Dr Inzipone, they remind me of the Fascists' round-ups. But if I have to take part in them, I'm certainly not going to put hungry people in jail.'

Inzipone threw up his hands, resigned.

'I've turned a blind eye to you many times, Bordelli. But this is happening a little too often.'

'What am I supposed to say? That I'll be a good boy? Which means, I'll get tough with the poor?'

'You have a way, Bordelli, of always saying the most irritating things.'

'Believe me, I don't mean to. Can I go now? I've got a couple of beggars to hang.'

Inzipone eyed him, clenching his teeth. He knew there was little he could do about Bordelli's methods, because he was, after all, an excellent inspector, he was loved by the entire department, and everybody knew that, in the end, he was right. There *was* too much poverty about.

* * *

Bordelli returned to his office. A few minutes later, Mugnai knocked again.

'Coffee, Inspector?'

'Yes, thanks. Listen, who wrote this?' he asked, waving in the air the stellar report he had found on his desk.

'A new guy, Inspector. Piras is the name.'

'Sardinian?'

'From head to toe.'

'Send him in to me, if you would.'

'Immediately, or with the coffee?'

'With the coffee.'

'All right, Inspector.'

Mugnai disappeared. Before returning to the report, Bordelli got up, opened the windows and half closed the shutters. As he did every summer, he thought it would be nice if all the holidaymakers decided en masse never to return to town. There would be everlasting peace.

He sat back down and picked up the report. He read it all in one go, quickly scanning the lines. It was about a car accident. Normally such matters were assigned to Vaccarezza, but in August the department was half empty. Bordelli took care not to take any time off during this period. He preferred battling the mosquitoes in the deserted city to finding himself alone as a dog on a crowded holiday beach wanting nothing more than to go home, where he might find a little peace. And this was why the report of an ordinary car accident had been put on his desk.

Somebody knocked again, and the door opened. On the threshold stood a lad Bordelli had never seen before, holding an espresso cup and saucer.

'You sent for me, Inspector?' The intonation was typically Sardinian: bouncy, proud, almost aggressive.

'Are you Piras?'

'In person.'

'Come in . . .'

He was young and handsome, with a bony face, two dark,

intense eyes, short but well built. On the whole, a likable sort.

'Mugnai told me to bring you this,' he said, indicating the coffee.

'Thanks,' said Bordelli, still looking at him. Piras set the little cup on the desk and remained standing.

'Where are you from, Piras? I mean, what part of Sardinia?'

'A little town near Oristano.'

'But what's it called? Come on, don't keep standing, have a seat.'

'Thanks, Inspector. I'm from Bonacardo.'

Bordelli leaned forward and looked him straight in the eye.

'Piras, from Bonacardo . . . Don't tell me your father's name is Gavino.'

'That's exactly right, Inspector. His name is Gavino.'

The inspector ran a hand over his face, shaking his head.

'It's not possible,' he said to himself.

'Is anything wrong, Inspector?' asked Piras, concerned. Bordelli didn't reply. He merely stared into space for a moment, looking absent. Then he opened a drawer of his desk and started rummaging through it with both hands, searching for something. At last he found it. A photograph. Setting it down on the desk, he spun it round with two fingers and pushed it towards Piras: three uniformed soldiers, framed from the waist up, leaning their heads together and smiling. Piras opened his eyes wide.

'But that's . . . my father!'

'Yeah, that's him all right,' said Bordelli, mimicking a Sardinian accent.

'So you must be . . . the Bordelli who saved his life!' Piras said excitedly. The inspector felt embarrassed, like a little kid. Piras picked up the photo and continued to look at it, incredulous. A faint smile played on his lips, parting them.

'When I tell my father about this . . .' he said.

'Send him the photo,' said Bordelli.

'Thank you, Inspector. My father will like that very much.'

Piras looked at the snapshot a moment longer, then put it in his pocket. Bordelli sighed.

'So, tell me, how is Gavino?'

'He's fine, Inspector, still strong as an ox.'

'I'm sure he's never told you, because he was always very modest, but he was one of the best. I always brought him along on my patrols. He was quiet and alert, like a cat, and we used to communicate with our eyes. He would sniff out the Germans as if he could actually smell them; he could see the Nazi convoys when the rest of us hadn't heard the slightest sound.'

The inspector also thought about the arm that Gavino had left behind in the nettles thanks to a mine, right at the end of the war. But he didn't know how to bring it up. He would have liked to know whether his old friend had any problems, whether there was any way he could help, but he didn't want to risk offending his son.

'And what is he up to these days?' he asked.

'He works as a caretaker at a school, but whenever he gets the chance, he runs off to his little patch of land so he can play peasant and talk to his animals.'

'What kind of animals has he got?'

'Pigs, sheep, chickens, rabbits, doves . . . There's even a turtle, and he talks to all of them as if they were people.'

Bordelli felt relieved.

'He liked animals back then, too. Has he ever told you he spent the last two years of the war with a mouse in his pocket? He even gave it a name—'

'He called it Gioacchino. He brought it home with him. It died when I was three.'

They talked about the past, the war and Gavino for a good half-hour.

Piras was eighteen years old. Apparently Gavino had wasted no time upon his return, promptly marrying his former girl-friend and getting straight down to the matter at hand. He certainly didn't need both arms to make babies, and after the first son, they had four more. As the conversation wound down, Bordelli sighed wistfully. He felt very old.

'Has your father got a telephone?' he asked.

'No, Inspector, I get in touch with him through the village priest.'

'Next time you talk to him, give him a hug for me, and tell him I would love to see him again.'

'Thanks, Inspector.'

For Bordelli, seeing Gavino Piras again would be like returning to the front lines. He felt at once very sad and very pleased. A gust of hot air filtered through the half-closed shutters, enveloping his face, and he felt his forehead bead with sweat.

'Now, to us, Piras.' He tapped the report with his forefinger. 'Did you write this?'

'Why, is there something wrong with it?'

The inspector scratched the back of his neck.

'No, on the contrary. It's very well done. I bet when you were a little kid you wanted to become a policeman,' said Bordelli, smiling. Piras remained serious.

'I've always liked discovering the hidden side of things, especially when everything looks completely normal on the surface.'

'I'm the same way, Piras. We're both cursed.' Piras gave a hint of a smile, with only his eyes. The rest of his face remained stony. It was probably a rare thing to see him laugh in earnest.

They remained silent for a few seconds, listening to a distant siren until its wail became confused with the buzzing of a restless fly. The heat was intense, the kind that slows the thought processes. Bordelli felt a bead of sweat drip down his side and bestirred himself.

'What do you want to do in the police force?' he asked the boy.

'Murder,' Piras said firmly.

'I guessed as much.'

'I should leave now, sir. I have to go somewhere in the car.'

'Have a good day.'

Piras thanked him and left the room with a firm step, not a drop of sweat on him. Bordelli's shirt, on the other hand, was wet and sticking to his back, and he envied the Sardinian with all his heart. He remembered the coffee and brought the cup to his lips. It was disgustingly lukewarm, but he drank it anyway.

Rodrigo lived in Viale Gramsci, in the nineteenth-century quarter that had sprouted up along the line of the Renaissance-era walls, after these were demolished. Broad avenues, no commerce. Inspector Bordelli rang the buzzer outside the main entrance and waited. His cousin worked at home in the afternoon and was usually loath to leave his desk. He taught chemistry at the *liceo* and saw the world through formulas. He was constantly assigning written exercises, then spent his afternoons correcting them. That was why he taught: so he could correct. In August, when everybody else was on holiday, Rodrigo was still correcting avalanches of homework that he would thrust into the faces of his pupils on the first day of class in October.

In childhood, he and Rodrigo had silently detested each other. Bordelli was two years older and used to frighten Rodrigo with the faces he made. In adolescence they ended up spending a few summers on the same beach. Their parents would send them out to sea together to fish, but all Bordelli could think about when they were on the water together was drowning his cousin. By age twenty, as fate would have it, they lost sight of each other, but on the first Christmas after the war, they met up again. And they shook hands and decided once and for all that they were different from one another. Neither had married, but for different reasons: the inspector because he was waiting for the right girl, and Rodrigo because he was afraid to spend too much, in every sense. Ever since that Christmas, they would seek each other out some three or four times a year, never for any particular reason, but as if, every so often, they both needed to see, with their own eyes, the abyss of difference between them, either as confirmation or for love of the challenge. And they would part, each pleased not to be like the other. For

Bordelli it was always a relief to realise that the whole world wasn't like Rodrigo, and Rodrigo always openly declared that Bordelli was not at all right in the head. But they didn't hate each other; they couldn't because they were too far apart. Actually, there was a sort of bond between them, though neither of them would ever have admitted it.

Bordelli rang the bell again, and at last Rodrigo came to a window on the fourth floor. Seeing his policeman cousin below, he stopped and looked at him, remaining provocatively immobile. The inspector gestured to him to open the door, but the other just stood there, staring at him. Then he saw Rodrigo disappear, and a moment later he heard the click of the electric lock on the door. Climbing the stone stairs, he detected the smells of old furniture and carpets, typical of that building. On the fourth floor he found the door open, but no one there to welcome him. He entered and noticed with pleasure that it was cool in the apartment. Rodrigo was sitting in the living room with pen in hand, obviously a red pen. He did not greet him or even look up from his papers. Bordelli sat down on the edge of the desk.

'Well? So how's Rodrigo?'

'You're sitting on the homework assignments I need to correct.'

'Oh, sorry. Where should I put them?'

'If I put them there, it means that's where they're supposed to be.' He spoke fast, correcting all the while, eyes fixed on the page. Bordelli stood up and put everything back in place.

'I'm going to make tea. Will you have some?' he asked politely.

'The housekeeper cleaned the kitchen a couple of hours ago,' said Rodrigo, still without looking up.

'So what? Does that mean you'll never cook again?'

'All right, all right, go and make your tea.' It seemed like a major concession.

'Lemon or milk?' asked Bordelli.

'Milk.'

'Sugar?'

'No sugar. There's honey in the cupboard on the right.'

'How many spoonfuls?'

'Two. Teaspoons, that is.'

'I got that.'

'I'd like a little silence.'

'I'll be silent as the grave.'

It was strange to talk to someone who was correcting papers without ever looking you in the eye. Bordelli thought about annoying him further by asking him what kind of cup he wanted, whether he wanted a napkin and what kind, paper or cloth, and other things of that sort, but thought better of it. He went into the kitchen to make the tea, trying to create as little mess as possible. He returned with cups in hand and found his cousin in the same position. Rodrigo seemed to have turned to stone. He was staring at a sheet of paper. He was only happy when he could make sweeping strokes of red ink. Bordelli set Rodrigo's tea down in a random spot on the desk, at the very moment his cousin was finishing a broad red flourish of the pen.

'Another mistake? Are they big mistakes or little mistakes?' he asked. Rodrigo finally raised his head and looked at him.

'Remove that wet cup immediately,' he said icily.

'It's your tea.'

'Get that mess out of here, it's making a ring on my agenda.'

'What's the problem? You're only going to throw it away at the end of the year.'

Rodrigo heaved a sigh of forbearance and decided to intervene personally. Setting down the red pen, he lifted the cup and wiped the cover of his agenda with a paper napkin, which he then rolled up into a ball and tossed into a wastepaper basket under the desk. Bordelli followed his every move with great curiosity. In a way his cousin's precision fascinated him; it looked very much as if it stemmed from some sort of madness. Rodrigo then straightened his back and gave a smile that was supposed to convey calm and serenity.

'Why are you here? Do you have something specific to tell me?' he asked.

'No, why? Does it seem as if I have?'

'I don't care. Why did you come?'

'For a chat.'

'All right, then. Let's chat.' Rodrigo folded his arms to show that he was interrupting his corrections. Bordelli sat down comfortably in a chair, and with his teacup balanced on his thigh, he lit a cigarette.

'So, then, how are things, Rodrigo?' he asked with a hint of a smile. Rodrigo stood up and opened his eyes wide.

'Put out that disgusting cigarette immediately,' he said, trying to contain his rage.

'I don't see an ashtray.'

'Do you know that it takes a week for the smell of smoke to go away?'

'I swear I didn't know,' Bordelli said, inhaling deeply, as if it were his last puff, asking again for an ashtray with his eyes. Rodrigo opened a secretaire and pulled out a small souvenir dish from Pompeii, set this in front of him, and immediately stepped back. Bordelli snuffed out his still-whole cigarette.

'So . . . aside from the cigarette, how are you? Getting along all right?' Bordelli asked. Rodrigo had sat back down at the desk, but seemed a little more inclined to chat, even if he had no choice.

'Yes, all right, not too bad. And yourself?' he said.

'Like shit, Rodrigo, I feel like shit . . . Oh, sorry, I know you don't like profanities.'

'It doesn't matter,' Rodrigo said, understandingly.

'In short, I feel like shit . . . I'm fifty-three years old, and when I come home there's nobody there waiting for me.'

'If you live alone, of course there's nobody waiting for you.'

'That's not what I meant.'

'So why don't you speak more clearly?'

'Jesus . . .'

'What is it now?'

'Nothing, nothing . . . Tell me something, are you still with that woman . . . what was her name?'

'What's she got to do with anything? And I don't like the way you phrased that.'

'Have you ever wondered why you like so much to correct other people's mistakes?'

'You're changing the subject again . . .'

'I was only curious as to why you like so much to correct other people's mistakes.'

'What's wrong with that?'

'Come on, try to be nice. I'm only trying to start a discussion.'

'What kind of discussion?'

'Any kind, provided it lasts more than two sentences.'

'Maybe we have nothing to say to each other.'

'Even two people who have nothing to say to each other can still talk.'

'That's an absurd statement.'

'Listen, why don't you tell me . . . I don't know, tell me what you do on Sundays, for example.'

'I try to rest.'

'You don't correct any papers?'

'And what if I do? I really don't see what you're getting at.'

'Nothing, I'm not trying to get at anything. As I said, I just wanted to have a chat.'

'Well, unfortunately, I have to work.'

'In August?'

'That's right, in August. Why not?'

'I have nothing to say.'

'Strange . . .'

'Tell me something, Rodrigo. Who do you vote for?'

'I vote for whoever I feel like voting for.'

'I don't doubt that. But are you satisified with the way things are going?'

'What do you mean?'

'I mean just what I said.'

Rodrigo sighed indulgently and started fiddling with his red pen.

'Italy used to be all wheat and sheep . . . and now prosperity is finally on its way,' he said.

'For whom, exactly?'

'For everyone. We used to be a nation of peasants, and now we all drive cars.' As usual, after a difficult start, Rodrigo was warming up to the idea of talking.

'The power of statistics,' said Bordelli. 'Do you watch a lot of television?'

'Why? Do you want to be left behind?'

'Left behind by what?'

'For now, we're still at the beginning, but before long, you'll be amazed.'

'I'm already amazed.'

'If each does his part, we'll all be fine.'

'I don't know why, but I don't like that statement.'

'Can't you see that you don't understand? You don't understand that everything is governed by the laws of chemistry, even man and society—'

'So it's all very simple, in other words.'

'Look, it's easy to see what you're thinking. You're one of those who think chemistry is only a cold science.'

'Ah, you mean I'm not alone?'

'You don't understand, none of you. One need only find the right formula for each thing. There are certain substances that can change the molecular structure of others. Some compounds are inert until they come into contact with a new agent that makes them explode . . . It's not magic; everything is governed by precise rules.'

'And where does prosperity fit in with all this?'

'Prosperity is the result of new combinations of elements that have always existed. Is that not chemistry? This is an important moment for our country . . . and Italians know this.'

'Italians? What do you mean by "Italians?"'

'I don't understand.'

'Which Italians are you talking about? The lawyer who lives on the floor below, or the day-labourer from Bari?'

13

'Everything's always a joke to you.'

'Look, I'm not joking. Which Italians do you mean?'

'You tell me something. How did you end up becoming a policeman?'

'Actually, it's a good profession. I've made a lot of friends as a policeman.'

'And a fine lot they are: prostitutes and thieves . . .'

'You should meet them some time, Rodrigo. They could teach you a great deal.'

'You are insane.'

'Right, I'm insane because I refuse to condemn the poor and I despise this dream-besotted country that believes in the Fiat 1100.'

'What are you, a communist?'

Bordelli shook his head.

'For now, it is easier to say what I'm not,' he said. Rodrigo raised the red pen and then dropped it on to the papers.

'As usual, you don't know what you want,' he said smugly.

'That's possible, but I don't like a poor little country that dresses up as if it's rich. It's asking for trouble.'

Rodrigo huffed and made as if to resume correcting papers. Bordelli finished his now cold tea and put an unlit cigarette in his mouth.

'Don't worry, I won't light it,' he said, raising a hand.

'I'm not worried,' Rodrigo muttered. Bordelli stood up, approached the desk slowly, then leaned on it with both hands.

'You know, Rodrigo, I really believe that, somewhere, there is a woman made just for me . . . Isn't that also a question of chemistry?'

'I don't like the way you put it.'

'Why, how did I put it?'

Rodrigo tightened his lips and said nothing. Snatching a paper already marked in red from the stack, he went back to work. Bordelli looked at his watch. He had a great many things to attend to, and here he was wasting his time doing nothing.

'I'll let you work,' he said.

'I've still got seventy more to correct.'

'That's a lot . . .'

'Have you anything else to say to me?'

'Let me think.'

Bordelli pulled out a box of matches and started to shake it as if it were some South American percussion instrument.

'You're making noise,' said Rodrigo, annoyed. Bordelli immediately stopped.

'You know something, Rodrigo? One day I'd like to take you to the forensics department and show you the corpses.'

'I'm not interested.'

'You're wrong not to be. You don't know how many things you could learn.'

'Make sure you shut the door on your way out.'

'Don't worry, I'll seal everything up.'

'Bye.'

'Goodbye, Rodrigo. Give my regards to Auntie.'

The inspector set his cup down on a stack of papers and left Rodrigo to his flourishes of red ink. As soon as he was on the landing, he lit his cigarette.

Three weeks of relative calm passed at police headquarters. But it was even hotter than before. The humid, motionless air ruled every corner of the city. The houses were saturated with the smell of *zampironi* and DDT. In that hazy summer solitude Bordelli often indulged in long monologues in his mind, especially at night in bed, before falling asleep. Or, perhaps more correctly, before sinking into that sort of laborious, memory-laden sleep which got him through the night. It was a kind of semi-consciousness peopled with overlapping images, where distant memories merged with absurd fantasies, and fatuous little dramas played themselves over and over to the point of obsession, tiring him out until they finally woke him up. At which point he would get out of bed, go into the bathroom, drink two or three glasses of water, then lie back down again, not bothering to cover himself with the sheet. Window still open, a pitcher of water with ice cubes on the nightstand. Sometimes he couldn't go back to sleep at all and would spend hours and hours in a confused state of mind, as if jumping from branch to branch like a restless monkey.

Rosa, for her part, had fled the city. But not before phoning Bordelli to invite him to join her and her girlfriends on their way to Forte dei Marmi. The old retired prostitute had the innocence of a pup.

'Come on, darling, drop everything and come with us. You'll have three women to yourself, all in love with you.'

Bordelli had made up some annoying chores that kept him hopelessly stuck in town. He really didn't feel like playing the stud with three ingenuous whores. Rosa had praised his heroism and asked him to keep an eye on her place.

'You know, with all the burglars about . . .' she had said. She complained that it was no longer the way it used to be, when she, the beautiful Rosa, was well known on the circuit and didn't need to worry. Things were different now; the new generations of burglars didn't look anyone in the eye.

'And don't forget the flowers, dear, don't let them wither like last year.'

'I won't.'

'Thank you, you're such a sweetie. I'll leave the keys with Carlino for you.'

Carlino was the barman at the corner café. He never closed shop.

'Have fun.'

'No need to tell us that, darling!' she said, sending a barrage of kisses through the receiver.

Bordelli sighed in the dark and turned on to his side. He closed his eyes, hoping to go back to sleep. All of a sudden he saw in his mind's eye the tattered bodies of Caimano and Scardigli, after they had stepped on an anti-tank mine a hundred yards away from him. They hadn't even shouted. One of their arms had to be taken down from a tree. Fucking war. In the morning you were sharing dishwater coffee with a friend, and that evening you were putting his body parts into a coffin.

Bordelli often thought about the war; he still felt it very close by. Sometimes it seemed as if he had stopped shooting at Nazis just yesterday. He could still hear the voices of his dead comrades, their laughter, each as distinct as a signature. He could still hear each one's personal verbal quirks and curses. If he had to name one good thing about the war, it was the way it had forcibly mixed people of every region together. One learned to recognise the different dialects and mentalities, the myths and hopes of every part of Italy.

Bordelli turned on to his other side and thought about the fact that he had nearly stopped smoking. This was a great triumph for him. During the war he had got up to a hundred cigarettes a day, the famously terrible MILIT cigarettes issued by the government. Once the Americans arrived, smoking no longer felt like torture. But Bordelli had kept smoking a hundred a day. Thinking about it now made him feel nauseated. Without turning on the light, he reached out and picked up a cigarette, his fourth. He propped himself up on one elbow and lit it. The ashtray was in the same place it had been for years; it was hard to miss. He smoked, still jumping from one memory to another, following no order whatsoever. Sometimes his head filled with many memories at once and they began to overlap, so that it became impossible to make any sense at all of the jumble. . . .

The telephone on the nightstand rang, and he groped in the dark for the receiver.

'Yes?'

'Is that you, Inspector?'

'I think so. What time is it?'

'Two.'

'Has something happened?'

Mugnai faltered.

'I don't know yet . . . I mean . . . well, a short while ago a woman phoned, saying she was worried . . . says some lady's not answering her phone, and she says that's unusual . . .

Inspector, do you by any chance know what a "lady companion" is?'

'I'm sorry, Mugnai, you'll have to start over again, from the beginning.'

'No, I'm the one who's sorry, Inspector. I probably shouldn't even have bothered you, but I'm here by myself, and you've always said that if I had any doubts about anything . . .'

'There's no problem, Mugnai, I'm listening, but try to make things simpler.'

'I'll try, Inspector, but nothing is clear, not even to me; I wrote everything down, otherwise I'd forget it . . . A little while ago a woman, called Maria, phoned saying she was the lady companion of a certain lady with two surnames . . . What's a lady companion?'

'I'll explain another time.'

'Does it have anything to do with whores?'

'Don't be ridiculous! Go on.'

'Sorry, Inspector. Anyway, this woman, Maria, I mean, says she spends the whole day with the lady, but then at eight o'clock she leaves because the lady wants to be alone at night. Every night, however, round midnight, she phones the lady to see how she's doing, because the lady is old and sort of sick.'

'You should say "elderly", Mugnai; "old" isn't very nice.'

'Whatever you say, Inspector . . . Anyway, so tonight Maria called at round about midnight, but there was no answer. She tried again a little later, but still no answer. She kept calling every fifteen minutes till one o'clock, and then she took a cab to go and check on the lady in person. She says she can see the light on inside, but the lady won't come to the door. So she called us.'

Bordelli had already started getting dressed.

'So why didn't she go inside?'

Mugnai slammed his hand down on the table.

'That's what I said, too, Inspector! Why didn't she go inside? And you know what she said?'

'What?'

'She said nobody else has got the keys to the villa, because the lady doesn't want to give them out.'

The inspector sighed.

'If she was so worried, she should have gone there with the woman's doctor and broken down the door,' he said. Mugnai practically ate the receiver.

'That's what I said, too, Inspector! And you know what she replied?'

'What?'

'She said the lady's doctor is so small that if he tried to break open the door he would break his shoulder.'

'Well, then the fire department.'

'I swear I said that, too. And so she says: "Well, at this point, there's nothing more to be done. The lady's dead."'

'Fine, I think I get the picture.'

'And you know what she said next, Inspector?'

Bordelli buckled his belt, holding the receiver between chin and shoulder.

'Go on, Mugnai, stop playing guessing games.'

'Sorry, Inspector.'

'Well, what did she say next?'

'She said the lady was murdered.'

'And how does she know that?'

'She doesn't know it. She only said she could sense it. Then she started crying.'

'Maybe she reads too many mysteries.'

Mugnai slammed his hand down somewhere else.

'That's what I thought, too, Inspector! So what are we gonna do?'

'Let me put on my shoes, and I'll be on my way.'

'Sorry about this, Inspector, but you always told me that—'

'Forget about it. I couldn't sleep, anyway. Give me the address.'

By half past two Bordelli was driving his VW Beetle up Via della Piazzola, a narrow little street in the hilly, posh end of town. The headlamps lit up the grey asphalt, which was full of potholes and patches. On either side of the street loomed the great façades of aristocratic villas and the monumental gates of villas hidden farther within. Against the black sky, the great, motionless manes of the trees stood blacker still. Bordelli felt an acidic bubble expand in his stomach and rise up into his mouth, prompting him to suppress, with some effort, the desire to light a fifth cigarette. He pulled up at number 110. The gate of Villa Pedretti-Strassen was closed. As the street was too narrow for him to park, he was forced to leave the car a hundred yards ahead, where the road widened. There wasn't a breath of wind. It was still hot outside, even at that hour.

He walked back down to the villa. Beyond the colossal cast-iron gate, at the back of a dark garden full of trees, he could make out the villa's dark silhouette. And, behind a towering hedgerow of laurel parallel to the house, the lighted rectangle of a window. Bordelli put an unlit cigarette in his mouth and suddenly felt all his accumulated fatigue. He wished he could lie down on the ground and savour the peace enveloping the villa, immobile, watching the sky and thinking of the past.

He tried to push the great gate open, but it was locked. It was also very tall, with pointed spikes on top. He had better find another solution. Walking along the enclosure wall, he found a small side gate. He pushed it open, forcing the accumulated rust in the hinges. The garden was in a state of abandon, but not completely, as if a gardener tended it perhaps three or four times a year. The villa, with its crumbling façade, must have been from the seventeenth century. Three storeys, five windows per storey, all closed except for the one with the light in it, on the first floor. Through the uneven panes he could see a frescoed ceiling.

Hugging the walls of the villa, he arrived at the rear. There was a large park with very tall trees and a small lane that vanished into the darkness. Beside the house, an enormous, age-old cedar thrust its bristling branches well above the roof. Bordelli threw his head back to look at it, then began to feel dizzy, losing his balance. He leaned against the wall and rubbed his eyes, to ward off fatigue. Returning to the front of the house, he rang the doorbell. He heard a gloomy trill beyond the great door, as in convents. He waited a minute, but nothing happened.

He lit a match and examined the lock. After an apprenticeship with his friend Botta, a petty thief who lived a stone's throw from his place in San Frediano, Bordelli could open almost any lock with a common piece of metal wire, and each time he did, it was a source of great satisfaction. Having burglars as friends had its advantages. But Botta wasn't only a thief; he was also a fabulous cook, having learned a variety of international dishes in the jails of half the world . . . But this was no time to be thinking about such things.

The lock resisted Bordelli's efforts for a good five minutes, then finally yielded. The inspector opened the door and was relieved to feel on his face a breath of cool air typical of old villas. He crossed the threshold and, once inside, called out the signora's two surnames. No reply. The light from a half-open door filtered out from the top of the stairwell. As his eyesight adjusted to the darkness, he began to look around. Some antique furniture, a Baroque mirror, many paintings. A monumental staircase in grey *pietra serena* ascended to the upper floors. A worn carpet of red fabric ran up the centre of the steps.

'Signora Pedretti, don't be afraid. My name is Inspector Bordelli, I'm with the police,' he called, slowly ascending the stairs towards the light. He stopped in front of the half-open door and knocked. No reply. He pushed it and felt a slight shudder pass over his face, as if he had walked into a spider's web: an elderly woman lay face up across a bed, her nightgown raised up to her belly. Bordelli approached, suppressing the impulse to cover her accidental nudity. The woman's wrinkled hands were round her neck, her eyes bulging in an expression of fear. Her narrow brow looked blackened round the temples. Her bony white feet, veined with blue, were suspended in air, just over the edge of the bed. On the sheet beside the woman's head was a glass, half overturned. The lady companion had guessed right: Signora Pedretti-Strassen was dead. On the bedside rug were her slippers, lined up straight, as well as a bottle of water, uncapped and half empty, and a book that looked as if it had been unceremoniously tossed aside. The inspector cocked his head to read the title: *Fatal Passion*. On the bedside table he noticed a small dark bottle with a black cap; without touching it, he bent down to read the label: Asthmaben. Fact number one: the lady suffered from asthma.

On the wall, an old Bakelite telephone, still plugged in. Bordelli took out his handkerchief and raised the receiver. The phone was in normal working order, and he availed himself of it.

'Diotivede, it's me, Bordelli. Did I wake you up?'

'I never fall asleep before three.'

'Good, grab a cab and come to 110 Via della Piazzola.'

'Should I bring pastries?'

'As always.'

'I'm on my way.'

Bordelli hung up and then phoned police headquarters. He asked for an ambulance and a couple of officers to take samples for evidence. He told Mugnai to track down Signora Pedretti's personal doctor and send him to the villa, asking him further to have Maria, the lady companion, come into the station. Then he went and sat down in a chair. Without knowing how, he found himself with a lit cigarette in his mouth. As he smoked it he studied the lady's sharp profile, her prominent, slightly hooked nose pointing up at the cherub-frescoed ceiling. He was practically powerless to look anywhere else. He cast his gaze into every corner of the room, following the cracks in the walls or the undulations of the spider's webs, but it always came back to that nose. He thought about Maria's certainty that this was a murder.

At first sight it looked like an unpleasant but natural death. A heart attack, perhaps, or a pulmonary oedema. Bordelli extinguished the cigarette against the empty pack, crumpled this up and put it in his pocket. Aside from the bed, the only other pieces of furniture in the room were a large black sort of armoire with glass displays obscured by yellow fabric, and a small open secretaire. All fairly tidy. He could rule out the possibility that anyone had come in and ransacked the place.

As if obsessed, the inspector turned round again to look at the signora's nose. From the dead woman's motionless, half-open lips a white foam that looked like snail-slime was trickling out. The little bubbles burst and then were followed by more bubbles. There was still some movement in that lifeless body. Then the spittle ceased, and the foam dissolved into two tiny droplets that rolled down her cheeks, drying before they reached the bedsheet.

Bordelli left the room and went back down to the ground floor. He turned on the lights to have a better look at the paintings hanging in the grand entrance at the foot of the staircase. Almost all were portraits, probably ancestors. High up on the yellowed wall, the severe figure of a cardinal leaned forward. He had the same nose as the signora, a cross in one hand and a book in the other, and a harsh glint in his eyes.

The inspector continued poking about. Pushing open a door, he entered a sizeable room with several glass-paned chests and a large round table in the middle. On the walls, a few fine melancholy, rustic landscapes. A pair of huge white oxen caught his eye, and he drew near. He wasn't mistaken: a Fattori. But the surprises weren't over yet. Farther ahead there were some Segantinis, a Nomellini, not to mention Signorini, Ghiglia, Bartolena, and others. Bordelli let himself be hypnotised by the colours, though every so often the dead woman's nose would reappear in his mind. He ran his hand over his face to wipe away the image, and went out of the room to continue his tour.

A large, very clean kitchen, a dusty sitting room, a tea room, bookcases, servants' quarters, a variety of strangely scented bathrooms. There was no end to the house. Going back up to the first floor, he opened every door, finding only spacious, half-empty rooms with ceilings frescoed in seventeenth-century naif style, enormous carpets and dust-laden crystal chandeliers. In the biggest room, a dark piece of furniture towered like a tabernacle against the shiny, yellowish plaster.

It was hotter on the second floor. All the rooms were completely empty but one, in which it seemed that all the furniture had been stored. Wardrobes filled to bursting with clothes wrapped in plastic, shelves with dozens of pairs of shoes, mouse-eaten armchairs, bedside tables, light fixtures, nightlights. On one chair was a wooden box with *Osborne 1934* written on it. It was full of old greeting cards. Too bad. Bordelli would have been glad to drink some strong alcohol. He squeezed the crumpled packet of cigarettes in his pocket, to convince himself it was truly empty. He felt like smoking again.

Wending his way through the chaos, he bumped a vase with his elbow, tried to catch it on the fly, but it eluded his grasp and fell to the floor with a crash, shattering into a thousand pieces. At once he was struck by the stillness in the house, which so contrasted with the noise a moment before. It was disturbed only by the creaking of the old furniture. Half closing his eyes from weariness, he sat down in the middle of an old sofa, spreading his arms like a Christ, then extending them along the edge of the back and dropping his head backwards. A faded frieze of intersecting lines ran along the upper parts of the walls, just below the angle of intersection with the ceiling. Bordelli wondered how many people had touched these walls, walked on these floors, used this furniture. There was nothing new, in short. He thought about all the babies that had been born in this big house, all the dead laid into their coffins. He noted that age-old walls had a solemnity that modern ones lacked. Then his thoughts grew less distinct, and he fell asleep as he sat there. A bit later, his head fell forward, rousing him. For an instant he didn't know where he was or why. Then he remembered the dead woman, and through the fog of sleep managed to look at his watch. He stood up with effort and began walking down the stairs. He passed the lady's bedroom without stopping, just turning round slightly, as if to make sure she was still there, and at that moment he had the clear impression that Maria was right: it was a case of murder. Then he shook his head and continued on down the stairs, thinking that fatigue played tricks on the mind.

He turned on the garden lights, two yellowing lamps hanging from the façade. Exiting the house, he went to the gate to wait for the others. The sky was overcast, the heat stifling. Lightning flashed silent on the horizon. A light rain began to fall, big warm drops bursting on the roof-tiles with the sound of pebbles. But it stopped almost at once. With a sudden intuition, he rummaged through his pockets and found two crumpled cigarettes. Straightening one out with his fingers, he lit it and inhaled deeply, trying to wake himself up. He had already smoked too much and he knew it, but at that moment his will was powerless. He couldn't get the image of the woman's corpse out of his mind. Murder, he thought. Leaning his back against the wall, he breathed deeply and looked up at the sky, seeking the moonlight behind the thick clouds.

The first to arrive was Diotivede, his white hair standing straight up on his head, his step still youthful despite his seventy years. He wasn't tall, but carried himself proudly, dangling the briefcase of his trade down around his knees. He paid the cab driver and, looking around, adjusted his glasses on his nose. Bordelli greeted him with a weary wave of the hand. The doctor walked up to him, lips curling slightly in the hint of a smile.

'You look pretty tired,' he said.

'Where are the pastries?'

'In here,' Diotivide said, tapping his case with two fingers.

'Come, let me introduce you to the lady of the house.'

They crossed the dark garden in silence. Diotivede looked around, sniffing the air like an animal. He followed Bordelli through the entrance; his sensitive nose was struck by the strong smell of old rugs and dust.

'Where's the body?'

'Upstairs.'

The pathologist stopped for a moment in front of the cardinal, then moved on, his mouth contracted in a childish pout. Climbing the stairs, the inspector made as if to take the briefcase from him, but the doctor gently pushed his hand away.

'I can manage alone, thanks,' he said.

'No offence.'

'No offence taken.'

They went into Signora Pedretti-Strassen's bedroom, and the doctor set his bag down on a chair. Changing his glasses, he approached the corpse. He studied it, sniffed it, touched it here and there, and said:

'Beautiful woman.' He took out a black notebook and, as usual, began jotting his first notes. Bordelli sat down in a corner and let him work, not saying a word. After five minutes of silence, Diotivede put the notebook back in his pocket, took a few plastic bags and phials out of his case, and slipped on a pair of rubber gloves.

'Seeing the medicine, one would think she died of a violent asthma attack,' he said. The inspector lit his last butt, squeezing it tightly between his fingers, to stop up a tear in the paper. He blew the smoke far away, as if to put a distance between himself and its poison.

'Can one die of asthma?' he said. 'I hadn't thought of that.'

'With a serious enough allergy, and a heart no longer young, yes, it can happen.'

Bordelli propped his elbows on his knees and rolled his head back and forth.

'It must be a nasty way to die.'

Diotivede drew near to the woman, bent down over her and, using two fingers, lightly lifted one of her shoulders, which yielded softly. He did the same with one foot. Then he went over to the bedside table, delicately picked up the bottle of Asthmaben and examined it carefully, holding it close to his eyes. He looked perplexed. He wrapped his fingers round the cap and opened it.

'Strange,' he said.

'What's strange?'

'The cap was screwed on perfectly. And rather tightly, I'd say.'

Bordelli instinctively stood up and approached the doctor, but his brain was heavy with fatigue.

'What's so strange about that?'

Diotivede looked at him askance.

'You're a policeman, aren't you?' he said.

'A policeman who hasn't slept.'

'You're excused, but for only that reason.'

'That's very kind of you.'

'Look around,' Diotivede began, pointing to things as he named them. 'An upended glass on the bed, an open bottle on the floor, a book thrown on to the carpet, and yet, here we have a little bottle of Asthmaben with its cap screwed on tight. And, as you can see, the screw threads are very long. In your opinion, would somebody gasping for air take the trouble to screw a cap back on?'

Bordelli scratched the nape of his neck and sat back down.

'Downright obvious,' he said.

Diotivede got down on all fours and started looking for something. In the end he peered under the bed and reached for something.

'Just as I thought.'

'What?'

'The cap to the water bottle. It was under the bed.'

'You could be a policeman.'

'That's all I need,' he said, sniffing the cap. Then he patiently got back to work. He dropped the bottle of Asthmaben into a transparent bag, picked up the glass from the bed and tilted it, looking inside. He poured the few drops remaining at the bottom into a sterile test tube with a hermetic seal, then put the empty glass into a bag, which he closed. He also took a water sample from the bottle, then put the cap back on and put this into a large bag. The book, too, got the same treatment. With great care he arranged everything in his case, putting the items into different internal pockets. Then he wrote something in his notebook again.

'She must have died at least five, maybe six hours ago,' he said.

'Oh, really?'

'I can tell you more precisely after the post-mortem.'

In the muggy silence they heard a car pull up, then another.

'Here they are,' said Bordelli, getting up from the chair with a groan of fatigue. He went down into the garden to meet the new arrivals, showing the way to two officers, Russo and Bellandi, and two ambulance attendants.

He went out on to the street for a little walk. He couldn't wait to lie down in bed. The sky had opened and the moon was visible. He stopped in front of the gate and looked at the villa from a distance, fascinated by the decay wrought by time. It pleased him to see that things, and not only people, suffered the wear and tear of age.

All of a sudden he felt somebody watching him and turned round. A very old woman, thin as a rail, was staring at him from the balcony of the villa next door, a great house whose façade gave directly on to the street. The woman stood immobile, staring, squinting as if she couldn't see well. She was wearing a white dressing gown and a night-bonnet.

'Are you here to buy the villa?' the woman shouted, pointing to the dead woman's house. Bordelli drew closer to her balcony.

'I was just looking,' he said.

'Well, it's not for sale.'

'It's a beautiful house.'

'They should give it to the nuns, I say . . .'

'Why do you say that?'

'Ooooh, don't get me going . . . don't start me talking,' she said, waving a hand in the air.

'Do you hear them?' asked Bordelli.

'How's that?'

'Are there ghosts?'

'Worse. Wait, I'll come down.' The old woman vanished indoors, and Bordelli went to wait for her in front of the house. Moments later, the front door on the street opened, and the woman appeared, panting, on the threshold. She was unimaginably thin, her clothes hanging as though draped on a coat hanger. She had a tiny face, all puckered round a mouth swollen with boils.

'A lot of people have been murdered in that house,' she said in a whisper, pointing to Villa Pedretti.

'Really?' said Bordelli, stunned. The old woman nodded, looking around with suspicion. She gestured to Bordelli to come closer.

'Strange things have always happened there.'

'Strange in what way?'

'The devil,' she whispered.

'The devil?'

'Shhh, speak softly,' she said, eyeing the dark street.

'Sorry,' Bordelli said in a whisper, giving her a complicit look.

'Ah, don't get me going,' said the woman. Bordelli looked behind her. On the other side of that door was a world that remained trapped in past centuries: massive black furniture, portraits on the walls, suits of armour, huge candelabras, dark carpets, a blue ceramic wood-burning stove. The air wafting out of that door smelled of old fabrics and burnt wood.

'Since apparently you've seen him, what does the devil look like?' Bordelli asked.

The old woman lowered her voice even more.

'I haven't seen him. But you do hear all kinds of noise,' she said slowly, in a solemn tone.

'What kinds of noise?'

'Do you really want to know?'

'Of course . . .'

'Wait, I'll call my mother.' The old woman turned round and screamed: 'Mamma! There's a gentleman here wants to talk to you!' Bordelli took a step forward.

'No, please, I don't want to disturb anyone.'

'Mamma! I said there's a gentleman here!'

'Never mind, signora.'

'No, no, here she comes now.' Bordelli saw a wraith flutter in the darkness of the room behind them, but at first glance she seemed not to advance an inch. It was Mamma. She took a very long time to reach the door. She was small, tiny, all bones. She stood as though hung from her neck, her voice almost inaudible.

'Who's here?' she said. There was a slight whistle in her voice.

'This gentleman, here, wanted to know about the villa next door,' the daughter said.

'Your daughter tells me you hear noises there,' said Bordelli.

'Where should I look?' the mother asked.

'She's blind,' the daughter explained. Bordelli took another step forward.

'I'm here, signora. Pleased to meet you.' The mother extended a tiny, skeletal hand. Bordelli held those little bones for only a moment, fearing he might break them. The old woman took three small, futile steps across a single tile, then regained her breath after that exhausting greeting.

'What is it you wanted to know?' she said, mouth quivering. Bordelli looked her straight in the eye. Her eyeballs were covered by white veils veined with capillaries.

'Your daughter was telling me you hear noises next door,' he said.

The old woman made a vague gesture, which must have corresponded to some expression of exuberance in her younger days.

'Oh, yes, yes. Many sounds, many, many sounds.'

'What sort of sounds, signora?'

'Many sounds. Many, many, many, many . . .'

'Mamma, do you understand? The gentleman wants to know what kind of sounds . . . Stop acting senile.' Bordelli wondered how he might extricate himself. His hand in his pocket fidgeted with his car keys. The transparent old woman joined her hands together and then pulled them tightly against her breast.

'At night, mostly. Many, many . . .'

'Not *when*, Mamma. The gentleman would like to know what sort of sounds.'

'Oh . . . all right . . .'

'Tell him about the screams you heard last February.'

Bordelli pretended to be keenly interested.

'What kind of screams?' the daughter persisted, jabbing her mother in the shoulder with her fingertips.

'Come on, Mamma, the gentleman is waiting.'

'Yes, yes . . . terrible screams, terrible, terrible screams . . . like animals . . .'

The daughter intervened.

'But they weren't animals, I'm sure of that!' she said very seriously, opening her eyes wide to emphasise the point. Meanwhile her mother seemed to have woken up and was eager to speak.

'I have a cousin who's mad, and I used to go and see him until '46,' she said.

The daughter gave a start at the sound of these words, taking such offence that she almost began to cry. She started slapping her mother lightly on the hands.

'Why did you say that, Mamma? Why did you say that now? Eh? Did you have to go and say that? Eh?'

'Let me speak . . . You see, sir, I so hate my sister . . . she drove my grandson mad.' The daughter clenched her dentures, growled, and stalked away as if she would never return. The mother continued speaking calmly.

'The only other place I ever heard such screams was in the madhouse. Now do you understand? Are you still here, sir?'

'I'm here.'

The daughter reappeared and stood behind her mother. She looked a bit calmer. Bordelli wanted only to run away.

'I'm so pleased to have met you both,' he said, holding out his hand. The mother started waving her hands in the air.

'Don't you want to hear about the shots?' she said.

'What shots?'

'They are so loud, so so loud, that they wake me up.'

'Pistol shots?'

'So, so loud.'

'Mamma! You don't understand! The man wants to know if they were pistol shots.'

'Ah, that's so nice of him . . .'

'No, Mamma, you don't understand . . .'

'. . . so, so nice.'

'Mamma!' the daughter shouted. Bordelli felt he should intervene, and made a slight bow towards the daughter.

'Please don't disturb your mother any further, I beg you. I've understood everything perfectly, thank you. Thank you ever so much. Goodbye.'

The mother took two tiny steps forward.

'Do come see us some time, sir, we're always here, all alone,' she said.

'Mamma, why do you say that? Why?'

'Because it's true,' the mother whimpered. Bordelli said goodbye again, loudly, so they would hear, and took to his heels. Behind him the argument continued. The daughter was furious.

'Did you really have to go and say that? Eh? Why did you say that? Tell me why!' she kept saying, enraged.

The mother wasn't listening to her.

'Adele, call the gentleman back here . . . we didn't tell him about the grunting noises . . .'

'Tell me why you said that! Tell me why! Why?'

The great front door closed, and silence returned. Bordelli was bathed in sweat, but at last he was free.

'The devil,' he said to himself. He would have given his right hand for a cigarette. It was possible that mother and daughter had heard only mating cats and sputtering cars, but still they had managed to give the villa an even stranger air.

He was about to go back into the garden when a white Fiat 500 pulled up. Stepping out of the car was a small, thin man of about sixty with a wrinkly mouth and a tiny skull that narrowed vaguely at the temples. He approached Bordelli with a hesitant step. Behind his enormous eyeglasses he wore a pained expression.

'I'm looking for Inspector Bordelli,' he said.

'I am he.'

'I am Dr Bacci, Signora Pedretti's personal physician.'

They shook hands.

'Poor woman. I still can't believe it,' said Dr Bacci, truly saddened. They walked through the garden and into the villa. Bordelli stopped at the bottom of the stairs.

'If you don't mind, I'd like to ask you some questions about your patient,' he said.

'I'm sorry, but I would like to see her first.'

'By all means. She's upstairs. I'll wait for you in that room over there,' Bordelli said, pointing to one of the sitting rooms. The doctor trudged up the stairs, head bobbing to one side. He returned a few minutes later and rejoined Bordelli. Stopping in the middle of the room, he stood completely still and stared into space. Bordelli had made himself comfortable on a sofa that smelled strongly of old velvet.

'Tell me, Dr Bacci, we know that the signora suffered from asthma . . . but to what degree?'

Bacci turned round, in a daze.

'What was that?'

'I was asking whether your patient's asthma was serious, or if, perhaps—'

'Ah, yes, of course. She suffered from tissual asthmatic allergy, a rather serious form of it, I should say.'

'Could it prove fatal?'

The doctor began to wander slowly about the room, hands at his sides, eyes darting from painting to painting. There was great sadness in his voice.

'The signora was allergic to many types of pollen. She sometimes had violent attacks, but never anything life-threatening.'

'Are you sure about that?'

Bacci turned to face the inspector. He looked bewildered.

'To tell you the truth, there was one plant that could be very dangerous,' he said. Bordelli waited to hear which plant. The doctor began to move again and stopped in front of the portrait of a judge dressed in ermine, hunching his shoulders round his head.

'*Ilex paraguariensis,*' he continued, 'commonly called maté, a typically tropical plant. Its pollen would have been deadly to Signora Pedretti.'

Bordelli coughed into his fist.

'You wouldn't happen to have a cigarette, would you?' he asked.

'I don't smoke.'

'So much the better. Tell me, Doctor, how did Signora Pedretti ever find out?'

'Find what out?'

'That she was allergic to that tropical pollen.'

The doctor took his eyes off the painting and returned to Bordelli. He said that from a very young age the signora had always travelled a great deal. A few years earlier, during a stay in Colombia, she had experienced a very serious attack and had to be rushed to hospital.

'They snatched her from the jaws of death. It was almost a miracle.'

The Colombian doctors discovered that the flowering maté had triggered the attack. The signora spent several days in hospital and recovered quite nicely in spite of everything. But the terrible experience had changed her, and after her return she hardly ever went out of the house any more.

'I used to say to her: Signora, you mustn't live like a recluse. Colombia is on the other side of the world. That plant doesn't grow here.'

'So, in short, that plant was the only thing that might trigger a fatal attack.'

Dr Bacci removed his spectacles, which were as thick as glass-bottoms, and pressed his eyeballs hard with his fingers. He resumed walking along the walls of the room.

The inspector stretched his legs, which had grown numb.

'As far as I know, yes, it was the only thing.'

'And what can you tell me about Asthmaben?' Bordelli asked.

'The signora always kept a bottle within reach. Luckily she responded well to it. Twenty drops, and in a matter of seconds, she could breathe again. That doesn't happen with everyone, I can assure you.'

'And what would happen if she didn't take it?' asked Bordelli.

'It's hard to say. Probably in normal cases she would have a few minutes of crisis, but I really don't think she would die.'

'With that tropical plant, on the other hand—'

'With maté it's almost certain that, without Asthmaben, she would die within minutes, especially after her previous crisis in Colombia.'

'And with Asthmaben?'

'Well, I have no proof, obviously. But I'm fairly convinced that with a double dose she would have been all right.'

The inspector sighed by way of conclusion.

'So, if I've understood correctly, seeing that there was a bottle of Asthmaben on her bedside table, we can rule out that she was killed by an asthma attack. Is that right?'

'I can't swear to it, of course, since asthma is a treacherous disease and can cause death by heart failure. The only thing we know for certain is that we are in God's hands.'

Bordelli remained silent, fingers pinching his chin, thinking of something. Then he stood up and held his hand out to the doctor.

'That'll be all for now, thank you. I'll ring you if I need you again.' They shook hands. The doctor was trembling a little.

'I am very grieved by this,' he said slowly. 'Signora Pedretti was not a very pleasant person, but I was fond of her. Very fond.' He said it in the tone of someone confessing to an unrequited love. His bloodshot eyes, huge behind their lenses, seemed to dance. Then he gave a sort of smile and left. Bordelli collapsed on the sofa again. He didn't like the look of this. Didn't like it at all.

A few moments later he heard the stretcher-bearers on the stairs and went back into the entrance hall. The stretcher with Signora Pedretti's mortal remains passed before him, covered entirely by a white sheet. Russo and Bellandi touched the visors of their caps to say goodbye to Bordelli, and left. Diotivede was the last to come down, his medical case swinging in his hand like a schoolboy's satchel.

'Could you give me a lift?' he asked.

They headed back to town together, with the Beetle back-firing and spitting flames out of the exhaust pipe. Someone had told Bordelli it might be a dirty filter or something similar. It was a Volkswagen, which was saying a lot, but now and then, it too needed a little medical care.

'What are your thoughts about this murder?' Diotivede asked.

'First we have to establish that she was actually killed.'

'You still have some doubt?'

'Well . . .'

'Then you really must be tired.'

'I've already said that.'

They fell silent. This happened often when they were in the car together; each ruminated as if he was alone. The Beetle advanced slowly, as if it, too, was thinking. The sky began to lighten; it was already past five. Bordelli's window and vent were both open, but he was sweating just the same. Diotivede had never had much trouble with the weather. Summer or winter, he never complained.

They descended into town, along Via Volta, and crossed the Ponte del Pino on their way to Diotivede's house. The only sign of life was a few stray dogs roaming about.

'I want to have a dinner party at my place. Feel like coming?' said Bordelli.

Diotivede rubbed his head with his hand.

'Why not?' he said.

The sun was already rising over the city, but Bordelli's night was not over yet. After dropping Diotivede off at home in

Via dell'Erta Canina, he went straight to police headquarters to have a chat with Maria, Signor Pedretti-Strassen's lady companion. By this point he was so tired he would never have been able to sleep.

The woman had been waiting for him for nearly an hour, sitting on the bench outside his office. She was in a whiny state, hands full of wet handkerchiefs, white hair gathered in a tidy ponytail. He had her sit down in front of his desk. She was a tiny little thing, with big round eyes and a lipless mouth. She looked like some sort of nocturnal bird. Bordelli offered her a glass of water and waited for her to calm down. Once the woman had stopped sobbing, he asked what made her think the signora's death was a murder. She waved her hands over her head and, starting to cry again, talked about the greed of the signora's nephews and their respective wives, whom she termed 'witches', emphasising the *tch* sound.

'They were just waiting for the signora to die, you could see it in the eyes of those two milksops and their whores!' she said, sobbing again. Bordelli objected that greed might be a sin, but it was not a crime. Maria twisted her mouth up.

'Wait till you see them in person; they're wicked. They killed her, I know it, I feel it.'

Bordelli felt a drop of sweat roll down his belly and stick to his shirt.

'What is Signora Pedretti's degree of kinship with these nephews?'

'They are the sons of a sister of hers, who drowned in the lake at Lausanne ten years ago.'

'An accident?'

'They called it a suicide.'

'What sort of work do these nephews do?'

Maria grimaced.

'They sell houses,' she said disdainfully. 'They have none of the Pedrettis' class.'

The inspector rifled through his drawers, searching again for a cigarette. He found two under a sheaf of papers and lit one.

'Tell me, Maria, what did Signora Pedretti herself think of her two nephews?'

'In their presence she never let anything show; but with me she would vent her feelings. She used to called them "the two worms".'

'And what can you tell me about her asthma?'

Maria confirmed that the signora's rare attacks usually subsided in a matter of minutes, thanks to the Asthmaben. Bordelli repeated what Dr Bacci had told him; that asthmatic allergy was a treacherous illness.

'They killed her . . .' she whimpered again.

'We shall perform a very thorough post-mortem,' said Bordelli. He then asked her to explain Signora Pedretti's difficult character, and she burst into tears again.

'She was a bit authoritarian, and not very generous, but, deep down, she was a very good person. Mostly, she was very, very lonely.'

'When did you see her for the last time?'

'Yesterday evening at eight. I always leave at that hour,' and down came the tears, the nose in the handkerchief. The inspector never knew what to do in front of weeping women. His first impulse was always to pat them on the shoulder and utter some trite words of encouragement, but he always ended up letting it drop and simply waited in silence for the tears to run their course.

As soon as Maria stopped sobbing, Bordelli asked her whether Signora Pedretti had any other close relatives. She pulled another handkerchief out of her purse and blew her nose, trying not to make any noise: first one nostril, then the other.

'There's a brother, who's half crazy. He didn't come to see her very often,' she said.

'What's his name?'

'Dante.'

'Do you know where he lives?'

'In an old house at Mezzomonte.'

'What sort of relations did he have with his sister?'

'They spoke over the telephone rather often. They would have long conversations, and sometimes I would actually hear the signora laugh,' she said, opening her eyes wide.

'Was it so unusual for her to laugh?' asked Bordelli.

Maria raised her eyebrows and bobbed her head up and down.

'Very unusual. She hardly ever laughed.'

'Whereas, with her brother . . .'

'With her brother she laughed a lot. And when she said goodbye, she would blow kisses into the receiver.'

Like Rosa, thought Bordelli.

'You haven't got this Dante's telephone number by any chance, have you?'

'I should have it, I think. Often it was I who dialled the number for Signora Pedretti.' She rummaged through her handbag for a long time until she found a little telephone booklet. Between the pages was a loose piece of paper.

'This must be it.'

Bordelli took the scrap of paper, glanced at it, and set it down on the desk.

'And where can I find the nephews?'

'Oh, those two! They're at the seaside villa, taking it easy. I'll give you their telephone number.'

'Thank you.'

'They always go on holiday together, the worms.' The woman recited the number in a quavering voice, then started crying again. Bordelli waited another minute as Maria sniffled. Then he stood up.

'Thank you ever so much. If I need to talk to you again, I'll let you know.'

'Throw them in jail, both of them,' said Maria, looking him in the eye.

'We will arrest the killer, I can assure you of that.'

Maria came up to him and clutched his arm with both hands, imploring him.

'Inspector, please do your best to find out whether Signora

Pedretti died by the hand of God or by. . . .' Chin trembling, she didn't finish her sentence. The inspector put his hand on her shoulder.

'Sleep easy, Maria, that's my job.'

'She was so alone, so very alone . . . And those four rascals . . .'

'Please don't worry.'

'Those disgusting . . .'

'I promise you that if they are guilty, they will not get off lightly.'

He accompanied the woman to the exit, then turned her over to a uniformed officer who would drive her home. Before she left, he asked her one more question.

'Aside from Signora Pedretti, who else had keys to the villa?'

'Nobody, Inspector. Signora Pedretti couldn't bear the thought of someone entering the house without her permission.'

'Not even Dante?'

'I have no way of knowing. But if Signor Dante does have them, I am sure he has forgotten where he put them.'

'Is he absent minded?'

'He is a very strange man.'

'Thank you again for your patience, Maria. Now go home and rest.'

'Mr Inspector, please, don't forget.'

'You can sleep easy,' Bordelli repeated, unable to think of any variations.

It was already seven o'clock. The inspector went back into his office and decided to call Dante, the brother, at once. The telephone rang for a long time. Bordelli was about to hang up when he heard someone pick up. A deep, warm voice replied.

'Dante here.'

'Signor Pedretti, please forgive me for calling at this hour.'

'Why? What time is it?'

'Just after seven o'clock.'

'A.M. or P.M.?'

'A.M.'

'Go on.'

'This is Inspector Bordelli. I have some unpleasant news for you.'

'Not over the phone.'

'When could you come in?'

'I'd rather you came here.' He gave Bordelli the address and hung up without allowing him time to respond. He had a beautiful voice, but perhaps Maria was right: he must be a bit strange. Bordelli thought that, in the end, a little drive in the country might not be such a bad idea. He scraped together all the cigarettes he could find in his drawers and left the station. He no longer felt tired; on the contrary, he seemed to be bursting with energy. The same thing used to happen to him during the war, when he was forced to stay awake for two or three days in a row. He kept going on nerves alone, relying on those mysterious powers that come into play when you least expect it. If he went home now, he wouldn't sleep a wink; he would only spend hours and hours tossing and turning in bed, sweating in the dark, in the clutches of the usual sad memories.

He got into his Beetle and calmly crossed the city, which was slowly repopulating. At Porta Romana, he turned on to the Via di Pozzolatico, which would take him up towards Dante's house. He drove slowly, enjoying the landscape. Mezzomonte was a tiny outlying ward on the hillside opposite the one where Signora Pedretti-Strassen lived. It was fairly wild countryside there. There were a few large aristocratic villas, but the rest were peasant houses, some still inhabited by old farmers, others half ruined and abandoned. The young were all fleeing the countryside to work in the city. Nobody seemed to want to live any more between the soil and the cow pats.

Bordelli pulled up in a clearing of beaten earth in front of number 117, Via Imprunetana, and got out of the car. He found himself in front of an open, rusty gate. On one of the gate's pillars was an old, terracotta plaque with the name: *Il Paretaio*, 'The Bird-Trap'. If this was the right place, Dante's house could just barely be glimpsed from the road, at the end of a grassy lane, hidden among the cypresses of an utterly neglected garden. Bordelli continued on foot and entered the garden, walking along a path of trampled grass which cut feebly through a jungle of shrubs and wildflowers. It was a two-storey house, but very broad. A sort of cross between a peasant house and a landowner's villa. On one side a sort of small, rather shabby turret had been built, apparently outfitted as a dovecote. Seeing the state of abandon of the entire property, it was hard to imagine it was inhabited. But that was the address. Bordelli approached the front doorway, which was open and as dark as a wolves' den, and pulled a sort of handle that looked in every way like a doorbell. In fact it was a mechanical ringer. He heard a clanging far off inside the house. By way of reply, he heard a muffled yell that sounded like it came from underground.

'It's open!'

Bordelli entered and proceeded in darkness along a disjointed floor. He didn't know what to do; he could see only one step ahead. He called Signor Pedretti loudly, then heard the same voice as before, shouting from inside the earth.

'Turn right, and at the end of the corridor you'll see an open door. Go down the stairs, but watch your step.'

The inspector followed these instructions and, groping along, came to a half-open door. He pushed this and found himself in front of a steep staircase that led below. At the bottom of the stair was a faint, flickering light. He descended the stairs, stepping carefully, and ended up in a vast, rectangular room the size of the house's entire floor plan. The walls were lined with old shelves full of books. Practically everywhere shone the flames of countless candles in large candelabra. At the back of the great room was a tall, fat man in a yellowish smock covered with stains. A white, woolly mane enveloped his head like a cloud of smoke. He was standing, busying himself over a long wooden workbench cluttered with a chemist's glassware and a thousand other strange tools and objects, including a pair of jugs with steam rising from their mouths. The workbench was at least ten metres long and one metre wide, but in that great space it looked like a pack of cigarettes on a desk.

'Are you Dante?' Bordelli asked, though there was no need for the question.

'I am.'

The inspector advanced, looking all around the room. It was as if he had entered another world. The floor was made of large wooden boards that creaked with every step. Dante didn't look up at the inspector until the last moment. After wiping it on his smock, he held out a gigantic hand to him, almost too big to shake. He had a broad, joyful face, like an enthusiastic baby's, with eyes ever so slightly veiled by sadness.

'Candlelight is so much more restful,' he said in his powerful voice.

'I agree.'

Dante looked at him as though sizing him up, from his height of six foot three inches.

'So you're a police inspector,' said Dante.

'I'm sorry to disturb you. What were you doing?' asked Bordelli, to buy time.

Upon hearing the question, Dante became as excited as a child.

'I am creating a substance that will revolutionise the world,' he said, smiling, as if he were talking about chocolate. Curious, Bordelli asked him what this substance was. Dante pulled a half-smoked cigar out of the pocket of his smock and lit it on a candle. He sat down slantwise on the workbench.

'It's a substance that will make mice happy,' he said with satisfaction.

'Mice?'

The inventor bared his huge teeth in a gargantuan smile.

'I love mice. I don't like that people kill them simply because they prowl in kitchens and frighten women. The powder I am creating will make them immune to all poison.'

'I see.'

'No, you don't. I can tell that you, too, think mice are trouble and full of diseases.'

'That's what we were always taught.'

Dante pointed a gnarled index finger at Bordelli.

'Would you like me to call them?' he said.

'Call whom?'

'The mice.'

'The mice?'

'But keep very still. They don't know you and might get anxious.'

Though Bordelli was already thinking that this man was simply mad, he felt perfectly at ease in that great, candlelit room. Maybe I'm mad, too, he thought.

'How many of them are there?' he asked.

'Don't worry. They're friends.'

Dante made some strange noises with his mouth, and a few seconds later the floor started to fill up with dark little creatures advancing with caution, sniffing the air in fits and starts. They approached the inventor. There were at least twenty of them. Dante knelt down and started whispering to them. The mice walked over his shoes without a care. He touched them with one finger, calling them each by name: Jeremiah, Attila, Erminia, Achilles, Desdemona.

Bordelli couldn't restrain himself.

'How can you tell them apart?'

Dante bit his cigar and spat out a wad of tobacco.

'To us the Chinese, too, look all alike,' he said. He took a piece of chocolate out of his pocket and started crumbling it on the floor. The mice ate the bits and went quietly home. Dante bid them goodbye in his basso voice, then turned to Bordelli.

'Coffee, Inspector?'

'I'd love some.'

'It'll be ready in an instant.' He went over to the workbench and began fidgeting with an alembic with a coiled pipe. He lit a flame under it and poured a handful of coffee grounds into it.

'A patented system,' he said. 'The fats evaporate and only the best part remains.'

Bordelli looked at the workbench, fascinated. It was crowded with incomprehensible gadgets, cogs and scattered test tubes. He had never seen anything like it in his life.

Dante put his big hands in his pockets.

'We inventors devote our lives to improving the lives of everyone. But I must admit we also have a lot of fun.'

There was a buzzing sound: the coffee was ready. Dante poured it into two strangely oval espresso cups.

'Another invention of mine,' he said proudly.

'I figured as much.'

'These cups are adaptable to every kind of mouth. Try drinking from it.' The inspector took a sip, and a large drop of coffee fell on to his shoes. The inventor frowned at him.

'You must turn the cup until you find the right place for your mouth,' he said.

The inspector spread his feet and tried again. He gave it his best, but it seemed impossible to drink from the cup without making it rain. And the coffee was bad into the bargain. The only thing special about it was that it had a strong taste of liquorice.

'I'll have to try again another time,' said Bordelli.

'Perhaps I need to modify the design,' said Dante, face darkening, and he started examining the cup from every angle, trying to find the defect.

'Signor Pedretti, as I was saying on the phone, I have some bad news for you,' said Bordelli.

'Tell me.'

'It's your sister.'

'Dead?' said Dante, staring at him.

'Yes.'

Dante did not react. He went over to a candle and relit his cigar, taking many consecutive puffs. Bordelli started to feel tired again and collapsed into a large armchair. The inventor remained standing.

'How did she die?' he asked.

'At first glance, it looks like a violent asthma attack; but we'll have to wait for the post-mortem to be certain.'

'So why are the police involved?'

'Because there's something fishy about it.'

Dante spread his legs and crossed his arms over his belly.

'Well, I can tell you now, I don't want to see her,' he said.

'You're under no obligation.'

'It's not that I would be shocked or upset. I am old, and I've seen my share of dead bodies. But I have no desire to see my sister for the last time on a slab at the morgue, sewn back up like a stuffed fish. I wouldn't like that. Another coffee?'

'No, thanks.'

Dante went and poured himself another cup, then continued.

'Life's funny, don't you think? I spoke with my sister by telephone just a few hours ago. She seemed rather well, in good spirits.'

He knocked back the coffee the way Russians do vodka. Then he tossed the empty cup on to the workbench and took a long, slow walk round the room, hands thrust deep into his pockets, making the floorboards suffer with each step. Slowly he came back to the inspector, eyes staring at an imaginary horizon.

'*We are like the leaves on the trees in autumn* . . . Who wrote that? Quasimodo or the other one . . . Ungaretti? Yes, it must be Ungaretti.'

Dante's voice was soothing, and his white, vaporous hair gave one a sense of peace, like the hair of the angels in heaven. Bordelli felt good, relaxed. The only thing missing was a bed. Dante stopped directly in front of him, looking bewildered, lips jutting out like Mussolini's.

'Dead . . . from an asthma attack . . .' he said softly. He stood for a moment in silence, head hanging on his chest. Then he raised it slowly, squeezing his eyes shut as if trying to remember something.

'Dead,' he repeated. Then he walked round the room again,

making the floorboards groan. He came to a stop again in front of Bordelli, who was practically falling asleep to the rhythm of Dante's footfalls.

'I know it's of no interest, but the same thing could have happened to me, you know. I think it was about a month ago, perhaps two, or maybe even last year—'

'Do you also suffer from asthma?'

'It's nothing to do with asthma. Do you want me to tell you about it?'

'Please.'

All of a sudden they heard a rustling noise. Dante opened his eyes wide and put his forefinger over his nose and lips.

'Shhh! Come,' he said very softly. Taking Bordelli's arm, he led him to the middle of the room, then brought his mouth to the inspector's ear.

'Close your eyes, Inspector, it'll be another few seconds.'

'Then what?'

'Shhh! Close your eyes.' The inspector obeyed, shuddering with excitement. Dante squeezed his arm.

'Now, Inspector! Keep your eyes closed and tell me what you feel.'

Bordelli sniffed the air and pricked his ears.

'What am I supposed to feel?'

'Shhh! Speak softly. Just tell me what you feel.'

Bordelli waited some more. He forced himself to feel something, but there was nothing. So he gave up.

'I'm sorry, I don't feel anything,' he said.

Dante was very pleased.

'Precisely. You feel nothing. And yet there is someone in this room, flying around us.' Bordelli thought Dante really was insane, and opened his eyes. All he saw were shadows chasing one another high up the walls and on the ceiling, and he instinctively lowered his head. Dante squeezed his arm again.

'Look over there, Inspector,' he said, pointing at a moving shape. A large bird was flying silently along the walls, without flapping its wings, creating as many shadows as there were candles in the room.

'What is it?' Bordelli asked.

'Isn't that a marvellous spectacle?'

'What is it?' Bordelli repeated, himself fascinated. Dante let go of his arm, still watching the animal, and raised his voice.

'That's Agostino, a barn owl full of gratitude. Three years ago, I put his broken leg in a splint and fed him for nearly a month. From time to time he comes to see me.'

Bordelli continued to follow the perfectly silent flight of the owl, which, after circling endlessly round the room, began to approach them. Dante raised his forearm, and the bird alighted on it. The owl wiped its beak two or three times on Dante's shoulder, then took flight again, circling the room once more before veering into the stairwell and leaving.

'Rebecca also loved animals,' said Dante, heading back to the workbench. Bordelli followed behind him and collapsed in the chair again. He felt a bit dazed. Dante relit his cigar on the nearest candle and put two fingers to his forehead.

'Now, what was I saying?'

'You were telling me about something that had happened to you.'

'Ah, yes. I had been working for several days on a revolutionary new detergent that would allow you to wash dishes without rubbing them, simply by immersing them in water. It's been an obsession of mine for many years. The challenge is to create a product that isn't poisonous, unlike DDT.'

Bordelli leaned forward.

'DDT is poisonous?' he asked, worried.

'Extremely poisonous.'

'I didn't know.'

'Now you are the second to know, I being the first. Who knows when everyone else will be told?'

Bordelli thought of the aerosol bomb he had on his bedside table, and how often he had inhaled its contents. Resigned, he lit a cigarette.

'Signor Pedretti, what do *you* do to keep the mosquitoes away?'

'I'm working on a device for that too, but it's going to take time. For the moment I use basil.'

'Does it work?'

'Not really, but I like the smell.'

'So, anyway.'

'Yes, I was talking about the detergent. After working out the formula, I was about to enter the experimentation phase. Do you know much about chemistry?'

'All I know is that water is written H_2O.'

'Then I shall skip the details and stick to the concept.'

'Thank you.'

Dante took his time, as if trying to find the right words.

'Let's see if you can follow. One night I lit the fire under the coil tube. I've always had a passion for mixing substances together; it's like glimpsing the secrets of the universe. I can only imagine what fun God must have had playing around with matter for those seven days . . .' Dante stopped short, his face turning serious. He started searching his pockets, then pulled out a folded piece of paper and a pen and began scribbling something.

'Sorry, but I have to make a note of something, otherwise I'll forget it.'

'By all means.'

Dante continued writing, muttering to himself all the while. When he had finished, he reread everything, shook his head, rolled the paper into a ball, and threw it away.

'A bad idea, needless to say.' He snuffed out the end of his cigar in a small dish, lit another and, clenching it between his teeth, resumed talking.

'So, on that famous evening, I needed a certain kind of nitrate, just a spoonful. And I went over to the shelf to get the bottle. As I was about to pour it into the receptacle, I stopped. I realised the liquid had no smell whatsoever, whereas the nitrate should have stunk. We chemists have a very keen sense of smell. It comes from our work, sniffing everything we get our hands on. Anyway, in the place of harmless nitrate I was about to pour some nitroglycerine. Do you know what would have happened? Boom! They would have found only a pile of ash,' he said, his head enveloped in cigar smoke.

'A moment of distraction?'

'The label on the bottle had the name of the very nitrate I was looking for. It's inexplicable. I'm a precise person, in my way. You see this room? At any moment, I know where to find whatever I am looking for, even the tiniest thing. I still wonder how that could have happened.'

Bordelli looked at the vast, chaotic room, the workbench submerged under everything imaginable, and thought he wouldn't have bet a single lira on Dante's precision.

The inventor's expression had changed. As he smoked, he kept spitting out big wads of tobacco.

'Do you have the keys to your sister's villa?' Bordelli asked him.

'I must have them somewhere. Is it important?'

'I don't know yet.'

Dante went over to the workbench and started rummaging through his ingenious debris. He moved aside stills and alembics and strange contraptions full of wheels.

'I thought I put them there . . .' He picked up bundles of papers and thick tomes and looked underneath them. In the end he gave up, put his hands in his pockets, and broke out in a smile.

'Here they are. I had them right here all along,' he said, pulling them out of his pocket and making them ring like a bell. The inspector remembered what Maria had said and decided not to give in just yet.

'Are you sure those are the right ones?' he asked.

Dante took a good look at the keys.

'You mean . . . they're for my house? Ah, I thought I had lost them . . .' he said.

'You can take your time looking for your sister's keys, but if you find them, let me know.'

'Yes, these must be mine. I'll put them right here so I won't lose them again.' He hung them from a nail and then stared at them a long time, as if to commit the event to memory.

'And what can you tell me about your two nephews, Dante?'

'Those two fools? They're in for a big surprise when they read Rebecca's will.' He broke into wild laughter.

'What sort of surprise?'

'My sister left everything to the Sisters of Monte Frassineto. Including the paintings, the embroidered napkins and the bedbugs. Brilliant, don't you think? I can't wait to go to the solicitor's office and enjoy the show.' He couldn't stop laughing.

'Are you sure your nephews don't suspect anything?'

Dante laughed again with satisfaction.

'No, they don't know a thing. Rebecca was very careful not to let on. She told only me.' He started laughing again, to the point of coughing, then went up to Bordelli, looming over him with all his bulk.

'It's the best trick in the world, because the person who plays it on you is gone, so you can't take revenge.'

'And you, Signor Pedretti, aren't you inheriting anything?'

The inventor made a sweeping gesture of the hand.

'Perhaps a few small gifts and souvenirs. But Rebecca knew I didn't want anything. I drew up my own will some time ago, and do you know to whom I shall leave my house, my laboratory and all my inventions?'

'The Sisters of Monte Frassineto?'

'To the Brotherhood of Orphans of Santa Veronica. I've already arranged everything. This house will become a school for disadvantaged children. It will be called the Collegio Dante Pedretti . . . But please don't misunderstand me, it's not for vanity's sake, but only to leave a mark. A silly consolation, but a human one.'

'Very human.'

'Do you have any children, Inspector?'

'No.'

'Do you regret it?'

'I think about it sometimes. Now I wish I had a twenty-year-old son; but I was never lucky enough to find his mother.'

'Right,' said Dante, who then reimmersed himself in his thoughts, wandering about the room and breathing noisily. He stopped in a distant corner.

'Do you believe in God, Inspector? Do you have the gift of faith?'

Bordelli stretched his legs, seeking relief.

'Those are difficult questions, and I confess I'm very tired.'

Dante wasn't the least bit tired. He paced slowly, stepping over the obstacles piled up more or less everywhere on the floor.

'What do you think? Is my sister watching us? Or has she vanished completely and for ever?'

'I don't feel like thinking about it right now.'

The inventor gripped the edges of his smock.

'I have always been curious about this question of faith. Personally, I think that those who have faith are fortunate, and those who don't are wretched.'

'Perhaps.'

'You have an odd way of conversing, my dear Inspector. I get the feeling you have a lot to say but for some reason you are careful not to say it. Am I wrong?'

'Maybe it's hard for me to say anything definitive.'

'Have you ever heard of Nicole d'Autrecourt?'

The conversation went on for a long time, and they spoke of many things. A bottle of grappa was brought out. In the heat, they began to sweat and unbutton their collars. The smoke of cigars and cigarettes stagnated in the air.

At ten o'clock that same morning, the inspector went to Careggi Hospital and parked his Beetle in front of the Office of Forensic Medicine. Entering Diotivede's laboratory, he found the doctor fresh as a rose.

'I see you haven't slept,' the doctor said.

'Have you?'

'I had a cup of coffee at home and came straight here.'

'You know what I think, Diotivede? I think you have a twin who takes your place when the going gets rough. At this very moment you are at home, sleeping, and I am speaking to your twin brother, who has slept twelve hours straight.'

Diotivede, who was preparing the instruments for the post-mortem on Signora Pedretti-Strassen, twisted his mouth.

'Twins, eh? And both pathologists?'

'It would be magnificent.'

The doctor had put on his gloves. He walked past Bordelli and looked at him askance.

'Keep away from me. If I were performing your post-mortem today, I would know, even before opening you up, that you've drunk a litre of grappa.'

'It's Dante's fault.'

'You can't always blame the poets.'

Bordelli leaned his back against the wall and crossed his arms.

'When can you give me some results on Signora Pedretti?' he said.

'I was just about to start on her.'

'As for dinner, would Wednesday be all right?'

Diotivede confirmed with a nod.

'Good, now I only need to find Botta. I hope he's not in jail,' said Bordelli.

'You could always get him out by Wednesday.'

'Don't overestimate me.'

The doctor went up to him.

'May I express a wish?' he asked.

'Go ahead.'

Diotivede lit up like a child.

'I would like bean soup *alla lombarda*.'

'In this heat?'

'I haven't eaten any for ages.'

'All right, soup it is.'

Diotivede smiled broadly, then approached the slab on which Signora Pedretti lay, and delicately drew back the sheet.

'If you don't want to look, you have only to leave.'

'Send me the results as soon as you can.'

'I'll ring you.'

When he reached the door, Bordelli turned round.

'Diotivede, did you know that DDT is poisonous?'

'I'm not surprised.'

The inspector waited to see the scalpel descend over the signora's abdomen, and then left.

As he stepped out of his car in the courtyard of police head-quarters, Bordelli thought again of his visit with Dante Pedretti and felt as if he had dreamt it all. He felt quite muddled, in fact. He must look pretty bad, he thought, since Mugnai stared at him for a long time and said nothing.

'I'm fifty-three years old, Mugnai, and if I go a night without sleep, it will naturally show in my face,' he said, a bit irritated.

'I didn't say anything, Inspector.'

'Sorry, I'm just a bit tired.' He walked down the corridor with Mugnai at his side.

'Did you know that DDT is poisonous, Mugnai?'

'I use *zampironi*, Inspector. They don't smell too good, but they work.'

Bordelli massaged his chin, which was rough with stubble.

'As soon as you see Piras, tell him to come to my office,' he said.

'Of course, sir.'

Bordelli entered his office and collapsed in his chair. The climate in there was tropical, and he felt a sharp pain burrowing through his head. The sweat on his skin had evaporated almost entirely, leaving it slimy. He lit what he defined as his first cigarette of the day and savoured it without haste. Since he was, in spite of everything, still quitting smoking, the 'few' he did smoke he smoked down to the filter. The last drag was disgusting. Crushing the butt in the ashtray, he searched his pocket for the little piece of paper with the phone number of the deceased's nephews. He found it balled up and opened it like a sweet wrapper. Normally the inspector didn't lend any weight to people's judgement of other people, since they were often intolerant and unjust, the fruit of personal malice. But Maria's doggedness and conviction gave him pause. He dialled the number, and a woman's voice answered.

'Hello?'

'Good morning, signora, this is Inspector Bordelli. I'd like to speak with either nephew of Signora Pedretti-Strassen.'

The woman at the other end held her breath.

'Has something happened?' she asked anxiously. Bordelli heard a long exchange of whispers, and then someone abruptly turned down the music playing in the background.

'I'm sorry, but I need to talk to one of Signora Pedretti's nephews. Is that possible?' he said. There was a moment of silence, then the woman summoned a clear, ringing tone of voice.

'Of course. With whom would you like to speak? Giulio or Anselmo?'

'It makes no difference.'

The woman called out loudly:

'Anselmo!' Then she said: 'He'll be right with you . . . Here he is.'

Through the receiver Bordelli heard a heavy step approach, some more whispering, then a nasal, masculine voice.

'Hello, who is this?'

'Inspector Bordelli. And you are Signor—'

'Dr Morozzi. Has something happened?'

'Dr Morozzi, I have some bad news for you.'

'What is it?'

'Your Aunt Rebecca passed away last night.'

Anselmo assumed a serious tone.

'Oh God, poor Auntie. I'm so sorry . . .'

'My condolences.'

'Thank you, Inspector.'

'I would like to have a little chat with you and your brother.'

55

Bordelli heard a sigh at the other end.

'About what?' said Anselmo.

'I'll tell you when I see you.'

'Is there a problem?'

'Perhaps.'

'Perhaps? Can't you tell me anything now?'

'I'm afraid not.'

Anselmo became compliant.

'All right, Inspector. Where should we meet you?'

'At central police headquarters. Let's say the day after tomorrow, at noon.'

'As you wish.'

Bordelli played the suspicious policeman.

'Aren't you going to ask me how your aunt died?'

'She was sick, Inspector. I'm not surprised she suddenly died.'

'I understand. Good day, Dr Morozzi.'

The phone call had been rather unpleasant. He didn't like the sound of Anselmo's voice or his shortness of breath, which crackled in the receiver. He tried to imagine the man, then let it drop. It was too hot.

'Hello, Piras,' said Bordelli, rubbing his bloodshot eyes with his fingers. 'I want to take you to see a villa.'

'Right now?'

'Yes. Bring along a book, a bottle of water, a glass, and a phial that looks like a medicine bottle. I'll wait for you in the courtyard.'

They set out in the Beetle. It was noon. The streets were nearly deserted because of the intense sun. After a short distance, they turned on to Via delle Forbici. The German vehicle's engine thundered between the walls, as in the towns emptied by warfare during the German retreat.

'Find everything I asked for, Piras?'

'Got it all.'

Bordelli downshifted, and the Beetle backfired.

'It's the carburation,' said Piras.

'I'll take her to the doctor's as soon as I can. Now listen closely, Piras. In a few minutes you're going to see the room where a woman of about sixty died. I'll try to sum up for you what we know so far.'

He told him about the allergy, maté pollen, Maria's suspicions, the brother Dante, and the will.

They entered the villa. The smell of old furniture and dust gently invaded their noses. In the bedroom Bordelli took the objects Piras had gathered out of the paper bag and arranged them one by one, reconstructing the original situation. He showed Piras how the woman was when he found her, miming the corpse's position, hands on his throat. Then he sat down and lit a cigarette.

'Let's play a game, Piras. You pretend to know for certain that it was a murder, in spite of the fact that the post-mortem shows that the woman died of a violent asthma attack. The question is this: how did the murderer kill the lady?'

Piras grinned.

'There's one thing I can tell you straight away, Inspector.'

'Tell me.'

'Are you sure you've put everything back the way it was?'

'Absolutely.'

Piras picked up the little bottle that was supposed to be the Asthmaben.

'The cap was screwed on?'

'Yes.'

'That makes no sense to me. All the other elements point to great agitation, whereas the cap . . .'

'Right.'

Piras put the bottle back in place and kept looking around. He went to the window and opened it, perhaps because the room was full of smoke. He paced about the room a little more. His dark eyes jumped quickly from one object to another. At last he stopped in front of Bordelli.

'Does the killer have an alibi in this game?' he asked.

'Let's pretend he does, since he did organise everything so he could kill without getting caught.'

Piras nodded, pensive.

'This is a tough one,' he said.

'That's why I called you. Do you feel like handling the case? Together with me, I mean.'

'That's fine with me. Could I ask you a question, Inspector?'

'Go ahead.'

'Is this an official assignment or your own idea?'

'It's all mine, Piras. But if we discover anything, you'll get the credit, too, and I'm sure you'll be promoted.'

'Another thing, Inspector. Do you already have a hypothesis, or are you sailing in the dark?'

'I have no idea of anything. I'm completely in the dark. I haven't even got the results of the post-mortem. It may actually come out that the lady died without anyone's help. But I don't like the look of this. There's a great big fly buzzing in my skull.'

Piras saw the weariness in Bordelli's face move up a notch.

'You need to sleep,' he said.

'You're probably right. You think about the riddle, in the meantime. We'll meet up again in my office tomorrow, let's say half past nine. I'll have the pathologist's results by then. I'd like to take stock of the situation before interrogating the Morozzis.'

'All right.'

They went out, leaving the window open. Piras didn't say a word the whole way back to the station. Deep inside, Bordelli was smiling. He felt as if he was back in the platoon with Piras's father. Same Sardinian silence, full of thoughts.

At nine o'clock that evening, Bordelli stripped down naked and got into bed. He had hardly eaten a thing. The heat gave no quarter. He tried to sleep, but in the absence of DDT the mosquitoes had an easy time of things. They were biting him mostly on the veins of his hands. He absolutely must remember to buy some *zampironi*. He put his raw hands behind his neck and stared at the ceiling. He thought about Dante, Maria and the intelligence of mice. He had read somewhere that for every man in the world, there were seven women and a million mice, and that, 'with such superior numbers, they could take over the world', but he couldn't remember whether that meant mice or women.

The following morning he awoke around midday, sweaty and aching, church bells clanging in his head. Even in August there was a priest to pull the clapper. He threw his legs out of bed and, once on his feet, felt a stabbing pain slice through his head like a knife through butter. His dry tongue stuck to the roof of his mouth. He felt old, but he wasn't, he told himself, he wasn't old at all. It was all the fault of those bad memories and the line of work he was in.

He dragged himself into the bathroom, pressing his temples hard with his forefingers. He wet his hands and face with cold water, and when he looked up, he saw a fifty-three-year-old man in the mirror with deep circles under his eyes and sagging cheeks. He leaned over the sink, supporting himself with his hands, and took a long look at himself. For consolation he thought of Diotivede at seventy, as lucid and light of step as a child. Seventy minus fifty-three made seventeen, not a bad number.

He shaved, hoping the weariness that had accumulated in his wrinkles like invisible dirt would be carried away with his beard. After a cold shower, he reheated the coffee of the previous morning and drank it in a hurry. Stepping out on to the pavement, he had to close his eyes halfway, so brilliant with sunlight were the streets. The soft, burning asphalt cast Saharan reflections.

It was one o'clock when Bordelli parked his Volkswagen in front of the Trattoria da Cesare, which had remained open for the dog days. It was rather eerie to see Viale Lavagnini completely deserted. Leaving the car windows slightly open, he headed into the restaurant. It was the only place he ever went to eat, and by now it was a bit like going to the home of friends. As soon as he entered, a number of hands rose in greeting. The tables were full of solitary husbands whose wives were at the beach, but Bordelli by now had his own reserved table in Totò's blazing kitchen, next to the ovens of the shortest cook in Europe. He sat down on his customary backless stool and leaned his shoulders against the wall.

'Ciao, Totò, I hope you're not going to give me wild boar again,' he said.

'Hello, Inspector! What have you got against wild boar?'

'Nothing, in winter . . .'

'All right, no boar. Today, for delicate souls, there's also panzanella.'

'I don't believe it.'

Normally Totò's dishes were swimming in fat. Even his fruit salads had something greasy about them. Panzanella. This was the first time he'd ever made panzanella. But Bordelli quickly discovered that Totò's version included an unheard-of amount of onions. He nevertheless served himself a heaped plateful, deciding not to eat anything else. Watching Totò juggle the skillets, he thought that spending the summer in the kitchen in front of eternal flames must be a kind of mission, which would make Totò a missionary. The heat there felt rather like a truncheon to the head. Mere breathing was an effort, though that didn't stop Totò from talking. The formidable cook was also a born talker, and he often told stories of his home town in the south.

'. . . Like that relative of mine, Inspector, who went to America in '32 to work as a labourer and now he's got more money than a lawyer.' This was followed by a thousand anecdotes that had a touch of myth about them. Sometimes he talked about thirty-year feuds that were still going strong. He would name all the dead, down to the last. People from his town would keep him up to date through letters and by telephone, giving descriptions of faces reduced to pulp by sawn-off shotguns and of goat-tied bodies. Bordelli gladly listened to him. He liked the musical intonations of his speech and his use of the plural *voi*, which in Totò had nothing to do with the Mussolini era.

'What was that wine you gave me, Totò!'

The cook opened his eyes wide.

'You don't like it, Inspector?'

'It's good, but it's thick as blood.'

Totò smiled broadly.

'It's from our grapes, Inspector. And if there's blood in it, that's normal.' Then he raised a lid and a bubble of greasy smoke rose slowly and stuck to the ceiling.

It was already two o'clock. Bordelli stood up from his stool and stretched as if he was getting out of bed. He squeezed the cook's shoulder by way of goodbye.

'Ciao, *bello*,' he said.

'Be well, Inspector.'

'I'll do my best.'

He exited Totò's lair feeling fairly light. It was the first time. He only had a halo of onion round his head. As he was about to get into his car, he felt someone touch his shoulder and turned round. Beside him stood a man of about seventy, with a nice, tired face and a small head that moved in jerks, like a snake's.

'May I? Cavalier Aldo Affumicato,' he said.

'A pleasure,' he said. 'Bordelli.'

They shook hands. The *cavaliere* had cold fingers.

'Could I have a minute of your time?' The *cavaliere* seemed a bit embarrassed.

'Actually . . .' said Bordelli.

'I don't know whom to talk to about this, and I've got some very important things to say. Do you have a minute?'

'All right,' Bordelli said, though he wanted to leave.

'You see, I worked at the Ministry of the Economy for sixteen years, and do you know what my job was?'

Bordelli waited in silence for the answer, but the man wouldn't speak.

'Aren't you going to ask me what my job was?' the *cavaliere* said after a pause.

'Sorry . . . What was it?'

'But, were you about to go somewhere?'

'It doesn't matter. Go ahead.'

'Oh, don't worry about me, sir, I have a lot of time on my hands,' the man said with an unhappy smile. 'Where was I?'

'You were telling me about your job at the ministry.'

'Ah, yes . . . and had you already asked me what my job was?'

'I think so, yes.'

'Good. My job was the following: I had to report, at the end of each trimester, the volume of sausages produced in a depressed area of Basilicata . . . Are you sure I'm not boring you?'

'Please, go on,' said Bordelli. They were standing in the sun at two o'clock in the afternoon, but the *cavaliere* seemed not to notice.

'I'm from a town near Turin, you see, but I won't tell you which because I'm sure you don't know it. To move house from there to the south was a big sacrifice, I can tell you.'

'I understand.'

'I had to submit my reports to the Central Office of the Ministry of the Economy. And I would type them up personally; I took my job very seriously.' The *cavaliere* looked him in the eye and spoke in a gentle voice. 'But one thing seemed very strange to me, and do you know what that was?'

'What?' asked Bordelli, ready this time.

'The fact that the ministry never once sent a reply, or any sort of communication at all. Absolute silence. Aside from my salary, of course, a little green receipt that alerted me that my postal account had been credited. That's all.'

'Really?'

'On my word of honour. Never a letter, never a phone call, and if I ever tried calling, the line was always busy. So, do you know what I did?'

'What did you do?'

'I did the following: one day I got on a train and went to Rome. I wanted to find out why I had never received any official communication . . . aside from my salary, of course, a little green receipt that . . . but I've already told you that, haven't I?'

'I think so, yes.'

'Anyway, I left for Rome and, without telling anybody, I went straight to the ministry's offices. They didn't want to let me in, because they'd never seen me before, and said I had to identify myself. In the end they let me go and look for the man in charge of production analysis for the south, and I found him doing the crossword! But that's of no interest. Do you know what I discovered?'

'What?'

'I discovered the following: that all my reports were there, still in their unopened envelopes, bound together by a strip of glued paper. Sixty-three envelopes, never opened. Can you imagine?'

'How is that possible?'

'The fact is that nobody had ever read even one of those reports. Just think!'

'I have no words.'

'When I asked for an explanation, do you know what they said?'

'What did they say?'

'They said the following: that those statistics were of no use to anyone, and that my studies were pointless. The reason for my job was something else, I forget what, something to do with politics. And so, do you know how I felt?'

'How did you feel?'

'Bad, very bad. I simply can't resign myself to the fact that I spent sixteen years doing a useless job.' The *cavaliere* gave a sad smile. 'And what do you do, Signor . . . Brodello?'

'Bordelli. I'm a police inspector.'

'A pleasure. Cavalier Aldo Affumicato. Could I have a minute of your time? I've got some things to say, and I don't know who to talk to.' He held out his cold hand, and Bordelli shook it.

'Listen, Cavaliere, why don't you just forget about everything and take a nice holiday?'

'Do you think I should?'

'I think it would do you good.'

'Then, you know what I'll do?'

'What?'

'I'm going to go to the ministry and ask them to give me an important assignment. What do you think? Should I do that?'

'I really don't know.'

'Yes, I think that's what I'll do . . . And what do you do, Signor Brodello?'

It was a difficult half-hour, but in the end the inspector managed to free himself. He got into his Beetle and drove off. The heat in the car took his breath away.

As Diotivede must be fairly well along at this point, Bordelli dropped in at Forensic Medicine. As soon as he walked into the laboratory, he felt revived; the temperature was decidedly pleasant in there. The doctor was travelling through the tiny, vast world of the microscope. He heard Bordelli come in, but didn't move. At the back of the room was the slab with the body of Signora Pedretti-Strassen. The sheet covering her had a dark stain over the belly.

'You know, Diotivede, if I had your job, I don't know if I could ever eat liver . . . or tripe.'

'I don't see why.'

'Don't tell me you can't imagine.'

Diotivede looked up from the microscope and saw the world life-size again.

'Haven't you anything to do at the office?' he said, glaring at him. Bordelli realised he was once again treading on delicate turf. Not that Diotivede was a touchy sort, but he did have trouble tolerating certain things. All jokes and clichés about those who made their living cutting corpses open irritated him. People had been trying his patience with such rubbish for decades. He felt that his job was like any other and, moreover, he liked it. He thought he was no different from a carpenter or a painter, and it irked him that others didn't realise this. Bordelli knew this and liked to rib him about it, just so he could see the vaguely childish vexation on the doctor's face. But he also knew when to stop, and so he immediately changed the subject.

'Have you got anything for me yet?' he said. The doctor continued to fiddle with his slides.

'Do you need to know right away or can you wait for the report?' Diotivede asked.

'You know I don't like to wait.'

The doctor sighed, abandoned his labours and came towards him, removing his gloves.

'The lady died about nine o'clock, from a violent asthma attack that triggered cardiac arrest. But the best part is that there was definitely Asthmaben in the Asthmaben bottle, but no trace in the drop I took from the glass.'

'Listen—'

'And that's not all. There was no trace of the medicine in her blood, either, nor in her stomach. Whereas there was a great deal on her tongue.'

'As if someone had poured the medicine into her mouth after she was already dead . . .'

Diotivede gave one of his rare, brief smiles, a sort of puckering of the lips that was decipherable only to those who knew him well, but wasn't necessarily the prelude to an amusing statement. Indeed, he said only:

'It's up to you to discover whether that's true.' He seemed glad not to have to concern himself with it.

The inspector snorted.

'Fingerprints?' he asked.

'A great many, all belonging to the deceased.'

'Have you analysed the pages of the book?'

'Nothing of interest.'

Bordelli bit off a fingernail. It had broken halfway and kept getting caught on the fabric of his pocket every time he stuck his hand in.

'Anything else?' he asked. The doctor went and washed his hands at the laboratory's tiny sink.

'At the moment, no, but I haven't finished yet.'

'Keep me posted. Now, I need to buck up and go back down to Africa.'

Diotivede gave a sly smile.

'Is it really so hot in your offices?'

'We're training for hell.'

'Well, in that case, I'll drop by from time to time.' Then he returned to Signora Pedretti's slab with a scalpel between his fingers. The inspector left him to his beloved work and climbed back into his Beetle to return to the office. He had a long, useless afternoon ahead of him. The only sure thing was his appointment with Piras at half past nine that evening, to discuss and take stock of the situation. When he pulled into the court-yard at headquarters, he was bathed in sweat. There wasn't a breath of wind; clothes stuck to the skin like leeches. Still, spending the month of August in the city also had its advantages: the corridors were less noisy, and Dr Inzipone was on holiday with his family.

Bordelli pulled up in front of Botta's place. The sky was becoming overcast; the humidity was unbearable. The only hope was that it might rain. Botta lived in Via del Campuccio, in a basement flat a few blocks from the inspector's. They had known each other for almost fifteen years. Bordelli wasn't yet forty years old at the time. Ennio Bottarini, the burglar known as 'Botta', had been caught lowering himself down the outer wall of a villa. Two policemen on bicycles happened to be passing by at the same moment, and Botta jumped down right in front of them. A case of very bad luck. They had found a bit of everything in his pockets: necklaces, a gold watch, a bronze statuette of a naked Venus, and even a glass ashtray.

At the station the thief had started philosophising, holding forth on certain injustices that nobody understood, and since he couldn't get so much as a dog to listen to him, he set his sights on Assistant Inspector Bordelli. He asked for him with such insistence, and with so many words, that in the end they gave him his way just to be rid of him. Even back then, Botta already bore the signs of a hard, wretched life on his face. Small and agile, he had the eyes of an ignorant genius, which won Bordelli's sympathy at once.

'Mr Inspector, I am pleased to meet you in person at last.'

'I'm still an assistant inspector.'

'Not for long, Inspector, not for long.'

'Why did you want to see me?'

'I'm called "Botta", Inspector. I just know you'll be able to understand me. My friends have told me that you're someone who sees things straight.'

'Which of your friends?'

'Gino Gamba and "the Beast".' Two smugglers.

'Go on,' said Bordelli.

'Look at me, Inspector. Do I look like a criminal? I haven't even got a jackknife on me. I break into the villas of millionaires, rich people whose knick-knacks could feed me for a year. And so I go in and take a couple of these stupid gewgaws just to get by; but if I'm caught, I get five years. Now, you tell me if that's fair.'

The assistant inspector knew that the little burglar was right.

'How many times have you been locked up, Bottarini?' he asked him.

'Not very many, at least not in Italy.'

'So you've worked abroad as well?'

Botta gave a start in his chair.

'You see, Inspector? You said "you've worked" and not "you've robbed" . . . I knew you would understand.'

'Not so fast, Botta, not so fast . . .'

They kept on talking a while longer of this and that. Botta started describing the peculiarities of various European prisons, the differences between Spanish warders and Turkish warders; it was a kind of anthropology lesson, an enriching experience. This was not just any common thief. In the end the assistant inspector had taken him home, and they dined together, tripe and onions, washed down with a foul wine that Botta knocked back by the pitcherful.

At the trial Bordelli had done everything possible to have him given the minimum sentence. In the end he got ten months, but was released after four for good behaviour. Ever since, they had remained friends of a sort. Sometimes they would dine together at Dal Lordo, in Via dell'Orto. Or else they would spend an evening together on the banks of the Arno, exchanging stories about the war. Every so often they would fall out of touch and then meet back up again. It was only a year ago, at Christmas time, that Bordelli had discovered that Botta was a born cook. The little thief had put together a French dinner that was hard to forget.

Bordelli tapped on the windowpane of Botta's basement with the keys to his Volkswagen.

'Are you there, Ennio?'

The window opened slightly.

'Inspector!'

'I hope I'm not disturbing you.'

'I'll be right with you.'

A good minute later, the front door giving on to the street opened up, and Botta appeared wearing a housewife's apron.

'Hello, Inspector, I was just making coffee.'

Descending the stairs into Botta's lair, Bordelli noticed a strange burnt smell.

'What are you cooking?' he asked.

'Nothing edible, Inspector. I'm doing a little job for a friend.'

'A "little job"?'

'Ancient coins. I boil them in mud to age them.'

'A swindle, in other words.'

'No, no, it's a way to make the tourists happy.'

'Well, when you put it that way . . .'

As they entered the flat the coffee pot started whistling. It felt better in there than on the street; the three steps down made all the difference. Botta's home consisted of two large, gloomy rooms, arranged with a certain care despite the modesty of means. One was the bedroom, with a bed and and an old wardrobe for clothes; and the other was a kitchen as well as sitting room, 'work' room and every other kind of room possible. Hanging on one wall was a framed photo of Fred Astaire in motion. Ennio had a burning passion for dance, never fulfilled for want of means. But, like all sentimentalists, he had many other passions as well.

Bordelli saw some ten or so half-dismantled wristwatches on the table.

'Looks like you're starting another "little job" the police ought not to know about.'

'Just changing the dial-plates, Inspector. That way, Forcella watches become Swiss.'

'I don't want to hear about it, Botta. Let's have this coffee.'

Ennio went and prepared the cups according to his personal method, with the sugar first, and any use of spoons forbidden.

'What brings you here, Inspector?'

'I was thinking about arranging a dinner at my place. What do you say?'

'When?'

'Got anything on for Wednesday?'

Botta reviewed his engagements in his mind, staring at the floor.

'Wednesday . . . Wednesday . . . Yes, I'd say that would be all right.'

'Good, I'll tell the others.'

'They'll be the same as last time, no?'

'Mind if I add a couple more?'

Ennio's face darkened.

'Policemen?' he asked.

'Don't worry, one is the son of an old friend, and the other is a scientist and friend to mice.'

'I've got no problem with that.'

'Okay, then, you're to make whatever you like. Just one wish, on the part of Diotivede.'

'If I'm up to the task . . .' Botta said, modestly.

'Bean soup *alla lombarda*. Just imagine, in this heat.'

Ennio brightened.

'Excuse me if I start drooling, Inspector, but that's one of my specialities. It doesn't matter if it's hot outside; I only have to find the right beans. And for the rest, I've already got something in mind.'

Now came the most delicate part of the operation, since Botta was a very sensitive man. Bordelli coughed into his hand and, with maximum nonchalance, pulled out his wallet, took out one ten-thousand-lira and two one-thousand-lira notes and laid them on the table.

'That should suffice,' he said.

Botta blushed.

'It's too much, Inspector. Take back the two thousand,' he said, putting the two notes back into Bordelli's hand. The inspector put them back on the table.

'You'll see, there won't be any change,' he said.

'You can tell a good cook by the way he shops, Inspector.'

'Well, if there's any left over, you can buy more wine.'

'Sooner or later, I'm going to buy you a fine dinner, I swear.'

Bordelli lowered his eyes.

'Never mind, Botta, you've already paid enough.' He patted him on the shoulder and left him to his watches with Swiss faces and Neapolitan hearts.

The heat in the street was ghastly. And there was no hint of rain. Bordelli tried to distract himself by thinking about the dinner and the guests. Was Dr Fabiani in town? He was an old, melancholy psychoanalyst who had made a strong impression on him. Bordelli had met him a year before, during the course of an investigation, and invited him to Christmas dinner with

Botta and Diotivede. It was a quiet, pleasant evening. Late into the night, each had told an old story from his past as they sipped cognac.

On his desk Bordelli found a handwritten note: *I must speak to you. I'll be back shortly. Zia Camilla.* Zia Camilla was Rodrigo's mother. Strange. She never called on him at headquarters. Bordelli expedited a couple of matters by telephone and finished reading the report of an arrest for murder. An unambiguous affair: a row, a knife, many witnesses. The killer was a young Calabrian male whose mother's virtue had been slandered. He had been in town for only a few days and didn't know that, in this part of Italy, slandering someone's mother was almost as common as saying 'Ciao'. A sad story of cultural misunderstanding. Bordelli got to the last lines: '. . . after which Bruno Pratesi addressed Salvatore Loporco with the words "son of a whore", whereupon Loporco took out a cutting instrument with a five-inch blade and set upon Pratesi, stabbing him repeatedly in the chest and abdomen, saying in dialect, "I'll teach you to talk about my dear mother that way". All witnesses concur in saying that Loporco etc . . .'

At that moment somebody knocked, and Mugnai's head popped inside the half-open door.

'Your aunt is here,' he said.

'Show her in.'

Zia Camilla was fat only from the waist down. She always wore a stunned expression and a hint of alarm in her eyes, but today more than usual. Bordelli got up to greet her.

'Zia, what's wrong?'

The woman set her shopping bags down on the chair in front of the desk and remained standing.

'I wanted to talk to you about Rodrigo. Lately he's been sort of strange,' she said in a worried tone.

'I saw him a couple of weeks ago, and he seemed fine . . . In the sense that he seemed normal.'

'It's only been these last few days . . .'

'In what way has he been strange?'

'He's just strange . . . A mother can feel these sorts of things.'
Bordelli sat down on a corner of the desk, thinking that Rodrigo
had always been a bit of a pill.

'Tell me more,' he said. Zia Camilla threw up her hands.

'He never goes outside any more, he doesn't shave, he
hardly ever answers the telephone, and when I call on him
he keeps me standing at the door and can't wait for me
to leave.'

'Wasn't it the same four years ago, when you gave his old
shoes to Father Cubattoli?'

'This time it's worse.'

'Really?'

'Why don't *you* pay him a call? Talk to him a little. Maybe
he'll confide in you.'

'Why would he do that?'

'You're his cousin . . . and you're a detective.'

'For him those are points against me.'

'Just pay him a little visit. Do it for me. I'm worried.'

'All right, Zia, I'll try ringing him later.'

'And what if he doesn't answer?'

'Then I'll go and see him at home.'

'Promise?'

'Promise.'

'Thank you, dear. God bless you.' She stood up on tiptoe
to kiss him and stroked his cheek with her fingers. Bordelli saw
her out, carrying her shopping bags for her.

'Ciao, Zia, give my best to Zio Franco.'

'Thank you, dear.'

'I'll phone you as soon as I've got any news.'

From the window the inspector watched Zia Camilla walk
briskly across the courtyard's flagstones. At seventy-three, she
was still strong and healthy. She was his father's sister, which
gave him hope for the Bordelli line. It would take an accident
to make him die young. Which was, in fact, what happened
with his father, Amedeo Bordelli, a big, burly man with the

broad, handsome face of a good-hearted boxer, who fell from a window while painting the shutter-latches.

The inspector returned to his office and saw that it was almost eight o'clock. His appointment with Piras was for half past nine. As he didn't have much appetite, he went out for a bite in the bar across the street and then bought a couple of cold beers. He put one in the bottom drawer of the filing cabinet and then uncapped the other with his house key. During the fifteen years he'd been working in that office, not once had he ever remembered to bring a bottle opener from home. Lighting a cigarette, he dialled Rodrigo's number. He let it ring for a long time, but there was no reply. He redialled the number half an hour later, with the same result. What a pain in the arse. Now he would actually have to go there. He had no desire to talk to Rodrigo, but since he'd promised Zia Camilla, he couldn't back out. Well, there were worse things in life than a peevish, pedantic cousin. Anyway, he was curious to find out what was behind this business of not shaving . . . He had never seen Rodrigo unshaven.

Round about nine o'clock the heat in his office became unbearable. It was like being caught between the fingers of a gigantic hot and sweaty hand. Bordelli didn't feel like going home. He lit another cigarette, his fourth or fifth, he couldn't remember. Not a bad tally, he thought. A few months ago, by that hour he would already have smoked a good thirty. There was still a little light outside. Clouds were still gathering, every so often you could hear some distant thunder, but still no rain. A good downpour would have made the night a little less asphyxiating.

Bordelli picked up the receiver and dialled Fabiani's number. The psychoanalyst was very pleased to be invited to dinner. He, too, always stayed put in August. He seemed in good spirits, though there was, as always, a note of deep sadness in his voice. When Bordelli had first met him, Fabiani was still tormented by remorse over a work-related incident that had ended tragically. It gave him no peace. They agreed on dinner and said goodbye.

Bordelli sat in silence, staring into space. Without knowing how, he found himself thinking about the woman of his life, the one he had never found. He tried to picture her, to imagine what she might look like, but he couldn't see anything. He had no precise idea of her, but he was certain that if she stood right in front of him, he would know at once that she was the one. And it would be a triumph. Then he realised that by now it was getting late. If he found her now, at fifty-three, it would only be a defeat. Maybe he'd done everything wrong. He had always been waiting for something special, the way little girls believe in Prince Charming, languishing in their illusions. Falling in love with the wrong women had only reinforced his desire to find the right one, making him more and more rigid and hard to please. Sometimes, just to escape the loneliness, he would throw himself into brief, sordid relationships with women who didn't understand him and only left him wanting to be alone. And now here he was, fifty-three years old, his only satisfaction that of having the same dream in his head, but with no hope of fulfilling it. He took comfort in the thought that he could never have done otherwise, and if he were reborn he would do the very same things. A heroic melancholy enveloped his head like a hot rag . . . Bordelli, the solitary knight, beloved of all women . . .

At 9.30 sharp, there was a knock at the door. Rousing himself, Bordelli felt ashamed of his silly dreams.

'Come in.'

It was Piras. He walked in and remained standing in front of the desk.

'Any news, Inspector?'

'One thing. But don't just stand there, sit down.'

Piras dropped into the chair, impatient for Bordelli to speak. Chasing the remaining scraps of dream from his head with the help of a sigh, the inspector readied himself to satisfy the Sardinian's curiosity.

'It's no longer a game, Piras. Signora Pedretti was murdered.'
And he told him in minute detail what he had learned from
Diotivede. Piras's mouth tightened.

'Interesting,' he said.

Bordelli denied himself another cigarette, pleased at such
willpower, and reclined in his chair, bending the springy back.

'Are you free Wednesday evening?'

'I get off work at eight.'

'I'm having a dinner party at my place, a little thing among
friends. Care to join us? I should warn you I'm the youngest
of the lot.'

Piras looked visibly pleased.

'That's fine with me, Inspector. I'll bring some Sardinian
pastries.'

'I'll bet they're *papassinos*.'

'How did you know?'

Bordelli smiled and recalled a cold morning in '44.

'Once, during a mortar attack, your father explained to me
in great detail how those biscuits are made, and I've been
wanting to taste one ever since. But I wanted to tell you another
thing. Tomorrow at noon, Signora Pedretti's two nephews are
coming to see me. I want you to be there, too. You can man
the typewriter and write the report, but mostly I want you to
try to figure out what's going through their heads.'

'That's fine with me.'

Piras left. After a few minutes of listless reflection, Bordelli
slapped himself on the forehead.

'Rodrigo,' he said. He immediately dialled his cousin's
number and let the phone ring for a long time, but it was no
use. Bordelli hung up and promised himself he would drop by
his cousin's place the following day. He was becoming seriously
intrigued by this business of not shaving.

A little rain fell around midnight, so sparse you could count
the drops. They were as big as eggs and splatted on the road
with a slapping sound, evaporating in seconds on the still-hot

asphalt. Bordelli had lain down in bed with a book by Fenoglio on his belly. Even immobile, he still sweated. A moribund fly kept going from one end of the room to the other, ceaselessly crashing against the walls in search of a way out. The mosquitoes were having a ball in the only apartment in town without DDT. Reading was impossible. It was easier to sink into the usual unwholesome melancholy. Warm gusts of wind blew through the wide-open windows, and still more mosquitoes, and the creaking sounds of old bicycles. Now and then a lone automobile, or a faraway train. Vito, known as Vinaccia, also passed by. He was an old alcoholic who talked to himself. He never left the San Frediano quarter. Bordelli recognised his stumbling, wine-sodden step. The drunk was muttering to himself, in the usual angry tone. The inspector set aside Fenoglio and turned off the light. He heard Vito stop to catch his breath. Then he suddenly raised his voice.

'They're all whores, the lot of 'em . . . nothin' you can do about it . . . all whores . . .'

Poor Vito. Bordelli heard him set off again with difficulty, cursing through clenched teeth. Then he stopped at the end of the street and started yelling the same things as before. He even banged on the steel shutters of a few shops, choked on his own voice, coughed to the point of fainting, and then, after spitting theatrically, resumed his grumbling. In the penumbra of the bedroom, Bordelli remembered another old madman from many years before, also an alcoholic who talked to himself. People called him Villoresi, but nobody knew his real name. Nor did anyone know how old he was. He had a monstrous nose exploding in the middle of his face like dripping wax, dilated pores as red as open wounds, two pale blue imbecilic eyes popping out of his death's-head as though blown out from within by force, and a rotten, perpetually open mouth. He dragged himself about, holding up walls with one hand, taking short little steps, like Vito, always speaking aloud to someone who wasn't there, question and answer in quick repartee, almost always angry, head dangling to one side. He would spit out insults at an invisible enemy and curse him for eternity. Whenever any women saw him approach, they would cross to the other side of the street, avoiding his gaze. Realising this, he would start yelling.

'Fucking whores! Yeah, you wish! Fucking whores is what you are! . . .'

He had a deep, hoarse voice, and the more he yelled, the more his imprecations stuck in his throat, his face turning red from the effort. Children were a little afraid of him and used to taunt him for the thrill of it. They would hide round street corners and shout a name at him – 'Bertolaniiiii!' – which functioned as a sort of magic word that, for obscure reasons, made him fly into a rage. 'Bertolani! Bertolaniiiii!' Villoresi would straighten himself with a start and look all around to stare down the culprit, screaming a litany of curses against the whole world: 'Damned pigs . . . sons of whoring sows . . . I'll kick your arses one by one . . .' The children would take to their heels, pursued by his oaths.

Almost everyone in the neighbourhood was fond of the old man. If a day went by without any sign of him, they would ask one another: 'Where's Villoresi?'

Bordelli swatted at a mosquito humming in his ear. It was even hotter than before. The weary buzzing of the fly had not ceased for a single moment. He closed his eyes, hoping to fall asleep, and before drifting off he saw a medieval village from the Marches region whose name he couldn't remember. To enable the Allies' tanks to pass through, they'd had to widen the streets by chiselling away the stones of the houses.

Anselmo was utterly unlike how Bordelli had imagined him: chubby, with beady, suffering eyes, a tuft of greasy hair atop his head. He had a troubled air about him and an oily face, and looked about thirty years old or a little less. He sat on the chair as if he was forever about to get up. He folded his sweaty hands, then wiped them on his trousers. He kept sticking his forefinger inside his shirt collar, as if he needed air. He genuinely seemed the anxious type, the kind who flush the toilet before they've finished pissing. One felt nervous just looking at him. Yet his voice was strangely calm and even. He was well dressed and wore a very serious-looking tie.

His brother Giulio was younger, also fat, also a 'doctor'. The same flabby face as Anselmo, the same pain-filled eyes, but a lot more hair and a more colourful tie.

The heat had reached dangerous levels. Anselmo was having difficulty breathing.

'Well, here we are, Inspector. Why did you want to see us?' he said with a cold smile. Bordelli looked over at Piras, seated at the typewriter across the room.

'Just a few questions,' he said.

'Very well.'

Bordelli sighed wearily and looked Anselmo straight in the eye.

'Signor Morozzi, where were you on Thursday evening between eight and ten o'clock?'

The sweat was dripping from Anselmo's chin. He took out a handkerchief and wiped his face.

'In what sense, Inspector? . . . I mean, why are you asking me this?'

'You're not the only one I'm asking. I also want an answer from your brother.' Giulio shuffled his feet on the floor.

'Me? On Thursday?' he said in a falsetto. Anselmo cut him off.

'We were at the beach,' he said.

'Where, exactly?'

'Cinquale.'

'Did you stay in or go out?'

'We ate out, then went dancing late into the night, at a club on the waterfront.'

Giulio confirmed the story with a nod. Anselmo rested one hand on the edge of the desk, leaving a wet imprint behind. He was panting softly.

'But, if I may ask, what has this to do with the matter of . . .'

He didn't finish his sentence, but just stared at the inspector, face shiny with sweat. Bordelli decided not to beat about the bush and to get straight to the point. He turned to Giulio, who was also sweating profusely.

'Your aunt was very wealthy, as you know. In cases such as these, it's always best to check whether any of the heirs tried to force the hand of fate.'

'The hand of fate?' said Giulio, eyes narrowing. He seemed weaker than his brother. Of the two, he was clearly the one who followed; he looked at Anselmo with admiration, under the sway of a charisma that he alone could see. Bordelli observed him carefully.

'You're direct heirs, aren't you?' he said.

The two brothers exchanged a quick glance. They moved about in their chairs, as if stalling. Giulio turned round to look at the inscrutable Piras, for only a second. Anselmo wiped his face again.

'There's also our uncle, Zia Rebecca's brother,' he said.

'Well, a good part would go to you. At least half, I believe.' Giulio looked shocked.

'That's certainly not our fault,' he said.

'No, but it usually constitutes a good motive,' said Bordelli.

Anselmo gave his brother a dirty look, then tried to set things right with a smile.

'But our auntie died of asthma, didn't she?'

Bordelli started drumming his fingers on the desk.

'Are you ready to start writing, Piras?'

'Ready.'

The inspector looked at one then the other brother – especially Giulio, who seemed more sensitive to psychological pressure.

'Good. Tell me the names of the restaurant and the night-club where you went to make merry, and the exact times of arrival and departure at both places.'

Piras's typewriter suddenly started clacking. Anselmo gulped and began to tremble slightly. He seemed deeply offended.

'What is the meaning of this? Why all these questions? Are we suspects? And what of? Our aunt died of asthma, didn't she?'

'It's not clear yet. I'm waiting for some test results. If it turns out your aunt died of natural causes, so much the better for everyone. But for now there are many doubts.'

'Doubts? What kind of doubts?'

'Dr Morozzi, I didn't say you killed her. I only meant that it may not have been an accident.'

'Then why all these questions?'

'Yes, why?' said Giulio, emboldened by his brother. Bordelli shrugged.

'You shouldn't worry too much about it. It's just a formality, a procedure we have to go through. I'm sorry.'

The typewriter had fallen silent. Giulio raised a finger to ask whether he could speak, as if at school.

'Should we call our lawyer?' he asked. The inspector threw his hands up.

'Do whatever you like, I don't mind. But I repeat, there's nothing to worry about. If this was a real interrogation, I wouldn't be questioning the two of you together, now, would I?'

Giulio looked at his brother, as if asking him to decide. Anselmo shrugged.

'Well, if it's only a formality . . .' he said.

Bordelli leaned lazily forward in his chair, resting his elbows on the desk.

'So, in the meantime, what do you say we have a beer?'

The two brothers nodded, then exchanged a look of surprise. The inspector glanced over at Piras.

'Will you have one too?'

'It's fine with me.'

Bordelli dialled an internal extension.

'Mugnai, could you go to the bar on the corner and pick up four beers? Just put it on our account and tell 'em I'll drop by later.'

Giulio pulled out a rolled-up handkerchief and started wiping his face. By this point Anselmo had two fingers planted firmly inside his collar, as if he were afraid of being strangled by his tie. They all sat in silence, as if they couldn't talk before the beers arrived. Bordelli leaned back in his chair and stared at the Morozzi brothers' ties, spellbound. He had always thought a tie was a very strange thing, a tongue of fabric that hangs from the neck . . . and when you reach out to grab the salt, it ends up in your soup. It had never made sense to him. He must have two or three of his own in a wardrobe somewhere, old gifts from women who hadn't really understood him and wanted him to be different from what he was. As he began to drift off into old memories, Mugnai knocked at the door.

'Your beer, Inspector.'

'You're as quick as lightning.'

Mugnai glanced in passing at the sweat-soaked brothers and walked out, waddling like a seal. Bordelli reached into a drawer and pulled out some paper cups, flipped off the bottle caps with his house keys and handed the brothers their beers. Piras got up to get his and immediately returned to the typewriter. All four took long, cool draughts. Giulio even shut his eyes in relief.

'All right, then, tell me the names of the restaurant and the nightclub,' said Bordelli.

'The restaurant is called Il Coccodrillo,' said Anselmo. 'We reserved a table. You can check, if you like.'

'I will, don't you worry about that.'

Anselmo looked offended. He was about to say something when Giulio impulsively cut in.

'And then we went dancing at the Mecca,' he said.

Bordelli let his eyelids droop, with the look of someone who has a long afternoon ahead of him and is in no hurry.

'What time did you get to the restaurant?'

'Half past eight. Right, Giulio?'

'Yes, yes.'

'And what time did you leave?'

'Roughly, about ten thirty . . . right, Giulio?'

'Yes, yes, about ten thirty . . . more or less.'

'And did you go dancing straight away, or did you do something else first?'

'Straight away.'

'And how late did you stay?'

'We were the last to leave . . . right, Giulio?'

'Yes, yes, the very last.'

Bordelli looked over at Piras.

'Did you write that down, Piras?'

'Certainly did, Inspector.'

'Good. What time does this Mecca close?'

'At five o'clock, right, Giulio?'

'Yes, five.'

'Were you alone?'

'We were with our wives, Inspector. But at the Mecca we ran into a friend, who was also with his wife. They're from Milan.'

'Yes, yes, from Milan.'

'And you all stayed there together until five o'clock in the morning?'

'No, Inspector, the Milanese couple left much earlier, round midnight, I think . . . They have a small child . . . Right, Giulio?'

'Yes, a little boy.'

Bordelli was beginning to think that at any moment the Morozzi brothers would take each other by the hand.

'And neither of you has any children?' he asked.

'Not yet . . . Why?'

'Just curious.'

Bordelli waited for Piras to finish clacking, then continued.

'What's the name of your Milanese friends?'

Anselmo took a deep breath.

'Salvetti. He owns a zip factory. In the summer they stay at the villa next to ours, at Cinquale.'

Bordelli started to massage his chin, looking pensive, like someone trying to grasp a hidden truth. The Morozzi brothers looked at him with suspicion.

'When did you last see your aunt?'

'A couple of weeks ago, before leaving for the coast,' said Anselmo.

And his brother: 'Yes, yes, a couple of weeks ago, a fortnight, more or less . . .'

The inspector was beginning to feel a powerful antipathy towards the two brothers. But he couldn't let this influence him. He was well aware that murderers are very often quite likeable.

'What sort of relations did you have with your aunt? I want you, Giulio, to answer me first.'

Giulio gave a start, as if he had just sat on a pin.

'What sort of relations? Well, I'd say . . . rather good relations. Eh, Anselmo?'

'Oh, yes . . . I'd say so myself, good relations . . . Quite good.'

Bordelli paused for a moment for Piras's sake, taking advantage of the lull to finish his beer, which had already gone warm.

'And what can you tell me about the inheritance?'

'In what sense, may I ask?'

'It's a whole lot of money. The villa alone must be worth many millions, no?'

There was a momentary flash of joy in Anselmo's eyes, but he quickly suppressed it. Tilting his head sideways, he threw up his hands.

'Well, what can we do about that?' he said in the tone of someone who has just punctured a tyre.

'It's certainly not our fault,' Giulio confirmed.

Bordelli felt almost fascinated by these two imbeciles.

'What sort of work do you do?' he asked.

'We deal in property. Why?' Anselmo asked, alarmed.

'Why are you getting upset? I only need it for the report.'

'I'm certainly not upset. Do I seem upset to you? Why should I get upset?'

'What kind of car do you drive?' asked Bordelli, ignoring Anselmo's questions.

'What's the car got to do with this?'

'Just to make conversation.'

Giulio gulped, sounding like the bathroom sink.

'A Fiat 600 Multipla,' said Anselmo.

'Me too,' said Giulio.

'But when we go to the coast we take only one car.'

Biting an unlit cigarette, Bordelli got ready to ask the final questions.

'And what can you tell me about your Uncle Dante?'

Both brothers smiled idiotically.

'Uncle Dante? He's a bit strange, someone with a couple of screws loose . . . Right, Giulio?'

'Yes, yes, a bit strange, very strange, in fact,' he said with a giggle.

Bordelli could no longer bear to listen to them or to see their faces.

'Strange in what sense?' he asked, looking at them with malice. Anselmo shrugged.

'He stays shut up in a great big room all day, mixing chemicals and building gadgets that are totally useless,' he said with a certain disdain. Bordelli remembered Dante's broad, unruly face and felt great compassion for the whimsical giant who jumped from one subject to another when he spoke. Talking to him was like entering another world, where imagination, play and intellectual freedom were more important than anything else. It irked the inspector to hear others refer to him as mad.

'Dr Morozzi, how long has it been since you last saw your Uncle Dante?'

'Maybe three months, maybe four,' said Anselmo.

Bordelli looked at Giulio.

'And you?'

'Me too, yes. We always go there together, to see my uncle.'

Bordelli gestured as if to conclude.

'Piras, could you read the transcript back to us, please?' he said. Piras stopped his clattering, pulled the sheet from the typewriter and stood up, scraping the legs of his chair on the floor.

Planting himself next to the Morozzis, he read the questions and answers in an indifferent voice, gave the report to the inspector, and returned to his post. Bordelli handed the transcript to the two brothers and leaned back in his chair.

'If everything's all right with you, please sign at the bottom.' The Morozzis hesitated for a moment, then signed, wetting the document with sweat. Bordelli looked first at Anselmo, and then at Giulio, staring long and hard at them.

'Good. Now we're all done,' he said. At the sound of these words, Anselmo's flabby face relaxed. But after a calculated pause, Bordelli added:

'. . . for the moment, that is.'

Both brothers gave a start. Giulio looked at Anselmo as if awaiting a reply.

'What do you mean, *for the moment?*' Anselmo asked.

The inspector tried to seem as polite and contrite as possible, as if wanting to apologise for the inescapable annoyances of bureaucracy.

'I'm sorry about your holiday, but unfortunately I must ask you not to leave the city until the investigation is over.'

'What investigation, Inspector?'

'You want to tell them, Piras?'

Piras stood up and planted himself beside the desk.

'The post-mortem results clearly show that Signora Pedretti-Strassen was murdered,' he said with great gusto.

Giulio grabbed hold of his brother's elbow, lower lip dangling like a ripe fig. Anselmo squirmed in his chair, and when he spoke his voice came out hoarse.

'No, I'm sorry, Inspector, perhaps I've misunderstood . . . First you said you didn't know anything yet . . . and that, actually, it was almost certain that . . . Aunt . . .'

Bordelli hunched his shoulders and made the face of someone who had to suffer the whims of fate.

'It's a nasty job, being a policeman. Sometimes we're forced to tell lies . . . though always with the best of intentions, of course.'

Both brothers stammered some half-formed words, opening and closing their sweaty hands like two newborns.

'But does that mean . . . we're considered suspects?' asked Anselmo, eyes popping.

'I'd say so,' Bordelli said serenely, fiddling with his pen. Anselmo made a weary gesture of rebellion.

'That doesn't seem right to me, Inspector. Why didn't you tell us that to start with? It just doesn't seem right. We're honest people. We work like slaves year round . . . And now you come and tell us that . . . we're suspects! This is really . . . unacceptable!'

Carried away and perhaps fascinated by his own voice and courage, he was about to slam his hand down on the desk when he looked at Bordelli and froze, hand in the air. Wiping away a drop of sweat from one eye, he said again, in falsetto:

'We're honest people . . .'

Piras intervened of his own accord.

'We merely need to confirm your alibis, nothing more. If you're innocent, you have nothing to fear,' he said, exchanging a complicitous glance with Bordelli. In the dead silence someone's stomach gurgled audibly. Giulio blushed and pressed a hand to his belly. Bordelli smiled coldly.

'You can go now,' he said, crossing his arms. Anselmo loosened his tie and stood up, gasping for air, lips moving like a fish's. He had left a sweaty imprint on the chair. He took Giulio by the arm and made him stand up.

'Let's go,' he said, looking deeply offended.

'Piras, see them out for me, if you would,' said Bordelli, lighting the cigarette he had kept unlit in his mouth for God knows how long.

The two brothers turned their backs and went out, escorted by Piras. Although the windows in the corridor were all open, the air was stagnant and stifling. Anselmo took laboured steps, dragging his feet, his brother panting behind him, staring at the back of his head. Their wives were waiting for them in the street, both blonde, in high heels and dressed for the beach, ready to return to the coast. Their stylish, oversized sunglasses made them look like two giant insects. They all climbed into a blazing Fiat 600 Multipla without saying a word, and drove off. All of Anselmo's rage could be heard in the way he shifted the gears.

Piras returned and, seeing the smoke rising to the ceiling, waved his hand to dispel it.

'So, Piras, what do you make of the dear brothers?'

Piras shrugged.

'Not exactly the most likeable pair I've ever met,' he said.

Bordelli started drumming his fingers on the transcript.

'Tomorrow dress in civvies. We're going to the beach.'

It was hotter than hell in Totò's kitchen. The oily, burning smoke stuck to the skin like glue, but the *baccalà alla livornese* was sublime, and the cool white wine went down without effort. Bordelli had rolled his sleeves up past the elbow. Totò was cleaning squid in the sink. He was in the middle of a monologue, telling another of his blood-curdling stories about home. It was difficult to stop him.

'. . . and so, next day, pardon the language, they found him in a straw hut with a fish shoved up his arse, one of those fishes with prickles on its back, the kind that go in easy but come out hard, if you get the picture . . .'

'You wouldn't happen to have a little more *baccalà*, Totò, would you?'

'Certainly, Inspector.'

'Just a little bit.' Totò went to get the pan and dished out another whole serving, with lots of sauce. It was like starting lunch all over again, wine and all. Bordelli didn't even try to protest; he knew it was no use. The only way to spare himself would have been not to ask for anything. Totò went back to skinning his squid and resumed his story.

'It took them all night to pull it out, Inspector. You can imagine the screams.' He recounted all the details of the procedure from A to Z, with due respect to the victim, of course.

Then he launched into another story, someone who had had his ear cut off.

'And then they made him eat it, just like that, raw. He had to swallow the whole thing.'

Bordelli swallowed his last bite of *baccalà*.

'Don't you know any nice love stories, Totò?'

'Of course I do, Inspector.' And while removing the bone from the squid, he told the story of a certain Antonino, some poor bloke who wanted to marry the daughter of a rich landowner. Naturally they told him to keep away and slammed the door in his face, and so one night, Antonino sneaked on to the landowner's property and set fire to the wheat.

'I was just a little kid, but I can still see it, Inspector. The smoke was visible for twenty miles around. People came from all the neighbouring towns to watch. There was a good sea breeze and the fire charged ahead like a stampede of horses. Not one grain of wheat was spared.'

Not waiting to hear what kind of end poor Antonino came to, Bordelli got up to leave.

'Duty calls, Totò.'

'You won't have a coffee?'

'I'll have it at the office.'

'Come back soon, Inspector.'

'Where else would I go?'

'I say it for your sake, Inspector. In the coming days I'm going to make swordfish my own special way.'

'I'll be sure not to miss it.'

Walking out on to the street, Bordelli ran into a wall of heat. It was half past two. The air quivered incandescently above the asphalt. A large yellow cat was sleeping open-mouthed on the seat of a Lambretta, undone by the heat.

Before getting into his Volkswagen, Bordelli opened all the windows. The plastic covering of the seats was soft and emitted a noxious, sickly-sweet smell. Down the street came a Motobécane racing bicycle, ridden by a man wearing only underpants and singing. Bordelli envied him with all his heart.

Then he summoned his courage and got into his Beetle. The side vents, opened all the way, deflected the wind on to him, but it made little difference. The steering wheel was so hot he could only manoeuvre it with one finger. The white wine he had drunk was behaving in the usual fashion: it goes down easily, but then suddenly your ears start ringing. It was impossible to visit Totò without endangering one's health. All the same, it was fun to sit down in his kitchen to eat and chat, watching the greasiest cook in the world at work, four foot eleven inches of peasant joy. Bordelli would definitely have included him in the hypothetical, impossible family he sometimes imagined for himself in his old age: a farmhouse in the vineyards, six or seven faithful friends, walks in the country, endless dinners and an avalanche of memories, listening to or telling stories of the past by the fire in winter, or under the pergola in summer, with the crickets filling your ears. And every so often – why not? – a round of *bocce* behind the kitchen garden. Diotivede, by then pushing a hundred, could care for wounded animals, Botta and Totò would be fixtures in the kitchen, Fabiani the shrink could attend to bouts of depression, and Rosa could brighten the cloistered life with her immaculate naivety. He could even imagine the visionary Dante there, who would charm everyone with gadgets for cutting mozzarella or peeling bananas.

Before going back to the office he decided to drop in on old Gastone in Borgo Tegolaio. He wanted him to hear the VW backfire a couple of times. Gastone's garage was where Tenaglia worked, a great big lad who couldn't buy a lucky break and for whom Bordelli had found a job at the garage to keep him out of jail. He still hadn't gone to see him at work, but he'd heard that things were going pretty well. Tenaglia wanted nothing so much as to get his hands on automobile engines. It was almost a disease for him. He loved plunging into the entrails of cars to find the illness to cure, it had always been his dream. But usually nobody wanted to take on a guy like him; a gigantic ex-convict usually inspired fear. And so he had kept on stealing cars and driving them down to Naples. Old Gastone, however, had faith in Bordelli. He hired the kid and every so often would phone the inspector to thank him for sending the big lug his way.

Bordelli turned on to Borgo Tegolaio and pulled up in front of the garage. He immediately spotted Tenaglia's silhouette struggling with a Fiat 1005. Gastone was in a corner, cleaning something with a rag. Seeing the inspector walk in, they both dropped everything and came towards him, greasy hands extended.

'So, Inspector, what are you doing still in town while everyone else is roasting their bum on the beach?' said Gastone.

'And what about you two?'

Gastone gave a half-nod and smiled.

'We're crazy, Inspector,' he said. And he pulled out a bottle of port and three tavern glasses. There was no way to say no; they would have felt offended. Tenaglia's forehead was dripping sweat like a fountain, but he looked happy.

'Any problem with your armoured car, Inspector?' he asked.

'It keeps backfiring, as if it's got digestive problems.'

'Lemme have a listen; noises are my speciality,' said the giant.

'That's all I'm asking.'

'Get in and we'll give her a whirl.'

Gastone intervened.

'Just go alone, Tenaglia. You don't mind, do you, Inspector?'

'Of course not.'

That's funny, thought Bordelli. A car thief driving a policeman's car. Tenaglia went and scrubbed his hands so as not to dirty the steering wheel, then hopped into the VW and pushed the seat as far back as it could go, though he still had his knees in his mouth. Then he drove off in a manner quite unlike Bordelli's, as if pulling out from the starting gate at a racetrack. The roar of the engine at high throttle could be heard fading down the narrow, hazy streets. At the first downshift, a kind of shot rang out, as the Beetle continued down the road towards diagnosis.

Gastone took Bordelli by the elbow and led him into what he called his office: two square metres of linoleum and a small table strewn with incomprehensible sheets of paper. Gastone seemed in a confidential mood.

'Don't tell him, Inspector . . . but I've got no relatives, I have nobody. I've already been to see the solicitor . . . I'm going to leave the garage to him.'

'You always did say you wanted to leave it to someone who knew the ropes.'

Suddenly they heard the German rumble of the Beetle returning to base. An entirely new rumble, generated by Tenaglia's driving. The giant pulled the car into the garage, gunning the engine one last time and stepping out of the car with a smile on his lips.

'It's the spark ignition, Inspector. The petrol's not burning up completely in the cylinders, and so it pops in the pipes.'

'Is it serious?'

'We just gotta fix the carburation; I can do it in a jiffy.' He went to get a screwdriver and lifted the bonnet. Bordelli watched him open a small, mysterious box and delicately stick the screwdriver inside. A minute later Tenaglia raised his head.

'Start 'er up, Inspector.'

Bordelli obeyed and, at the giant's orders, revved the engine for a good minute. Tenaglia then lowered the bonnet with a thud.

'All taken care of, Inspector. If it happens again, I'll eat my hat.'

Bordelli turned off the engine and got out of the car.

'Thanks,' he said.

'Any time.'

'How much do I owe you, Gastone?'

The old mechanic raised his hands.

'Don't even mention it, Inspector.'

Bordelli went up to Tenaglia.

'How much do I owe you?' he said, pulling out a thousand-lira note. The young man spread his arms, as if to move them away from the money.

'I don't want anything,' he said.

'C'mon, Tenaglia, it's like you pulled an aching tooth from my mouth.'

'A thousand lire is too much, Inspector.'

'It's not a thousand lire. It's a way to say thanks.'

He entered his office, pulled the shutters to, and lay back in his chair as best he could. His intention was to reread the transcript of the Morozzi interview. But, as usual, it was too hot. He sent Mugnai for coffee and a couple of beers. While waiting he started thinking about his fifty-three years of life, how brief they had been and yet how full. A very long time ago he had asked himself how and when one realises one is old. Now, perhaps, he knew. One day he had happened to think about the past, and in so doing, he had felt very melancholy. That must have been the exact moment when he turned old. Before that, memories had only been faraway images, more or less faded, a weightless train of events; but after that day they had become something entirely different, something hard to define, part consolation, part resignation.

Mugnai knocked. He had two puddles of sweat under his armpits.

'Here you are, Inspector. Coffee and beer.'

'Thanks. Just put it right down here.'

'Need anything else?'

'No, thanks.'

Mugnai wiped his brow with the sleeve of his uniform.

'Half an hour ago a man called for you, sir, a certain Dante.'

'What did he say?'

'He said he'd call back later.'

'Good.'

Mugnai went out and Bordelli lit what he defined as his second cigarette of the day. But perhaps he was cheating. He smoked it while drinking his coffee and thinking about the war.

He was unable to forget those years; they were still with him, as present and real as his own hands. August 1944 had been hot; and their dirty uniforms stank of sweat. He had gone out on patrol with Piras Sr, machine gun slung over his shoulder, finger on the trigger. The Germans were in the vicinity, as always, just over the hill, quartered in small villages abandoned by all but a few old, terrorised peasants. Piras and he walked along shoulder to shoulder, scanning the horizon with their eyes. The countryside lay fallow; mines had taken root in place of grain, but the wild flowers didn't give a damn about the war and still blossomed everywhere, filling the valleys with colour. In an abandoned farmhouse they found an almost whole ham of prosciutto hidden under some straw. It was like a vision. They ate it in big hunks, cutting it with their daggers, then put it back in its place. When they returned to base after dark, their throats burned from the salted meat. Next day the thought of the prosciutto drove them back to the abandoned house, this time with a piece of stale bread. Crawling through the high grass all the way to the door, they entered carefully, preceded by the machine-gun barrel. There was nobody there. But they quickly discovered that the prosciutto had been partly eaten, almost certainly by some Nazi patrol. A good chunk of it was gone. They sat down, backs to the wall, and pulled out the bread. It seemed like a dream to be able to eat the stuff. It reminded them of the snacks their mothers used to make for them, centuries before.

As they chewed their last morsel, he and Piras looked at one another. They had to decide what to do with the remaining ham. They now knew not only that they were not the only ones eating it, but that the others were Nazis. In the end they quietly smiled and put the prosciutto back under the straw. When they returned the following day, again the ham had been eaten. By this point it became clear that the Germans had caught on. It went on this way for several days: one Italian bite, one German bite, down to the bone. It was almost touching, but mostly it was absurd. Tomorrow they might shoot a Kraut and dispatch

93

him to the next world, though he might be one of those with whom they had shared the prosciutto.

Bordelli crushed the butt of his cigarette in the ashtray and remained pensive for a few minutes. Then he stood up with a sigh, got in the car and went to Forensic Medicine to see Diotivede. The heat didn't reach the lab. Aside from the stink of disinfectants, it was a kind of paradise.

The doctor was preparing some slides for the microscope, humming through his nose, which was rather unusual. Diotivede never sang. Bordelli went up to him, hands in his pockets.

'You in a good mood?' he asked.

Diotivede looked at him askance.

'Why do you ask?'

'You're singing.'

'I don't see the connection. Black slaves used to sing, too.'

'Well, I've never heard you singing before.'

'Actually, I wasn't singing.'

Bordelli realised the conversation was going nowhere and therefore changed the subject.

'So, the dinner's all set for Wednesday,' he said.

'Have you asked your friend about bean soup *alla lombarda*?'

'He said it's one of his specialities. He must have spent a holiday in San Vittore.'

'And they say you never learn anything in prison.'

'It's a question of character, dear doctor. There are those who go to university and remain ignorant, and there are those who become cultured behind bars.'

The doctor put his slides in place and began his magical journey through the world of living microorganisms. He started droning again as before. It must have been an operatic aria, but it remained unrecognisable.

'It that *Carmen*?' asked Bordelli.

'*Barber*,' said the doctor, still humming.

The inspector felt like arguing.

'So you *are* singing . . .'

'Call it whatever you like,' said Diotivede, who kept on

humming. When he was focused on his microscope, he was able to stand as still as a statue. If Bordelli ever sculpted a monument to him, he would portray him like that, hunched over his microscope.

All at once Diotivede tore himself away from the microscope and went up to a slab, raising the sheet, exposing a stocky body with a bloated belly. It was a man of about fifty whose skin had turned grey. Round his dry, nearly blackened lips was a layer of coagulated, yellowish saliva.

'What are you going to do?' Bordelli asked. Diotivede had rubber gloves on his hands and was poking the corpse's belly, seeking the right point to begin cutting. Fascinated, the inspector followed those expert hands as they traced a path from the navel to the ribs. 'You going to open him now?' he asked the doctor.

'I'm running late. They wanted it done this morning.'

'Why don't you request a helper?'

'I've tried. The ministry said that when yours truly checks out, they'll send a new doctor,' Diotivede said bitterly.

'How thoughtful of them.'

'It's probably better that way. Who knows what kind of person they would send?'

'Such faith . . .'

Diotivede interrupted his work, turning serious.

'When I die, make sure nobody opens me up, all right?' he said.

'Maybe I'll die first.'

'Don't change the subject. Will you prevent them from cutting me in two? I want an answer.'

'I'll do what I can.'

'I don't want some youngster learning the ropes on my mortal remains. Swear that you won't let them do it.'

'There are certain circumstances in which—'

'Swear it,' Diotivede interrupted him.

'You know perfectly well that it also depends on the cause of death.'

'I don't give a damn. Swear it.'

'And what if I'm unable?'

'Just swear to it. At any rate, I'll never know.'

'I swear,' said Bordelli, sighing. Diotivede finally seemed satisfied and returned to the corpse. He sank the tip of his scalpel into the hollow of the dead man's stomach, going deeper and deeper. They heard a snap, then a burst of air. Smelly gas came pouring out as the stomach deflated. The blade slowly continued along its path, without so much as a single drop of blood oozing from the lips of the cut. Setting down the scalpel, Diotivede widened the aperture with his hands.

'Who is he?' Bordelli asked.

'Some poor bloke they found dead in the middle of the street.'

'Murder?'

'Looks more like a heart attack.'

'I hate those words.'

'I could call it cardiac arrest, if you prefer.'

'You're a true friend.'

'Would you hand me that basin, please?' Diotivede had extracted the liver and held it in his hands, waiting to set it down.

The moment had come to pay a call on Rodrigo. Driving through the streets, Bordelli started quibbling with himself: Why was he going to see Rodrigo? And for whose sake? For Zia Camilla's? For Rodrigo's? Or for his own? And if he was doing it for his own sake, what was the reason? So as not to feel guilty in his auntie's eyes? To do his moral duty? Or was it merely for curiosity's sake? There was no question that he found Rodrigo's spinsterish bitterness terribly amusing. Maybe, all things considered, that was the real reason.

He parked his Beetle a couple of streets away from his cousin's flat and continued on foot. It was always best to get a breath of air before visiting Rodrigo. When he got to the main entrance, he instinctively looked up to the fourth floor. The building was not very pleasant to look at, overloaded with monumental motifs as it was. Rodrigo's shutters were closed. Bordelli rang the intercom, but no one answered. He rang again, repeatedly, with no result. Finally he squashed the button and held it down a long time, and suddenly the lock started clicking frantically. Bordelli climbed the stairs to the fourth floor. Finding Rodrigo's door closed, he knocked.

'Who the fuck is it?' he heard someone call from behind the door. Strange. Normally Rodrigo never used certain words.

'Is that you, Rodrigo?'

'No, it's the big bad wolf.'

'Could you open the door?'

'What do you want?'

'To have a little chat.'

'I really don't feel like it.'

'All right, I'll go. But I'm going to come back tomorrow, and the day after tomorrow, and the day—'

He heard a click, and the door slowly opened. Rodrigo was in his underpants, a week's growth of beard on his face. He stood in the doorway, as if guarding the flat.

'It's nice to see you finally dirty and debased like the rest of humanity,' said Bordelli, genuinely pleased.

'What do you want?'

'Would you let me inside?'

'What do you want?'

'Shall we have a drink?'

'I hate it when people answer a question with a question.'

'Then let me in.'

'Mamma sent you, didn't she?'

'I haven't seen Zia Camilla for a month. Anyway, why would she send me to see you?'

'You're a liar.'

'I'm a policeman.'

Rodrigo sighed with irritation, stepped aside, and flung open the door.

'Come in.'

The flat was dirty. On the floor near the entrance were some strange shards pushed up against the skirting board and, high up on the wall, a large, sticky-looking stain. The air smelled musty. The telephone was unplugged. Bordelli followed his cousin inside, eyeing his naked legs. Rodrigo looked good for fifty: no fat, no hanging skin. They entered the study, and Rodrigo went over to the window, opened it brusquely, and stood in front of it in his underpants. He started watching the few cars passing along the avenue below.

'Find yourself a place to sit down,' he said. What had once been his study now looked like a chicken coop. Bordelli took off his shirt and tossed it joyfully on to a chair. He really liked this situation; it was like finding a friend who had fallen into the hands of the Germans. He managed to find a spot on an armchair by removing a tray covered with leftovers. The sofa was nearly invisible under a layer of dirty clothes.

'Nice little mess you've got here,' said Bordelli, looking around. Rodrigo made a guttural sound, lingered for another minute in front of the window, looking out, then closed it and left the room. When he returned he had a pair of trousers on and a glass in his hand.

'What are you drinking?' asked Bordelli.

Rodrigo looked into the glass.

'I don't know. Want some?'

'Just a drop, thanks.'

Rodrigo shuffled off and returned with a bottle he dropped between Bordelli's legs.

'Find yourself a glass,' he said. Bordelli glanced at the label. Triple Sec, a sweet liqueur they used to get drunk on in childhood. So as not to seem unfriendly, he went into the kitchen to wash a glass. Returning to the chicken coop, he poured himself some of the sugary glue.

'Tell me something, Rodrigo. Do you remember the last time I dropped by to see you?'

'Yes, I think so . . . years ago, it seems . . . you really got on my nerves.'

'No, not years ago. It was a month ago, at the most.'

'A month . . . Yes, maybe you're right . . . I threw you out, if I remember correctly . . .'

Bordelli heaved a long sigh, deliberately, for rhetorical effect.

'All right, Rodrigo, now tell me what's going on.'

'What the fuck do you mean by "what's going on"?'

'I mean, if you're ready to talk, I'm ready to listen.'

Rodrigo freed up the couch, throwing everything on to the floor, and lay down on it.

'Talk about what?'

'Take a look around. Tell me, how does a man so finicky and neat to the point of obsession turn his house, from one day to the next, into a magnificent pigsty? Don't get me wrong, I say this with admiration.'

'This is my house and I'll do whatever I like with it.'

'Good answer. A child couldn't have said it better.'

'Why don't you just leave me alone?'

Bordelli took a sip of Triple Sec and repressed his disgust.

'You shouldn't be so mistrustful.'

'What's that got to do with anything?'

'If you'll spill the beans, I promise it won't leave this room.'

'You talk like a cop.'

'I appreciate the retort, but only because I didn't think you capable of it.'

Rodrigo took a long swig. For a moment his face shrivelled like a fist; he looked as if he had stomach pains. Then he suddenly burst out laughing uncontrollably and slid off the sofa, chest heaving. He spilled his Triple Sec all over himself, which made him laugh even harder. He could hardly breathe, and tears rolled down his face.

At that moment, for the first time in his life, Bordelli felt sympathy for his cousin. Seeing him writhe in laughter on the floor, he felt like giving him a big kiss on the forehead. It was beautiful. He thought that whatever it was that had happened to Rodrigo, it had given him a chance to become freer. The results, for now, were a bit strange, but still better than before. Perhaps Rodrigo was suffering like a dog, but at last he was able to let himself go. One could only hope it didn't end soon.

Bordelli finished his Triple Sec in one gulp and pulled out a cigarette. He could have easily resisted, but he didn't because he wanted to see what would happen. The old Rodrigo would have goggled his eyes and screamed at him to extinguish 'that disgusting thing' at once. He lit the cigarette and blew out a nice big mouthful of smoke, waiting for his cousin's reaction. Rodrigo slowly stopped laughing and, still lying on the floor, looked at Bordelli thoughtfully.

'Could I have one of those?'

'Shall I toss it to you?'

'I'll come and get it.' He crawled on all fours to the packet, extended five dirty fingers and took a cigarette. Bordelli lit a match for him, and Rodrigo thrust his whole face towards it, singeing an eyebrow, though he was too busy lighting the cigarette to notice. After the first puff, he coughed for a good minute. With each hack, smoke came out of his mouth. He nearly lost his voice.

'How the hell can you . . . smoke this . . . this stuff?' he said, eyes red. Bordelli decided to take him by surprise.

'It's about a woman, isn't it?' he said.

Rodrigo took three puffs in a row, without coughing. His voice, however, was stuck in a gravelly timbre.

'She's a monster, not a woman,' he said.

Bordelli decided not to press the issue, at least for the moment.

'What are you doing for the holidays, Rodrigo?' he asked.

'What have the holidays to do with any of this?'

'You're not taking any time off?'

'In what sense?'

'Never mind.'

Rodrigo extinguished the butt on the floor and rested his chin in his hand.

'A monster,' he muttered.

'Want to come to my place for dinner on Wednesday? There will be four or five of us.'

'Give me another cigarette.'

Bordelli tossed him one, followed by the matchbox.

'What do you do all day long, Rodrigo?'

'I watch TV. Did you see Celentano the other day?'

'Has she dropped you?'

Rodrigo lit his cigarette and pushed away a pile of detritus with his foot, remaining seated on the floor. He tore a page from a newspaper, rolled it up into a ball and aimed it at a vase across the room.

'I should never have met her,' he said through clenched teeth. He tore out another page and did the same as before; the ball hit the neck of the vase and rebounded far away. He started laughing again, from the effect of the Triple Sec, losing control and burning the sofa with his cigarette in his convulsions. Bordelli rather enjoyed watching him; he'd never seen him in such a state. Then Rodrigo stopped laughing and turned decidedly gloomy.

'I want her . . . the witch,' he said.

'What'd you say?'

'I said I want her. She's very beautiful.'

'And what about her? Is she as far gone as you?'

'I think so. And that's what scares me.'

'Scares you?'

Rodrigo changed expression and sat up.

'You want to know the real reason I've been holed up at home for two weeks? Do you?'

'Absolutely.'

'Because every time I leave home I go immediately to her place and we make love all day for two days straight. Now do you understand?'

'Is that all? And to think I was worried about you.'

'You're right to be worried.'

'Well, there are worse things in life.'

'But don't you understand? Joy, happiness . . . they're ghastly.'

'Don't worry, happiness doesn't last very long.'

'Well, I'm scared stiff of all that. Do you think it's easy . . . just like that, overnight?'

'I don't know what you mean.'

'I'm afraid, terrified – I'm entering a world I know nothing about, and yet I can't help but enter it. Is that a little more clear?'

'Crystal clear. But what world are you talking about?' asked Bordelli.

'I can sit there and look into her eyes for hours and hours, and when I hold her in my arms, I don't give a damn about dying . . . Does that seem normal to you?'

'Sounds like the usual lovey-dovey stuff to me.'

'Of course, except that this time it's happening to me, which is another matter entirely.'

'I think that's fantastic, don't you?'

'I feel like I'm being swept away by a river in spate, I no longer know what I feel . . .'

'Perfectly normal.'

'Not for me. I've tried to stop and think, to try to understand what is happening to me.'

'And have you understood?'

'Only one thing: that the wall I had built around myself, brick by brick, has collapsed, like the house of the three little pigs. There's nothing left standing.'

'Magnificent.'

'What the hell is so magnificent about it? I'm trying to tell you I'm shitting my pants!'

'Throw yourself into it, Rodrigo. I'm telling you for your own sake. You're over fifty, and life is shorter than the time it takes a mouse to piss. You're still in time to throw it all overboard.'

Rodrigo was tense, continually wiping his face with his hands.

'Why me, of all people?'

'If I were in your place, I would dive straight into that river in spate and gladly drown. You can sort things out later.'

Rodrigo kept staring at the floor, long faced. He was puffing on the spent butt like a madman. Bordelli decided it was time to go and stood up. His cousin had to think this through alone, and probably needed to slap himself in the face a few times. He looked around for his shirt. Rodrigo turned abruptly to look at him.

'Are you leaving?' he said.

'It's late.'

'I won't see you out.'

'Doesn't matter.' Bordelli put on his shirt.

'Would you do me a favour on your way out?' said Rodrigo.

'Sure.'

'Would you plug the phone back in?'

'If that's what you want.'

Bordelli left him lying there, staring at his own feet. In the entrance hall, he bent down, plugged in the phone cable, and went out. He hadn't descended the third stair when he heard it ring. He turned back to eavesdrop. The seventh ring was interrupted halfway through, and then he heard Rodrigo's voice.

'Hello, Beatrice . . . no, it's nothing serious, don't cry . . . Let me explain . . .'

At nine that evening Bordelli pulled up at Dante's gate in his Beetle. He got out and paused for a few minutes to look at the countryside. The sun was low on the horizon. A cool, mild wind had risen and now caressed his face. The thought of spending a little time with the inventor made him feel better. He pushed the gate open and walked down the lane. A family of cats lay spread along the rim of a waterless fountain. He liked this house, drowning as it was in a sea of wild vegetation. It had a peaceful atmosphere. As he walked along, spikes of brome grass remained embedded in his trouser legs near the bottom, prickling his ankles. In the silence he could hear the soporific hum of an aeroplane overhead. He would have liked to lie down in the tall grass and go to sleep.

The front door to the villa was wide open, and by now

Bordelli knew his way around. He went downstairs to the great room where Signor Dante spoke to mice. He found him standing in the middle of the room, enveloped in a cloud of cigar smoke. He was still wearing the same white smock, open over his paunch. The inspector threaded his way through the piles of books stacked on the floor. The inventor made a gesture of greeting without breaking his train of thought.

'Did you phone me?' asked Bordelli.

'Possibly,' said Dante, distracted. He shook some ash to the ground, went to get the bottle of grappa, and filled two small glasses, passing one to Bordelli. Then he extracted a photograph from his pocket.

'You've only seen her dead. I wanted you to see what she really looked like,' he said gloomily. It was a photo of Rebecca as a girl. She was very beautiful. Smiling, with a lock of hair in her mouth.

'She always used to do that,' said Dante.

'Do what?'

'Put a lock of hair in her mouth.'

'My mother used to do that, too,' said Bordelli.

'Do you ever think of death, Inspector?'

'At night sometimes, before falling asleep.'

'What exactly do you think about?'

Bordelli took a sip of grappa and suddenly felt all the weight of the day on his shoulders.

'They're rather vague thoughts,' he said.

The inventor waved his index finger in the air.

'I often think about it myself, and I don't like it one bit. Death is unacceptable, disgustingly unacceptable . . . unless there really is such a thing as an immortal soul, an eternal consciousness of oneself.'

'I agree.'

Dante dropped his hands into the pockets of his smock. A deep furrow formed in his brow.

'And what about the resurrection of the flesh? What do you think about that?' he said.

If it hadn't been so hot, Bordelli might have tried to reflect on this. Dante chewed his spent cigar and began to pace in silence through his ingenious debris. The rhythmical sound of his footsteps very nearly managed to put Bordelli to sleep. A few minutes later, Dante was standing in front of him again.

'The great themes, Inspector . . . It's the great themes that drive me mad. Death, consciousness, life . . . Take life, for instance. A spermatozoon plunges headlong into an ovum, and immediately a long-term project is set in motion. The cells proliferate at a dizzying rate, clustering, diversifying. Out of that initial, infinitesimal particle will grow a beating heart, hands, fingernails, hair, glands, and a brain with the power to think of itself . . . And it's already all written down, from the position of the liver to the composition of the cartilage. But from time to time nature, too, gets things wrong, and so you'll have six fingers on one hand or one leg shorter than the other, or else she may construct a brain incapable of understanding the simplest things . . . And the reason for this? A simple mistake? Or is there a design? And why, if I know I can't answer these questions, do I continue to ask them? . . . A little more grappa, Inspector?'

There was no point in answering. Dante was already headed towards the bottle. He returned, clutching it by the neck, and filled the two little glasses to the brim again. Emptying his own, he dropped his head, chin resting on his chest.

'Always the same questions: Why does God allow evil? Is history the work of man, or does it have an independent force of its own? And what about time? What is time?'

'Before I forget, would you like to come to my place for dinner on Wednesday?'

They left early in the morning to avoid the heat, car windows open all the way. Bordelli was in shirtsleeves, driving with one hand and enjoying the air blowing over him. He could still smell the nauseating odour of Dante's grappa in his nose. He hadn't shaved, and every so often ran his hand over his stubbly face. He wondered where Rodrigo might be at that hour. Maybe he was walking about naked in his flat, declaiming Byron to his woman, also naked, in a smoke-filled room, both drunk and happy after a night of sex. At any rate, his disagreeable cousin was becoming much more agreeable to him.

Piras was in civilian dress and looked rather like a penniless student. Bordelli turned to face him and raised his voice to make himself heard above the German growl of the car.

'Got any cousins, Piras?' he asked.

'Dozens.'

'Do you get on all right with them all?'

'I don't even know them.'

They sat in silence for a while, hypnotised by the Beetle's noise, a dull rumble with a sort of whistle inside. Piras sighed.

'Aren't we going to interrogate these Morozzis? I mean seriously interrogate them,' he said.

'Of course, Piras, but not right away. I would like first to have something more definite in hand.' Piras nodded and rested an elbow on the window rim. Bordelli took his hands off the steering wheel, holding it steady with his knees as he lit his first cigarette of the day. He blew out the first puff without inhaling it, since it tasted like sulphur.

'So, what do you think, Piras? Have you managed to solve the riddle?'

'Theoretically, yes, but the facts still elude me.'

'Explain.'

'It's a question of mathematics. You gave me a problem to solve, an equation with an unknown. It's all very easy on paper; the hard part comes later, when you try to apply theory to practice, you know what I mean?'

Bordelli pressed his lips together.

'Go on.'

'Let me think it over a little longer. Sooner or later something will come to me.'

It seemed to Bordelli that Piras hadn't explained a thing, but he let it drop.

By the time they got to the coast, the sun was high in the sky. The heat was more bearable than in the city. Bordelli parked the car along the seafront.

'What are we going to do?' asked the Sardinian.

'It's been so long since I last saw the sea, Piras.'

The beach at Marina di Massa was covered with people. Too many people. The countless rows of deckchairs ended just a few feet from the water. There was something unpleasant about the constant movement of all those half-naked bodies on the sand. Under the grating music of the radios one could hear the distant chirruping of children playing in the surf. As they made their way through the countless umbrellas, Bordelli tried to imagine a deserted beach, going swimming in the nude and then lying down at the water's edge with eyes closed, listening to the sounds of the sea, the cries of the gulls, without a thought in his head.

He stopped to wait for Piras, who had fallen behind while removing his shoes and socks. He walked towards Bordelli over the scorching sand, shiny black shoes dangling from his hooked fingers. His bony face gleamed in the sun like a copper pot. The inspector resumed walking towards the sea, and Piras picked up his pace until he was at his side again.

'You should take off your shoes, too, Inspector. It makes it much easier to walk.'

Bordelli took a cigarette out of his pocket and lit it.

'Never mind, we're only staying a minute.'

When they reached the water's edge, Bordelli heaved a melancholy sigh. His head was full of memories. He saw himself as a toddler again, playing in the wet sand, his mother playing cards and gabbing with her friends, his dad never losing sight of him, his old aunts from Mantua sitting next to one another with shoes on their feet and purses in their laps, coconut vendors walking quickly by, kicking up sand with their heels. It was all a very long time ago, when women's bathing suits started at the neck and went all the way down to the knees.

*   *   *

The waiter at the Coccodrillo remembered the Morozzis well. They had arrived at half past eight and stayed until 10.30.

'Good people,' he said in a serious tone, which led Bordelli to think that they left generous tips. Piras had pulled out a notebook and was writing everything down. It was almost noon and there was a great deal of commotion in the kitchen. The dining room was still empty, however. As he answered Bordelli's questions, the waiter continued slowly setting the tables, stretching across them to arrange glasses with the ease of habit. He was short and slightly hunchbacked. Despite an oversized nose, his face looked empty. He called to mind the comic books of Signor Bonaventura. He circled round the larger tables, exasperatingly slow, making endless adjustments as he lined up the cutlery. Bordelli and Piras followed him around with the feeling that they were bothering him.

'Do they eat here often, the Morozzis?' the inspector asked.

'Yes, they do. They've been coming here for many years.' A bit farther away, a little girl with bruises on her knees was spreading out the last tablecloths, smoothing out the wrinkles with her open palms. Bordelli glanced at the fake fish hanging on the wall and felt a great weariness come over him.

'So you're sure they left here at half past ten.'

The waiter stopped, a fork in his hand.

'Absolutely sure, Inspector. But has something happened to these gentlemen? Some misfortune?'

A fat woman with a thick fringe of blonde hair over her forehead came out of a door. She had to be the restaurant's owner.

'Gigi! Haven't you finished yet?' she said.

'I'm almost done. These gentlemen are with the police.'

After a moment of confusion, the woman gave a forced, lipstick-painted smile.

'Can I get you anything?'

'No, thank you. We'll be on our way in a minute.' The owner raised a hand to say they should wait, then went and stuck her head inside the kitchen door.

'Gisella, bring two vermouths, quick,' she ordered.

'Please don't bother, we were on our way out,' said Bordelli, irritated by her false smile.

'Oh, no bother at all, just a little glass . . . So, has something happened?'

'We just wanted to ask Signor Gigi a few questions, which we've already done.'

The woman seemed relieved. She folded her hands and let out a little giggle. Gisella arrived with glasses in hand, and the owner sternly ordered her back to the kitchen to fetch a tray.

'These young girls are a disaster,' she said.

'There wasn't any problem,' said Piras, giving her a dirty look. Gisella returned, red in the face, eyes lowered under a thick black fringe. She held the tray out for the policemen. Bordelli would have liked to decline; at that moment his stomach really wasn't ready for vermouth, but he felt sorry for the girl and so took the less full glass. Piras grabbed his and smiled broadly at Gisella, who practically ran away. Bordelli wanted to get out of there as quickly as possible and downed the glass in one gulp. A flash of heartburn immediately rose up his oesophagus and into his throat. The Sardinian emptied his glass and couldn't restrain a grimace. The owner kept smiling, her face shiny with sweat.

'Another little drop?'

'We really must go, thank you.'

The inspector grabbed Piras by the elbow and led him towards the exit. Once outside, Bordelli put a hand on his stomach.

'Pure poison.'

'Do you mean the woman or the wine?'

'Both, Piras, both.'

They parked the Beetle under a great palm along the seafront. Piras stayed in the car to eat a panino. Bordelli had already crossed the street and was knocking on a locked door under a green sign that said: *La Mecca – Dancing*. Nobody answered.

The inspector turned to face Piras and threw his hands up, then crossed the avenue again and got back in the car. He bit into the panino he had left half eaten and said something with his mouth full, which Piras didn't understand.

'What did you say, Inspector?'

Bordelli swallowed.

'I said it looks like we're going to have to hang around here till this evening,' he said. Piras looked back towards the Mecca.

'Maybe not,' he said, gesturing towards the nightclub door. A dishevelled blonde head had popped out of the now half-open door. The girl looked around, yawning, then came out into the sunlight and stretched. She looked very young, and pretty too. She was wearing a bathrobe too big for her. Bordelli quickly rewrapped his panino in its paper and raced back across the avenue. He reached the girl just before she could close the door behind her.

'Excuse me, miss, I'm Inspector Bordelli, police. If you don't mind, I'd like to ask you a few questions.' The girl looked at him askance, a soft wrinkle appearing on her broad, smooth brow. She still had one hand on the door, as if waiting to decide what to do. Bordelli looked down and saw her bare little feet, slender and tanned, the toenails painted bright red. He thought: she really is pretty.

'Do you work here?' he asked.

'Why do you ask?' She had a northern accent, proud, intelligent eyes, and a stubborn air that made her seem even prettier. She shifted one foot forward and curled the toes, leg slightly bent at the knee, which jutted forward out of the bathrobe. Bordelli smiled.

'Want to tell me your name?'

'Elvira.'

'Do you work here?'

The girl shrugged.

'I'm a waitress, but only in summer. The rest of the year I'm a student.'

'Were you here last Thursday evening?'

'I'm here every day. But why are you asking me all these questions?'

'Do you happen to know two brothers by the name of Morozzi?'

Elvira shook her head, a blonde lock falling over her face.

'I don't know anyone,' she said. Bordelli didn't know what else to say, but was unable to leave. With every second that passed, Elvira looked more and more beautiful to him. She radiated something magical that fascinated him. It had been a very long time since he had last felt such things. Then he realised she could be his daughter and scratched his head in embarrassment. The girl rearranged her hair and burst out laughing.

'What's wrong, Mr Policeman? Have you lost your voice?'

'No, it's that . . .'

'You can't keep me all day at the door like this. If you want to know more, come inside. I need some coffee.'

'Of course.'

Bordelli turned towards Piras and gestured for him to wait. He crossed the threshold and found himself in an entrance hall full of pitiless mirrors. Seeing himself next to the beautiful young girl, he felt even older than he already was. He followed Elvira into a very big, dark room illuminated only by a red light hanging from the ceiling. In the middle of the room was a circular dance floor surrounded by the dark shapes of empty sofas. The girl walked across the room, her bare feet making a slapping sound. She parted a heavy velvet curtain, holding it open for Bordelli to pass through, then headed down a narrow corridor that led to a small, disorderly room, half bedroom, half kitchen, with an unmade bed and a small gas cooker in the corner. The blue-tiled floor was covered with a light veil of sand. High up on the wall was a half-open window that gave on to the sea, beaming with sunlight. A chair was completely buried under a layer of clothes, and atop the pile was a pair of white knickers. Seeing them, the girl grabbed them and stuffed them into her pocket.

'Please sit wherever you like,' she said.

The only thing available was an old wooden chair. Bordelli flopped down into it and felt the legs sway. A shaft of light speckled with floating dust filtered down through a crack in the ceiling. Turning her back to the inspector, Elvira busied herself making the coffee.

'Will you have some too?' she asked.

'Yes, thank you.' Bordelli gazed admiringly at the girl's legs and sinewy feet, not looking away until she turned round.

'I'm all yours, Mr Policeman. What would you like to know?'

'Just a bit of information,' said Bordelli. Elvira put the coffee pot on the burner and went and sat down on the bed. She raised her knees to rest her arms on them, causing the bathrobe to slip down and uncover her legs.

'What are you doing, looking up my dress?' said the girl, without covering her legs.

'No . . . forgive me. You're very pretty, Elvira.'

'Forget the compliments, Inspector. They make me sick. That's all I've ever heard my whole life.'

'I'm sorry,' said Bordelli, who in his mind was thinking: *Old fool, get out of here as soon as you can!*

The girl started picking at an old scab on her ankle until it finally came off. Bordelli was sweating. He didn't know where to look. He felt happy when he heard the coffee start to bubble up in the pot. Elvira stood up, rearranging her hair, went to get two espresso cups in the sink, and rinsed these off, wiping the inside with her fingers. A blonde lock of hair fell on to her face and she blew it away.

'How many sugars?' she said.

'One, please.'

'So you really don't want to tell me what you're looking for?' she said as she handed him the coffee. The handle on the little cup was broken, and Bordelli burnt his fingers. Still, it was easier than drinking out of one of Dante's cups.

Elvira remained standing in front of him, bathrobe hanging loose, and looked at him. Her eyes were big, green and full of irony.

'I'm investigating a murder,' said Bordelli, blowing on the hot coffee in embarrassment. He felt awkward and silly, and wished he had never come inside. Elvira tightened the bathrobe round her body.

'And who was killed?' she said, without emotion.

'A very rich lady.'

'Then it wasn't my mother,' she said, shrugging her shoulders. With a grim smile she went and sat back down on the bed, espresso cup in hand, and folded her legs like a fakir. Bordelli set his scalding cup down on the floor and pulled out his cigarettes. He offered the girl one, and she gestured for him to throw it to her. He got up anyway and handed her the pack, then lit a match and leaned over her so she could light hers. Mingled with the odour of burning sulphur he clearly smelled the scent of her blonde hair and tanning lotions and felt as lonely as a dog. She inhaled and smiled, revealing a mouth of perfect little teeth.

'Your hands are shaking, Mr Policeman.'

Bordelli hid his hands and stepped back.

'Watch out for the coffee,' Elvira said, pointing at the floor. Bordelli missed the little cup by a hair, staggered for a moment, and then leaned against the wall to keep from falling. This was the height of embarrassment. He really didn't understand what was happening to him. This girl made him feel uneasy as nobody had ever done before. He picked the cup up off the floor, emptied it in a hurry and went and set it down in the sink. He would have liked to light his cigarette, but he felt too ashamed of his trembling hands, and so he left it in his mouth, unlit. He didn't understand why he had ever agreed to come inside. It made no sense. And now he felt he couldn't leave. He stood stiffly in the middle of the room, lacking the courage to sit down. He didn't know what to say, and his silence weighed heavily on him. He had never felt so humiliated in all his life. And yet he was a police inspector aged fifty-three, and Elvira not much more than a little girl. She watched him, a knowing smile on her lips, then set down her cup and collapsed on the bed, lying back in complete inno-cence. She extended her legs, crossed her ankles, and then took a lock of hair between her fingers and started looking for split ends.

'And what's the Mecca got to do with this dead lady?'

'What's that? . . . Ah, yes, of course . . . it's still a bit early to say. I just need to verify a few things.'

Bordelli described the Morozzi brothers to Elvira in great detail, pleased to have at last something specific to say to her. This calmed him down a little. The girl held out her hand, her finished cigarette between her fingers.

'Would you put that out for me, please?' Bordelli took the butt from her fingers and looked around for an ashtray.

'Just throw it in the sink,' she said. She turned on to her side, propped herself up on one elbow, and rested her cheek in her open hand.

'Yeah, I remember them. They were really revolting. And there were two women with them who looked like whores.'

Bordelli took advantage of the moment to look her straight in the eye.

'What do you mean, revolting?'

'They'd drunk a lot and were trying to be cute. One of them even put his hand on my bottom. Disgusting! And the two geese did nothing but laugh!'

'Can you tell me what time they arrived and what time they left?'

'They didn't leave till closing time. I remember it well, because they were stinking drunk and could barely stand up. But don't ask me what time they arrived, because you have no idea how chaotic this place gets.'

Bordelli thought again just how beautiful Elvira was. Subtle and wild at the same time.

'Is there anyone who might remember what time they arrived?' he asked.

'I really don't think so. As I said, it's too chaotic here. By nine o'clock this place is a zoo.'

'I see.'

Elvira extended her arms and stretched for a long time, closing her eyes and arching her back with obvious pleasure. Then she sat up and put her feet on the floor.

'Are we finished? Because, if you don't mind, I've got some things to do,' she said. Bordelli felt a pang in his chest. Only now did he realise he'd been hoping she liked him, at least a little, and that she'd be sad to see him go. Stupid old codger, he thought.

'Yes, we're done,' he said, trying to smile.

'Are you all right?' she asked, surprised by his grimace.

'It's my ulcer . . .' he lied.

'I'll show you out.'

Elvira got up from the bed and stopped for a moment to look at herself in a make-up mirror hanging from a nail. She made an expression as if to say: You are so ugly. Then she turned to Bordelli.

'Shall we go?'

They headed towards the exit. Bordelli remained one step behind her, to watch her walk. Her blonde hair left a sun-scented wake in the air. Hold your nose, old moron, he said to himself. When they were at the door, she held out a warm little hand.

'Well, goodbye,' she said.

'Thank you, Elvira. See you again some time.'

She smiled.

'I really don't think we'll ever see each other again,' she said. 'Goodbye, policeman.' She closed the door and Bordelli found himself singing a song by Celentano. He crossed the avenue slowly. The pavements were full of mothers and prams. Back in the Beetle, Bordelli found Piras bare-chested and asleep. Hearing the car door open, the Sardinian jolted awake, sat straight up, and started putting his shirt back on.

'So, Inspector, how did it go?'

'How did what go?'

* * *

Bordelli breathed in very deeply through his nose, and the smell of the sea brought him violently back to a very distant past. In his mind he saw again, as in some mythic remoteness, the house at Marina di Massa where his Mantuan aunts, rich old maids, used to spend their holidays, an art nouveauish little villa of grey stone, nobly spotted here and there with dry, greeny moss. It looked like a miniature castle ensconced in a magic garden, shady and private, full of very tall, slender pines and big dark plants. Resting on the brown, fertile ground was a broad basin full of slimy water with goldfish in it. A table of travertine stone glowed almost white under an arbour of passion-flower, site of grown-up conversations. He saw again the great marble staircase, the tea-room with its lead-lined windows, the cast-iron spiral staircase that ascended mysteriously towards the ceiling and up to a room he was not allowed to enter. He was, however, allowed to eat chocolates, which were always old and stale, and the maid's own home-made biscuits. And he was allowed to play with the cat, but not to hurt it. After lunch there was the usual nightmare: he had to take his nap. This was a terrible sacrifice for him: outside the sun was beating down, hundreds of lizards were waiting for nothing more than to be chased, while he was forced to lie in bed between Mamma and Papà, doing nothing. All he could do was think or follow the blurry, colourful shadows of passers-by on the ceiling, cast by the sun through the slats of the closed shutters. But as soon as Papà began to snore, he would get out of bed. Mamma was his accomplice and would gesture to him to be quiet, and he would go downstairs. The house was all his: silent, in semi-darkness from the partially closed blinds, and full of shadows. He used to slither across the floors on his belly, sliding under the furniture to escape the monsters who wanted to eat his feet. Round about four o'clock he would hear his mother's footsteps upstairs, as she went into the bathroom. A bit disappointed and a bit glad, he would come out from under the sideboard and go and sit on the big red couch, already at the beach in his mind . . . Sea, sun, playing in the sand, diving, hearing Mamma call from afar: 'That's enough now, come out of the water.' Then, after the last swim, a warm focaccia, taking big bites while shivering under his bathing-wrap. The sun, big and red, sinking into the sea before his eyes, an infinity of unfinished thoughts cluttering his head, turning him pensive, serious. The aunties used to say under their breath that 'the little one' was a melancholy child, and so they smiled and coddled him more than was necessary, and gave him presents. Poor aunties. They had died quite a while ago. He saw them again, seated one beside the other on the beach, dressed as if in a sitting room, with gold brooches and necklaces. They would look out at the sea, making useless comments or discussing projects for their vast farm in Argelato. Zia Cecilia, with her tiny head and a face like a night-bird; Zia Vittorina, with a black hairnet over her head and a walking stick with a silver knob at one end; Zia Ilda, white and transparent as a ghost, with her big, untroubled eyes, deep-set in her skull; and lastly, Zia Costanza, tiny and round, with her always cheerful face and gravelly voice. She gave off a sickly-sweet smell and loved to kiss everyone. A future friend of Il Duce and a famous medium, often chosen by the spirits of the long dead to be their voice for a few minutes among the living. Images of a vague, time-worn past, made all the more remote by the profound differences between those times and now, as distant from each other as a horse-drawn carriage and a Lancia Flaminia . . .

Under the spell of these thoughts, Bordelli had stopped eating his ice cream, which was now melting and dripping down the sides of the cup. A baby's scream woke him up, and he found himself sitting in a café mobbed with people in bathing suits. Piras was looking at him, a curious expression on his face.

'Inspector, can you hear me?'

'Sorry, Piras, I was distracted.'

'I said it's already two o'clock.'

Bordelli ran his hands over his face to wipe away the memories. He pushed away the cup of ice cream and lit a cigarette.

'Well, Piras, it seems the Morozzi brothers told the truth. What do you think? Shall we go look for these Salvettis anyway?'

'Why not?'

Bordelli paused for a moment to reflect, then took out his wallet to pay.

'Then let's go straight away, so we can catch them before they go to the beach.' When he stood up, he felt slightly dizzy, and in his mind he saw Elvira, clear as a photograph.

'Signor Salvetti?'

'Yes, I'm Salvetti. Who are you?'

'Inspector Bordelli. This is Piras. Would you mind if we asked you a few questions?'

'About what?'

'It'll only take a minute. May we come in?'

Salvetti looked as if he'd just got out of bed. He was dishevelled and a bit irritable, wearing swimming trunks and a shirt with the sleeves rolled up. His thin black moustache cut his face into two equal parts. He glanced at Piras and opened the gate.

'Is it all right if we stay here in the garden? My wife is asleep.'

'As you wish.'

They crossed a large, just-mown lawn in silence and went to sit under a pergola of honeysuckle about fifty yards from the villa. The chairs were made of cast iron, softened by colourful cushions. There wasn't a breath of wind, but it felt divine under that little roof of leaves. Salvetti rested his elbows on the armrests of his chair and folded his hands with an air of irritation. Piras was agitated and looking at the Milanese man with antipathy. Bordelli hated to ask questions in such a tense atmosphere, and so he tried to find a way to lighten the situation. Turning round to look at the villa, he nodded his head in admiration.

'Beautiful house. My compliments.'

The Milanese changed expression and also turned towards the villa.

'My grandfather bought it in 1912 for a song. It's a famous

villa, you know. It's been featured in many books with big bright colour photos. Just imagine, even D'Annunzio slept here.'

It was indeed a very unusual villa, at once solid and light. All marble and brick. At one corner it featured a square sort of turret with mullioned windows on all four sides. Salvetti kept gazing at his house with a certain joy, a smile of satisfaction broadening his mouth. Piras also seemed calmer. Good. Now they could start asking questions.

'You know the Morozzi brothers, is that right?' he asked.

Salvetti pointed to a smallish, modern house beyond the hedgerow.

'They live right next door.'

'Yes, we know.'

The Milanese looked amused.

'What have those two blockheads been up to this time?'

'We just need to corroborate a few things. Are you very close friends with them?'

Salvetti smiled and threw up his hands without taking his elbows off the armrests.

'How shall I put it, Inspector? We've known one another since childhood, but we only see each other in summer. I don't know if you could really say we are friends . . . You know what I mean?'

'Of course. Tell me, when did you last see them?'

'Yesterday morning. They left rather early, and we greeted them from the garden. I'd thought they had things to do around here, but then I haven't seen them since. Don't tell me they . . .' He raised a hand and traced a cross in the air. Bordelli shook his head.

'No, nothing like that. Signor Salvetti, where were you last Thursday night at eleven o'clock?'

'Thursday? I went out dancing with my wife. Shortly after we got there, the Morozzis showed up with their wives.'

'At what establishment did you go dancing?'

'At the Mecca. It's right here, on the seafront. Aren't you going to tell me what happened?'

'For the moment I can't. At what time did you leave the Mecca?'

'I'd say midnight, more or less.'

'Why so early?'

Salvetti appreciated the observation.

'When we go dancing we leave our little boy with some friends here in the neighbourhood, who also have a ten-year-old boy. And normally we come and pick him up at midnight.'

'What about the Morozzis?'

'What do you mean?'

'Did they leave with you at midnight?'

'No, they stayed.'

'Do you remember at what time they arrived?'

'They came in around eleven, more or less.'

The alibi was airtight, and Bordelli began to feel bored. He exchanged a glance of understanding with Piras. The Morozzis' version of events had been confirmed, point by point. He would have to start all over again. The two nephews had nothing to do with their aunt's death. Perhaps the motive wasn't the inheritance at all, but something else which nobody suspected. The only sure thing was that she had been murdered. Period. And yet there was something that eluded him, like a fly buzzing inside his head without letting up. He felt tired, very tired. He couldn't wait for night to come, so he could lie down and sleep. Maybe even die . . . to die, to sleep . . . to be or not to be . . . to dream . . . to dream or die . . .

'Is there anything else, Inspector?'

Bordelli snapped out of it and ran a hand over his face. Salvetti was staring at him.

'That'll be all, Signor Salvetti, thank you. Sorry to have bothered you,' he said. He was about to rise from his chair, but Piras asked permission to ask a question himself. Bordelli nodded assent, and the Sardinian turned to the zip king.

'At the Mecca, did you run into the Morrozis by accident, or had you arranged to meet there?'

'Neither. My wife and I go there every Thursday night, and

the Morozzis know this and sometimes drop in to see us there.'
Salvetti glanced at his watch and asked whether that would
indeed be the last question. Bordelli rose by way of reply, and
Piras followed. At that moment they heard a rather shrill female
voice call out from the villa.

'Artemioooo! Who are you talking tooooo?' A woman in a
dressing gown leaned out from a first-floor window. Salvetti
waved at her, then raised his voice so she could hear.

'Ciao, darling! . . . I'll explain later!' Then he turned and said
softly to Bordelli, 'That's my wife.'

The woman yelled louder:

'Whaat diid youu saaayy?'

'Laaater! . . . I'll tell you laaater!'

'Is Giacomo there with youuuu?' she persisted. Salvetti shook
his arm in the air.

'Nooo, he's still at the Consaaaalvooos'.'

Bordelli put an unlit cigarette in his mouth, promising himself
he wouldn't smoke it until the drive back to Florence.

'Is Giacomo your son?'

'Yes. Every day after lunch he goes to stay with those friends
I mentioned, to play with Matteo, their boy. He should be back
by now. In a few minutes we'll be going to the beach.'

Salvetti's wife had disappeared from the window and reappeared on the lawn. She was wearing a gauzy little sundress
covered with giant butterflies, her shoulders bare. She walked
towards them with a rather studied step, planting the tapered
wooden heels of her clogs into the grass with the nonchalance
of habit. From afar she looked rather attractive, more plump
than slender, hair full of airy curls. When she was under the
arbour, she noticed the empty table.

'Artemio! Haven't you offered these gentlemen anything?'

'Sorry, it didn't occur to me.'

The wife gave him a playful little slap on the back of the
neck but appeared to have miscalculated, striking him rather
hard. Salvetti took it quite badly, but his wife paid no heed.

'You're always so impolite! Isn't that so, signor . . .' and she looked at Bordelli, holding out her hand. The inspector shook it and immediately felt as if his own had been greased up for life.

'Inspector Bordelli, pleasure.'

'Piras,' said Piras, barely rising.

When she realised they were policemen, the woman got scared.

'Has something happened to Giacomo?' she said, alarmed.

Her husband snaked a hairy arm round her waist.

'No, no, dear, there's no need to worry. They only wanted to ask me a few questions. I'll explain later.'

'My God, what a fright!' she said, putting a hand over her heart. She was indeed attractive. A bit too made up for Bordelli, but attractive, all in all. She soon recovered her smile and asked what the two nice policemen might want to drink.

'No need to bother, signora, we have to leave,' said Bordelli.

'Won't you have a glass of *orzata*? Or mint?'

'Come on, Giovanna, can't you see these men are in a hurry?'

'Don't be such a bore, Artemio! Come now, Inspector. What can I get for you?'

Bordelli looked at Piras and bit his lip.

'An *orzata* would be fine,' he said.

'And this handsome young man, what would he like?'

'That would be fine for me too, thank you,' said Piras, his dark eyes staring hard at her. Signora Salvetti excused herself to prepare the drinks and walked away, swaying on her pretty clogs, followed by Piras's analytical gaze. The three men sat back down, at a loss for words. Piras pretended to tidy his hair but was actually having a last look at Giovanna before she disappeared into the house. Salvetti noticed and felt annoyed. He crossed his legs, shaking the top one furiously, as if trying to make time speed up.

'I really would like to get to the beach before dark,' he said, seeming a bit on edge. Piras was looking at him harshly, as if wanting to rearrange his face. Bordelli couldn't stand the tension any longer and got up out of his chair.

'Signor Salvetti, we're going to go. Please give our regards to your wife.'

Salvetti was already standing, pleased to put an end to the encounter and particularly pleased to be rid of this Sardinian who was undressing his wife with his eyes. But Giovanna reappeared in the distance with a tray full of glasses and bottles. The husband sighed and fell back into his chair, resigned. As the woman approached, smiling, they all heard the clanging of an iron gate and then saw the two little boys appear on the lawn with their bicycles, excited and sweaty. They rode up to the arbour and skidded on the grass when they stopped.

'Papà, papà! Can we go and drive in the garage?'

Salvetti raised a hand to shield the sun from his eyes.

'Before anything else you must say hello to these gentlemen,' he said.

'Hello . . . Can we go now?'

'All right, but be careful.'

The boys turned their bikes round and sped away, pedalling madly. Signora Giovanna poured the *orzata* into the glasses and smiled at Bordelli.

'They're going to play in the car . . . You've removed the keys, dear, haven't you?'

'What a question!'

Giovanni handed the two policemen and her husband their respective glasses, then served herself some mint and sat down with the sun directly on her face, not wanting to miss a single ray. She started talking about how much she had always loved the sea, from childhood.

'I assure you, Inspector, when we come here I have a better appetite, I digest better, sleep better, breathe better – in short, I do everything better, ev-ery-thing . . . Don't I, Artemio?' She squeezed her knees together and giggled in a way that her husband found irritating.

'Please, Giovanna . . .'

'Why, what did I say?' and she laughed again, slyly, hiding behind her glass of mint. Bordelli couldn't wait to be liberated, and he finished his milky *orzata* in one long draught that bordered on the impolite. He glanced at Piras, hoping he would do the same. His assistant got the message and drank hastily, darting lightning-quick glances at Signora Giovanna's legs, her fancy gold-rimmed clogs, and her naked, sunburnt, peeling shoulders. Salvetti, if he could have, would have killed him.

Signora Giovanna kept on talking, saying how much she adored the hot sand, how wonderful it was to lie and roast in the sun, how much she loved to take the rowing boat out to sea so she could finally take off her bathing suit and get some sun on her breasts and bottom. She had a beautiful smile, did Salvetti's wife. Bordelli pictured her naked on the boat, covered head to toe in tanning oil, breasts in the sunlight, and at the same time he pictured people who had nothing, who toiled all day in order to eat just a little, who didn't even know that lotions to prevent sunburn existed. Clenching his teeth, he rose with a sigh.

'We really must go, thank you so much,' he said. Salvetti didn't wait for him to say it twice, but shot up like a spring to show them out of his territory. Signora Giovanna beamed a panoramic smile and, remaining seated, offered her hand to the policemen.

'Well, see you soon, Inspector. Ciao, young man.'

Piras and Bordelli politely said goodbye and headed out across the lawn, struggling to keep pace with Salvetti, who was practically running. Piras stared at the Milanese's neck with a disagreeable look on his face. At the gate, the three men very quickly shook hands. Bordelli and Piras were about to leave when Giacomo, Salvetti's son, came running from the garage.

'Papà, papà, the car's been scratched!' he cried with the proud intonation of someone delivering bad news. Salvetti's eyes opened wide and he turned round abruptly, losing his balance, and would have fallen had Piras not caught hold of his arm.

'What do you mean, "scratched?"' he yelled, brusquely yanking his arm out of the Sardinian's grip.

'We didn't do it, it was already there! It was already there!' Giacomo screamed cheerfully, before running back to the garage. At the far end of the garden, Signora Giovanna waved her arm to say goodbye again to the policemen, wondering why they were lingering at the gate. Salvetti, meanwhile, had disappeared into the garage, and Bordelli didn't know whether to leave or to wait for him. He leaned against a gatepost and looked at his watch. The sweat was flowing down his back. It seemed the afternoon would never end.

At last Salvetti emerged from the garage. He looked quite upset.

'Jesus bloody Christ, is that any way to act?! That scrape's going to cost me a good two hundred thousand! The least they could have done is tell me!'

Bordelli threw up his hands.

'Well, we'll be off now,' he said, ready to flee. For his part Piras had taken a step forward and was staring at Salvetti, who was gesticulating and shaking his head as he approached. The Milanese seemed angry and was talking to himself.

'Is that any way to act? *La madonna!* They could have told me at least, dammit! Is that any way to act?'

Piras waited until Salvetti was beside him, and then asked:
'Who are you talking about?'

Bordelli wasn't expecting this sort of question. It actually seemed a bit intrusive on Piras's part. But the Sardinian looked so serious that the inspector let him continue. Salvetti had stopped and was scratching his cheek and staring into space.

'What pricks!' he added.

Piras persisted.

'Who are you talking about?' he asked, eyes fixed on Salvetti.
'Who? Why, those wretched Morozzi brothers, damn it all!'

Bordelli came away from the gate and back into the garden.
'The Morozzi brothers?' he said.

Salvetti was fuming.

'I'll never let them borrow it again, so help me God!' he said, shaking his hands wildly in the air.

'I'm sorry, but when did you lend them your car?' Bordelli asked. Salvetti looked at him as if he'd just realised he was there.

'What did you say?'

'Your car . . . when did you lend it to the Morozzis?'

'How should I know! They wanted to go for a drive in the hills, the show-offs! So much for trusting your friends! . . . Two hundred thousand that scrape's going to cost me! The cunts! Have you any idea how much a car like that costs?'

Piras gestured towards the garage, where one could still hear the sounds of the two little boys pretending they were driving.

'Could I see it?' he asked. Salvetti ignored him and walked in the direction of his wife, cupping his hands round his mouth.

'Giovannaaaa! The Morozzis have scratched the caaaaar!' he yelled.

'Whaaaaat?' she shouted back.

'The caaaar! They scraaaaatched it! The Morozziiiiis diiiid!'

The wife then yelled at the top of her lungs.

'Yes, I know, they waaaaashed it! They're soooo sweeeeet!' and she started waving her arm again. The husband was hopping from one foot to the other.

'What did you saaayyy?' he yelled.

'They're sooo sweeeeet!'

'It's scraaaaatched!'

Signora Giovanna gestured with her hand as if to say she couldn't understand. Meanwhile Piras had gone into the garage and was already on his way back. He came up behind Salvetti.

'Signor Salvetti, when, exactly, did you lend your car to the Morozzis?'

'What? What's my car got to do with any of this?'

Bordelli was right there beside him.

'Please try to remember; it could be very important,' he said in a serious tone.

'Oh, really?' Salvetti looked first at one, then the other, still in the grips of his tantrum. 'They wanted to go for a drive through the hills. I think it was last Friday.'

Piras butted in.

'Did you lend it to them Friday morning?'

'Yes . . . I mean, no. I must have given it to them Thursday afternoon; that nincompoop Giulio came by to pick it up.'

'Are you sure it was Thursday? Think it over carefully.'

'Yes, yes, of course it was Thursday . . . because that morning we went early to the beach, whereas they normally don't go out until ten, the bums. And so I let them take it the day before. A fine way to behave, bloody hell. They scrape your car and then don't tell you! Neither of them, the pricks!'

'It's a pretty nasty scrape, Inspector,' Piras commented. 'Looks like they clipped a tree.'

By this point Salvetti was out of control, stamping his feet and cursing between clenched teeth.

'Never mind washing it, they shouldn't have scratched it. Bloody hell. The little boors!'

Bordelli tried to summon forth the least irritating tone possible.

'Oh, so they washed it?' he asked.

'Yeah, they washed it! To thank me for the favour. Bloody hell!'

Signora Giovanna couldn't understand what was going on. She'd been waving for the last fifteen minutes, and still nobody had left. Finally she got up and started coming towards the three men with her fashion-model walk, legs popping out of her beach cover with each step. Piras's eyes were glued to her. She realised this and pretended not to notice, but did so in such an obvious way that Salvetti raised his eyes to the heavens and sighed. Bordelli was fed up with the whole situation.

'We have to go, Signor Salvetti, thank you ever so much,' he said, grabbing Piras by the arm and dragging him away. The Sardinian, however, managed to turn round one last time to look at Signora Giovanna's legs and smile.

When they got into the broiling Volkswagen, Bordelli turned to Piras.

'So?'

'Beautiful woman.'

'Aside from that.'

'It's an Alfa Romeo Giulietta Sprint, Inspector. It can do a hundred and ten no sweat.'

Bordelli wanted to see the sea again. They sought out the least crowded beach and went and sat down on an overturned *pattino*. Neither of the two said a word about the Pedretti murder, as if wishing to ruminate for a while alone.

A sun-blackened lifeguard dozed on a deckchair under a vast umbrella, beside him a bottle of beer within arm's reach, buried up to the neck in the sand, and, on the other side, a crumpled newspaper with a pack of cigarettes on top.

A pleasant breeze had risen, lightly ruffling their clothes. Bordelli chased the image of Elvira from his thoughts and studied Piras's wooden face. The young man's pitch-black eyes, with their veil of ancestral nostalgia, seemed able to look past the horizon.

'What are you thinking about, Piras?'

'I'm not thinking about anything.'

The inspector half-closed his eyes and looked at the sun setting slowly into the sea.

'They say it's impossible not to think about anything,' he said. Piras did not reply. He picked up a handful of sand, letting it flow out of his closed fist. They both remained silent, each with his own thoughts, listening to the regular yet ever-changing sound of the surf. Bordelli again remembered Piras's father . . . Sometimes they would sit on the ground, back to back, looking up at the black sky and its infinite points of light, not saying a word, while the others played cards or wrote letters that might never reach their destinations.

'What do you say we leave, Piras?'

'It's your decision, Inspector.'

'All right, then, let's go. I need to have a little chat with Diotivede.'

'You want me to drive?'

'Sure, why not?'

Bordelli dozed the whole way back, hands between his legs, head swaying to and fro against the seat.

'I'm going to close my eyes a little, but not sleep,' he said.

'Do whatever you like,' said Piras.

'I'm just a little tired.'

Bordelli closed his eyes and started to snore. Piras pulled into the courtyard at headquarters in Via Zara and turned off the engine. The inspector stirred, opened his eyes but then immediately closed them again to stop the burning. He pulled himself up with a grunt and shook his head, as if to throw off the cobwebs of sleep. Piras patiently waited for him to wake up fully.

'You want me to take you home, Inspector?'

'No, thanks. I can manage. First, however, I want to drop in on Diotivede for a minute. You want to come too?'

'That's fine with me.'

'I'll drive. It'll help wake me up.'

'As you wish.'

They both got out of the car to trade places. Bordelli staggered. A stabbing pain in the back made him groan. He yawned at the wheel all the way to the Forensic Medicine lab, running a red light and clipping a kerb, but Piras remained unflustered.

They entered Diotivede's lab together, and Bordelli immediately sat down in the only available chair.

'This is Piras, he'll be joining us on Wednesday,' he said.

Diotivede made a gesture of greeting to the lad and then looked Bordelli up and down, slipping white rubber gloves off of his small, slender hands.

'Don't you think you'd better go and get some sleep?' he said.

'I shall, a little later. Listen, Diotivede, don't get offended if I ask you something I've already asked; it's just to be thorough.'

'Be my guest.'

'Are you sure Signora Pedretti died round nine o'clock? Couldn't it have been later? Or much earlier . . .?' He ran a hand over his face, unable to say anything else.

The doctor shot a quick glance at Piras and took a step forward, stiff as a tree trunk.

'No offence taken, but if I was unable to establish that sort of thing, I wouldn't do the work I do.'

'But *errare humanum est*, no?'

'Science is not human. If you'd brought me a body that had been dead for a month or a year . . . then I might have trouble determining the hour and day of death. But in this case . . . there are very precise stages, and there's the science to back it up. It's as impossible to make a mistake as it is to make a hole in water.'

Bordelli looked convinced.

'All right, then, I promise I won't ask you again. I was only hoping to make some progress, and instead I'm back to square one. Oh well.'

Piras squirmed as if wanting to say something, but remained silent. Bordelli got up, one hand on his back, and waved goodbye to Diotivede with the other.

'See you Wednesday,' he said.

'Bye,' said Diotivede without looking at him.

Bordelli insisted on driving again, and Piras said not a word. The car windows were completely open but only hot air blew in. One way or another, they arrived at headquarters. Bordelli's eyes were bloodshot and lifeless. Walking through the corridors like a drunk, gesturing hello to the various cops on duty and trailed by Piras, he went and sat down at his desk. He pressed his eyes with his fingers.

'Listen, Piras. I'm too tired and really don't feel like talking. But I wouldn't mind hearing you say something. Were you able to make anything of all this?'

'Are you sure you want to hear it now?'

'Absolutely.'

'And you promise to go to bed afterwards?'

'Promise.'

Piras asked whether it was all right if he paced about the room. Bordelli assented by drooping his eyelids and nodding ever so vaguely. He was trying, in the heat, to keep his exertions to a minimum. Piras came to a stop in the far corner. Bordelli followed him with his eyes, waiting for him to begin. To aid concentration, he was about to give in and light a cigarette, but the phone rang. It was Zia Camilla, asking after Rodrigo.

'Did you go and see him? How was he? All right?' she asked anxiously.

'Oh, quite all right, I'd say. He's just a little upset over—'

'Oh my God, has something happened?'

'No, no, nothing serious. Or maybe yes. He's in love, head over heels, like a teenager.'

'Oh, the poor dear. He's certainly not used to that. He must be in terrible shape.'

'You can rest easy, Zia. Rodrigo is only a little confused.'

Zia Camilla hung up, and Bordelli turned his eyes back to Piras.

'I'm ready,' he said.

'Do you mind if I start at the beginning?' asked Piras.

'Take all the time you need.'

Piras resumed pacing, with short, slow steps. He cast a glance at the photo of the president behind Bordelli, then made a fist and raised his thumb.

'Point number one: Signora Pedretti died of an asthma attack.' He raised his index finger. 'Point number two: only maté pollen could have ended her life that way.' He raised his middle finger. 'Point number three: maté doesn't grow here.' And he brought his three fingers together. 'We know that somebody killed the signora by triggering a lethal asthma attack through the use of the pollen of a tropical plant. A murder by the book. Furthermore, the cap of the Asthmaben bottle was screwed on too tight, which leads to the hypothesis that someone came into the room after the lady was already dead. Everything clear, so far?'

'Perfectly.'

'Good. We know the Morozzis are telling the truth – that is, that at the exact time their aunt was dying, at nine p.m., they were at a restaurant. One could conclude they are innocent.' And he gestured as if to put this hypothesis in a drawer. 'Now let's pretend we know for certain that it was they who killed Signora Pedretti. The mechanism, in the abstract, is easy to grasp: they found a way to make their aunt inhale that pollen while they were miles away. You see, Inspector? The theory is easy. But how the hell did they do it? That's the hard part.'

'Maybe they paid somebody.'

'So they could be blackmailed for the rest of their lives? No, and anyway, they're a couple of milquetoasts; they would never know where to find someone to do a job like that.'

'Go on,' said Bordelli.

Piras continued to explain the dynamics of the murder of Signora Pedretti-Strassen, speaking in a clear, clipped voice, succinct in every respect.

'Let us recapitulate in another fashion. A lady suffers from allergic asthma and I want to kill her, but of course I want it to look like an accident. I know that maté pollen can trigger a fatal attack, but I also know that her medicine, in most cases, even this one, can save her. The goal is to make her inhale that tropical pollen without giving her a chance to take her medicine . . .'

Bordelli got more comfortable in his chair and lit a cigarette, promising himself he would put it out halfway. He was anxious to hear Piras's conjectures, but he would rather have listened to a long, perhaps fictionalised exposé, so he could sit there comfortably for a few hours, listening to someone tell a story. He wished it would pour outside, to give some hope of a cooler night. Piras didn't seem to have such problems; despite the torrid heat, he looked cool and, most importantly, didn't sweat. He resumed talking, his eyes looking up at the corners of the ceiling.

'The first thing I need is the keys to the lady's house. This takes some doing, but in essence it's easy. All I have to do is make a cast, or else take the keys on the sly and get copies made.'

'Right.'

'Then I have to procure the pollen. I've done some research and found that they have a variety of specimens of maté at the botanical gardens.'

'In the greenhouse?'

'Of course. I need only pluck a few flowers when nobody's looking.'

'Right.'

'But I have to arrange things so that the signora will inhale some pollen, but without arousing any suspicions, either in her or anyone else.'

'Exactly.'

Piras stopped in front of the window and looked out at the rows of rooftops.

'There *is* a way to do this; the point is to find it. But this is not the only problem. I must also find a way to prevent the signora from taking the medicine she always keeps within reach.'

'Go on,' said Bordelli, staring at a big black fly walking on the windowpane. Piras turned to face him.

'That's easier. You replace the real medicine bottle with an identical one containing only water.'

'How?'

'I have copies of the keys. In a house of that size I can easily hide, and when Auntie is on the ground floor, I can go into her bedroom, switch the medicine bottles, and put the pollen where I need to put it.'

Bordelli rested his chin in his hand.

'And what if the police find the bottle with water instead of medicine in it?'

'Good question. For this reason, I return in the middle of the night and put everything back in its proper place. I put a couple of drops of medicine in the signora's mouth, so that it looks as if she did manage to take some, then I put the real bottle back in its proper place . . . But I'm very nervous and I forget to unscrew the cap.'

Piras fell silent for a moment, pinching his lip between thumb and forefinger, then continued.

'That blessed cap,' he said.

Bordelli sighed.

'If that's really the way things went, all we need to do is find out who did it and how,' he said ironically.

'The most likely thing is that it was one of the heirs. A murder of this kind goes through a long period of maturation and is organised with great care. But there must be a good motive, and money is an excellent motive, at least for some.'

Bordelli found himself with another cigarette in his hand but didn't light it. He offered one to Piras, who refused politely but with a certain disgust. Apparently he never smoked.

'All right, Piras. Let's pretend you're right. The killer is here before me, I know he did it, I have no doubt about it. Now, however, we need to find proof, otherwise there won't even be a trial.'

'Before anything else, we need to uncover the mechanism of the murder.'

'Right. The mechanism.' At this point Bordelli could wait no longer to light his cigarette, and took two deep puffs, immediately shaking away the first ashes.

'How the hell did they do it?' Bordelli repeated, talking mostly to himself.

Piras not only didn't smoke, he couldn't stand smoke. Stepping back instinctively, he started waving his open hands in the air to dispel it, as if only now finding the courage to vent his dislike. Bordelli pretended not to notice.

'All right, let's begin the game again,' the inspector said. 'Let's pretend we have the killers here before us. We know they did it, and they know we have no proof. What, at this point, would you do?'

'I think it would be totally pointless to apply any pressure on them before having first demolished their alibi. In short, we must figure out how . . .' All at once he stopped to swat away the smoke in the air around him, assumed a very serious expression and pointed to the pack of cigarettes on the table. 'Did you know, Inspector, that every one of those things shortens your life by one hour?'

Bordelli was well aware of this, but like all smokers he calculated only the damage done by a single cigarette, without ever tallying the final sum. He crushed the still-long butt in the ashtray, if only so that Piras would stop waving his arms in the air in disgust.

'I know it's a stupid vice, Piras, but it's not so easy to quit. I started during the war.' Piras was satisfied with the destruction of that cigarette and resumed his lecture.

'I was saying we need to work out how they managed to kill her from afar.'

'We've been circling round it for an hour.'

'Let me finish. The killers feel protected by their alibi, and they're right, in a sense. But once we discover their trick, we'll strip them down to their underwear by showing how flimsy their alibi is. And at that point we can try to make them confess.'

'Think so?'

'We can try, I say. If they lose their alibi, they'll get scared. I don't see any other way.'

Bordelli remained lost in thought for a good minute, chin in hand, eyes trained on Piras's wooden face. Then he looked at the sky outside the window as a breath of wind blew in, at long last. A distant rumble of thunder revived his hope for a good storm. It was almost nine, always the most melancholy time of the day for Bordelli. Down on the street, somebody called after his dog. The swallows were gobbling up insects, flying low and screeching between the buildings.

The inspector sat there for a long time staring out of the window, lulled by a string of vague thoughts, which often happened to him at that hour. He wasn't thinking of anything specific, but was rather in a state akin to daydreaming. The screeching halt of a car snapped him out of it. He stuck another cigarette in his mouth and reassured Piras with a hand gesture.

'I'm not going to light it. It's just to console myself.'

Piras said nothing, but his silence was as eloquent as his father's had been. His indignation and bitterness over this sordid killing could be read in his eyes.

'Let's rack our brains a little, Piras. We need to wipe out this damned alibi.'

'I'm doing my best, Inspector, but it's not a game. It's like trying to understand the composition of water by watching the rain fall.'

Piras could see that Bordelli was running out of steam and asked him again whether he wanted to be taken home, but the inspector refused.

'Thanks, Piras, but I can make it on my own.'

'As you wish.' They parted with a look of understanding.

Bordelli settled a couple of matters and then tried to phone Rodrigo – for the hell of it, just to find out how things were going with his belle – but there was no reply. He imagined his cousin half naked, clinking glasses with his woman, properly drunk and happy to be so, the flat a shambles, a splendid layer of filth on the bedroom floor, the phone ringing and ringing with neither one of them paying any mind, the once untouchable desk covered with dirty dishes.

He turned off the light and sat for a while in his office, watching the sky turn slowly red. At last he lit the cigarette he'd been craving for the past half-hour.

It wasn't quite eleven when Bordelli lay down in bed and turned out the light. The air smelled of *zampironi*, but the mosquitoes continued to buzz round his face. He lit his thousandth cigarette and smoked it, sweating and thinking of Elvira. He concentrated all his thoughts on her, in the hope of forgetting her more quickly that way. Perhaps it was only his fatigue, but he pictured her on the beach, next to his aunts from Mantua, then lying on the marble floor playing with him at two o'clock in the afternoon. Maybe it was because she looked like some-body else from long ago and who-knows-where. He saw Elvira's bare feet again, her pink mouth standing out on her tanned face . . . She was smiling at him, looking him straight in the eye as she lay back in bed, opening her arms, and he ran to kiss her, caressing her fragrant blonde hair, holding her tight until her bones began to crack . . . Maybe that was it . . . She resembled someone else from half a century before, during a summer with his aunts, a sixteen-year-old housemaid who seemed like a grown woman to him at the time. What was her name? Mariolina, Giannina, Annina . . . something like that, a name that ended in *ina*. Maybe Annina, yes, blonde with big green eyes and an imperfect little nose that he loved to death. He was about eight years old at the time, give or take a year, with eyes wide open, curious to see the world.

'I can scrub your back for you. Would you like that?'

'Yes.'

Annina leaned over him, smiling. She began running her hand up and down his back, all the way up to the nape of his neck. He felt the waves of warm water on his skin and closed his eyes in pleasure.

'Do you want the sponge?' he asked.

'No, I don't need the sponge,' she said, letting her soapy hand slide over his little neck and shoulder, over his chest and then down, under the water, over his belly . . . And this became a little game . . . Who knows how it started, or why . . . a shudder down his spine and butterflies in his stomach. Then he arched his whole body so that his little thingy came out of the water, and he held it with his fingers so that it would stand up straight.

'Look! There's an enemy periscope!' he shouted. She laughed and reached into the water.

'I'll take care of it,' she said. And she took the periscope between two fingers and squeezed it gently. He shuddered and plunged back into the water, feeling as if the space around him had expanded.

'Do you want to see it again?' he asked in a daze.

'No need. I know where to find it,' she said, smiling. And she rolled up her sleeve and immersed her arm in the water to look for the submarine. She found it at once, and with a complicitous smile she splashed all about down there. He just stared at her, not moving, as his periscope began to change form. It became hard and straight and almost hurt at the tip. He couldn't see it, but could feel its weight. It had grown so huge, it seemed to him, he was afraid to look at it. At last a flash of heat burned his neck, and his lips started trembling, hot and tingly. The periscope turned red hot and seemed to explode, and he started bucking like a colt with a strength completely unfamiliar to him, splashing water all over the floor. Annina was laughing for joy. She continued fondling the submarine for a few more seconds, then took her hand out of the water and caressed his wet hair.

'Did you like that?' she asked, drying her hands on her skirt. She had a face like the Blessed Virgin. He looked at her with eyes half shut and a great desire to sleep. She put her hand on his head, shaking it affectionately.

'Hey, little submarine, don't go telling your aunties about this, or they won't let us play any more. It's a secret, okay?'

He nodded yes and grabbed the rim of the tub to keep from sinking into the water.

'I mean it, okay? Don't tell anybody.'

'I promise,' he said, finger over his lips. Annina blew him a kiss and opened the door to leave.

'Annina!'

'What is it?'

'Can I ask you something?'

'Make it snappy.'

'Can I take a bath every day?'

Annina burst out laughing.

'Well, won't that make your aunties happy!' she said. She

blew him another kiss and left, singing to herself, leaving him to dream about the new game he had just learned.

As of that day, he started bathing very often, and his aunties were indeed happy.

'What a good little man, always so clean,' they would say.

Annina would slip into the bathroom and play the periscope game with him, her hand under the water and a smile on her lips. Afterwards, he would kiss her cheek, or bury his face in her blonde hair, breathing a scent of sun and the kitchen.

One evening he lay in bed, unable to sleep because that morning Annina had whispered into his ear: 'Tonight I'll come and see you in your room, and I'll read to you. Would you like that?'

He lay there with his head under the covers, listening to every sound. It seemed an eternity. When at last he heard the door open, a cold shudder ran up the back of his neck to his head. Someone sat down on the edge of the bed and pulled back the sheets. He felt the touch of coarse linen on his face and then, in the shadow, saw Annina's smiling face, a restless glint in her eye. A blonde braid brushed his ear. He pulled himself up and leaned back on the pillow. Annina was wearing a white, almost glowing nightgown.

'Let's be quiet.'

'Okay.'

'So, what shall I read you?'

'Ahhh, I dunno!'

She held a half-broken book in the air.

'Do you know *Moby-Dick*?'

'The whale?'

'Would like me to read it to you?'

'Yes.'

Annina rested the book on her lap, holding it still with her open hand. With her other hand, she went searching under the covers for his periscope and started playing with it with her fingertips. After she had read barely a page, she stopped.

'Can I come into bed with you?' she said. He nodded yes.

Annina dropped the book on to the floor and jumped into bed, lying down beside him and pulling the covers over her.

'Come on, little torpedo, come on top of me so we can cuddle.' And she slipped a hand under his back and gently rolled him on to her. He nearly sank into that large, female body. Burying his face under Annina's chin, he felt his lips against her smooth collarbone. A hot vein in his neck was throbbing fast. Anna was fiddling with his periscope, doing something he didn't understand, and then he felt her other hand slide down to his bottom and pull him towards her. His periscope plunged into a warm sea, and it felt as if his whole body were submerged in a hot tub. Annina began to move about and breathe heavily, then grabbed his hips and made him move with her. Raising his head, he saw her smile, eyes closed, as she stroked his hair and arched her head backwards. Her braid lay across the pillow beside her face.

'Kiss me, kiss me,' said Annina, pulling him by the shoulders. He thrust his lips forward and covered her cheeks with kisses.

'Yes, yes, lots and lots of kisses, kisses, kisses, kisses . . .' He kept kissing her, on the nose and eyes, then the ears, mouth and chin. His periscope aflame, all at once he felt a hot wave run deep through his flesh from the lower back to the nape of his neck, then many waves all together, rapid and deep. He grabbed her tight, almost in fear, fast exhaling all the breath he had left in him, as she pulled him tightly towards herself and whispered words he couldn't understand into his ear, caressing his head with both hands. He felt so good he almost wanted to cry.

Then peace.

'Now sleep,' said Annina. He collapsed on top of her, sinking into that vast, scented sea. Still feeling a few shudders under his skin, he fell into a deep sleep until morning. Waking up, the first thing he noticed was the smell of Annina's skin on the sheets.

A few days later, Annina was summoned home by her family.

They had found her a job with a seamstress in a town near by. He stood in the doorway of her room, watching her pack her suitcase. Every so often she would turn round and make a face.

'Little monster,' she said to him in play.

Before she had finished, he ran away, into the garden and under the pergola where his aunts were taking tea. Annina then came down carrying her suitcase and bowed faintly in greeting. The aunts, however, all stood up together and went to kiss her.

'Dear Annina, we wish you all the very best, do stay in touch . . .' He stood there beside them, not moving. He felt strange. The world had changed. Annina bent down to say goodbye to him, kissed him on the cheek and, before raising her head, whispered in his ear:

'Bye-bye, little torpedo.' Her lips were so close that her words echoed in his head, and he was worried that his aunts had heard. He blushed and stood there as Annina walked briskly away. He followed her with his eyes, waiting for her to turn round again, but she never did. The last he saw of her was the blonde braid bouncing on her bare neck.

'A registered letter for you, sir, from Rome.'

'Thanks, Mugnai, just set it down here. Do you know where Piras is?'

'I'll send him to you straight away, sir. I saw him just a moment ago.'

Mugnai disappeared and Bordelli opened the letter. As he leaned back in his chair to read it, his fingers searched his pocket for his cigarettes. He'd just been promoted to chief inspector. Old Giuseppe Ierinò had reached the end and was retiring. Bordelli chased away a fly that kept trying to land on his wrist, then lit his cigarette and, with a wrinkle of concern on his face, picked up the intercom to the office of the Assistant Commissioner.

'Dr Cavia, this is Bordelli.'

'Hello, Bordelli, did you get the news?'

'I certainly did.'

'You deserved it, don't you think? You can move straight into Ierinò's office this morning, if you like.'

'Well, that's what I was calling about. I'd rather stay where I am.'

'Why? Ierinò's office is bigger and brighter, and gives on to the street.'

'I'd rather stay where I am, believe me.'

'I really don't understand.'

'I don't either, but that's my preference, I assure you.'

'As you wish, Inspector – I mean, Chief Inspector.'

'Thank you, sir.'

As Bordelli was crushing his cigarette in the ashtray, there was a knock at the door.

'Come in.'

'You asked for me, Inspector?'

'Sit down, Piras. We need to take stock of the situation.' A wisp of smoke rose from the not quite extinguished cigarette in the ashtray, and Piras looked at it with concern. Bordelli noticed and snuffed it out. As he was about to speak, he slapped himself on the forehead.

'Damn!' He'd just remembered Rosa's flowers. He sprang to his feet and spread his arms. 'I'm sorry, Piras, but I have to go somewhere very quickly.'

They left the room together. In the doorway, Bordelli turned round to look at what had been his office for the past fifteen years. By now it had become his home. He could eat and sleep there as easily as in his apartment. Not even a salary increase could persuade him to move upstairs. Let alone the fact that it would have disturbed him to see someone else sitting at his desk. It would have made him feel old.

'I'll see you later, Piras. Meanwhile, give some thought to our next move.'

'My brain is mush today, Inspector, but I'm not giving up. I can sense that we're close.'

'It's always good to be optimistic. See you later.'

Bordelli ran out, hopped into his Beetle and raced to Rosa's place. He could already see the devastation, the plants withered all the way down to the roots after a long agony. He imagined Rosa's expression. She certainly wouldn't start yelling, since that wasn't her style, but she would wear a long face for quite a while.

He parked on the pavement in front of Carlino's bar, to pick up the keys. Carlino Forzone had been a resistance fighter in the Piedmont with the *azzurri* and had met Beppe Fenoglio. After the war he had seen things he didn't like, and had placed a few 'righteous' bombs here and there – that is, bombs that didn't kill anyone – just to let people know that not everyone was ready to take it up the arse.

Even before getting out of the car, Bordelli saw him through the window, leaning over the bar, reading the newspaper with a butt between his lips, hollow cheeked, fingers yellow with nicotine, an old partisan always ready to rant polemically against the Christian Democrats and just about everyone else. The inspector entered the bar and raised a hand in greeting.

'Ciao, Carlino. Rosa was supposed to have left you the keys for me.'

Carlino guffawed and clapped his hands above the newspaper.

'You're just the man I was looking for, Inspector. Listen to this: *the minister asserted that we need to forget the past . . . the country needs a positive response . . . Italy has emerged, with some effort, but with head held high, from a fratricidal war . . . and all that matters now is the future . . . he praised the industriousness of all categories of workers, who in only a few years . . . tremendous growth for the country . . . prosperity . . . a home . . . I am committed to enforcing respect for . . .* and blah blah blah blah blah . . . I've heard this claptrap before, been hearing it for years, an' it makes my hands itch so bad that if I start scratching I'll scratch myself down to the bone.'

'Stop tormenting yourself, Carlino. We've already done our part, now it's time to let the young people try. You'll see, sooner or later the bad guys'll get a spanking.'

Carlino rolled up the newspaper and went over to the espresso machine.

'Coffee?' he said.

'No thanks. I've already had two.'

'The young are only interested in having fun, Inspector. What the hell do they care about the blackshirts and the war?'

'Don't take it personally.'

'They only see us as senile fools with a nostalgia for bombs.'

'They may be right, Carlino.'

'I'd like to see these brats fight the Nazis and the Black Brigades, for Christ's sake!'

'Sooner or later they'll learn what happened, you'll see.'

'At least one of those pricks up there needs to have the balls to tell the truth, Goddamn it all! After the war was over they let all the Fascists out of jail only to make room for us partisans. Don't you think it's time they explained why?' He took Rosa's keys out of a drawer and walked round the counter. 'Goddammit! If we don't change this world, we who have seen what we've seen . . . if we don't do it, then nobody will. I'd bet my family jewels on it.'

Bordelli smiled.

'I'd love to change the world,' he said. 'But I can only change it by doing my job well.'

Carlino gave him a funny look.

'Sometimes I wonder how someone like you manages to stay in the police force, in the service of *those guys*.'

Bordelli sighed.

'I'm not in anybody's service, Carlino. I'm a policeman. I try to find out who killed whom. Politics has nothing to do with it.'

Carlino shook his head.

'Wrong. Everything is political, Inspector, even . . . even taking a piss,' he said. He dropped Rosa's keys into Bordelli's hand.

'Well, Carlino. I've really got to go now.'

'Take care, Inspector. And drop by some time.'

Bordelli left the bar and walked briskly towards Rosa's building, as if getting there a few seconds earlier might save a few plants. He climbed the stairs, opened the door and rushed through the sitting room towards the terrace, but then stopped halfway. He had clearly heard a noise coming from Rosa's bedroom.

'Anybody here?'

He heard a door creak. He cautiously approached the room and turned on the light. Everything looked to be in order, but one of the wardrobe doors was ajar.

'Is that you, Rosa?'

He turned off the light and went back into the hall. He reopened the front door and then closed it again, remaining inside the flat. Then he tiptoed into the kitchen and waited, looking towards the sitting room through the half-open door. About a minute later, there appeared a short, thin man with the sad face of a comic from a warm-up act for a variety show. The stranger tiptoed his way towards the front door. Bordelli came out of the kitchen and walked up to him, shaking his head.

'Canapini! What are you doing here?'

The little man's jaw dropped, and he nearly fell from fright. 'Inspector . . . it's you!'

'Yes, but you still haven't answered my question.'

Canapini stood there in the middle of the room without moving. He threw up his hands, his face turning sadder than ever. Bordelli flopped into an armchair.

'How can you possibly be so unlucky, Canapini? A lady friend of mine lives here.'

The burglar grew animated and ran up to Bordelli.

'I swear I didn't know, Inspector. Anyway, all I took is this.' He removed a small statuette of yellow glass from his pocket, dusted it on his shirtsleeve. 'An' I'm going to put it right back.' He set it down on a console. 'There,' he said. 'I swear I didn't know.'

He looked at Bordelli with the expression of a beaten dog.

'At ten in the morning, Canapini!'

The little man shrugged.

'I'm in a bad way, Inspector. If I don't find something to sell to Zoppo today, I won't eat.'

'When did you get out?'

'Yesterday, Inspector. This is the first flat I've broken into.'

Bordelli stood up, knees cracking, and headed towards the kitchen.

'Give me a hand watering the plants,' he said. The little burglar followed Bordelli on to the terrace, which looked out over the roofs of Santo Spirito, and together they gave drink to the thirsty – geraniums, azaleas, tulips, rosemary, lavender, and all the other species of plants and flowers Bordelli didn't recognise. Luckily they had survived the heat, and the moment they felt the water, they began visibly to revive.

'Canapini, let's not beat about the bush. First of all, strike this address from your list.'

Canapini was about to promise, but Bordelli raised a hand as if to say he took his word for it.

'Secondly, take this . . . and I don't want any fuss.'

He put a ten-thousand-lira note in the little man's hand and then put his finger over the other's mouth.

'Don't say anything, Canapini. I just got a raise today.'

'But I can't accept this, Inspector.' He had tears in his eyes, holding the note with two fingers, as if it were diseased. Bordelli lost patience.

'I don't want to hear about it, Cana. Take it or I'll arrest you, and I'm not joking.'

Canapini wiped his eyes with his fingers.

'Thank you, Inspector. If all policemen were like you . . .'

'You'd be out burgling every single day. Is that what you were going to say?'

Canapini blushed and twisted up his mouth. He seemed on the verge of sobbing. Bordelli put his hand on the man's neck.

'That's enough, Canapini, for Christ's sake! You're the unluck-iest burglar I've ever met! Why don't you change professions?'

'What would I do?'

'Listen, why don't you come for dinner at my place tomorrow evening? I've invited a few friends. Botta's doing the cooking.'

The little thief lit up.

'Botta? I haven't seen him for months.'

'You must spend your holidays in different places.'

'And Botta . . . knows how to cook?'

'No, he doesn't know how to cook, he's a born cook. It's different.'

'Well, well.'

'You remember my address?'

'Of course, Inspector, I've got it printed up here,' he said, pointing a finger to his forehead. Bordelli thought a poor bloke like Canapini deserved a tombstone with a carved inscription at the very least. He belonged to a generation of thieves who put honour above money, a species that was slowly but inexorably dying out.

They descended the stairs together. Out on the blazing pavement, Bordelli had an idea.

'Listen, Cana, I'm supposed to come here every day to water the flowers, but I'm terribly busy.'

Canapini understood at once. His lips curled as if to smile, but his face became sadder than ever.

'I'll take care of it, Inspector, don't you worry, I can do it.'

'Thanks, that takes a load off my mind. Here are the keys.'

As he held them out to him, Canapini raised his hands.

'I can't take them, Inspector. I'm afraid I'd lose them.'

'Then how will you get in?' Bordelli realised at once what a silly question he had asked, and only shook his head, smiling.

'If God created flies, there must be a reason,' somebody had written, though at that moment he couldn't remember who. His thoughts drifted off, searching his memory for things he had read in his youth, but he still couldn't remember . . . and slowly they turned to other flies, in April of '45, in northern Italy, the flies swarming round the face of the last

Nazi he killed. He had taken aim from afar, and from above, as the German ran by below the embankment. He had set the machine gun for single fire and kept shooting until the target fell to the ground. The Nazi was a blond lad of about seventeen, eyes open wide to the heavens above. His helmet had rolled ahead of him, and Bordelli had picked it up and felt something like a blow to the stomach. On one side was a swastika painted in white, with a large X painted over it in red. Above, at the top of the helmet, was the bullet hole, which passed right through the first N in the name ANNA, written in white paint beside a heart, also white, its point slanted to the left. Bordelli felt the vomit rise into his throat. He had killed a blond boy in love with an Italian girl, not a Nazi. He sat down on the grass and lit one of his hundred daily cigarettes. He had kept that helmet ever since, stowed away in a wardrobe. He never killed anyone else after that, never felt like firing any more. The notches on the butt of his machine gun stopped at thirty-seven.

He ran a hand over his face, and for the first time felt as if the war had taken place a thousand years ago.

Piras's face appeared inside the half-open door.

'Am I disturbing you, Inspector?'

'Not at all, Piras. Come in.'

The Sardinian remained standing in front of the desk. He chased away a fly that had landed on his cheek. He had a grave expression on his face.

'I wanted to ask you what we're going to do about the Morozzi brothers,' he said.

'You seem to be taking the case very much to heart.'

'We should interrogate them again, but separately. And I would do the same with the wives.'

'You want to upset them, I guess.'

'Exactly. And it doesn't matter that we don't yet have a clear sense of things. What do you say?'

Bordelli mulled it over. He swatted at two flies making love on his arm.

'Piras, do you remember who wrote: "If God created flies, there must be a reason?"'

'Saint Augustine, Inspector. In the *Confessions.*'

Bordelli nodded, as if he'd known all along.

'All right, Piras, I agree with you. Let's interrogate them all, one at a time.'

The Sardinian looked quite pleased.

'Then I'll have them summoned,' he said.

'Yes, take care of that yourself. And have them come tomorrow.'

Piras left, and Bordelli sat there, reflecting, amid a dozen or so frantic flies. The case was still at the same point. They needed to work out how it was possible to kill someone from sixty miles away. And they had to do it in August, the hottest August in memory.

But what if the Morozzis were in fact innocent? Who could have killed that woman, and why? For revenge?

Bordelli thought with envy of Rodrigo, so full of hope and novelty. Perhaps he had found the right woman, which was saying a lot. And he was two years younger than him. One could only imagine what kind of nights he was spending with his mysterious lover.

The interrogation was a painful affair. Bordelli consoled himself with the thought that Botta was already at the cooker. He had left him a short while before, chopping onions.

The Morozzi brothers did nothing but whimper the whole time. They wiped away their sweat with their handkerchiefs, repeating everything they had already said. Their wives resembled one another like sisters. Gina and Angela. They had the same unpleasant mannerisms, the same whorish make-up, and both gave off a strong smell of chestnut flour. They too repeated everything their husbands had said, with a long-suffering expression that inspired only antipathy. The only concrete result of the interrogation was to make them all upset, as intended.

After they left, Bordelli started pacing about his office.

'So, Piras, how did they do it? . . . And what is that smell?'

'That's all I can think about, Inspector, but I still can't come up with an answer.'

Piras, of course, was referring to the first question. Bordelli crossed his arms over his paunch, continuing to sniff the air with irritation, then got up and opened the window wide. Piras sat stone faced, thinking, trying to put the pieces together. It wasn't so difficult, after all. By now the dynamic of the murder was more or less clear: Salvetti's Alfa Giulietta Sprint, the switched medicine bottles, the copied keys. All that remained to be unravelled was the business of the pollen, nothing more, and then the rest would be like taking candy from a baby. Bordelli circled round his desk and plopped down in his chair.

'Today's the funeral, Piras, then they all go off to the solicitor's to read the will.'

'Was Signora Pedretti very rich?'

'Very. But she left it all to the nuns.'

Piras smiled wickedly.

'Good for her,' he said.

'If the Morozzis did it, it was all for nothing,' Bordelli said.

Piras started walking about the room, index finger over his lips, gaze wandering up and down the walls. The inspector drummed his fingers on his cigarette pack, also thinking. He glanced at his watch and saw that it was already one o'clock. The nauseating smell was still in the air and made his head ache.

'I'm going to get a bite to eat, Piras. See you tonight, at my place.'

'All right.'

On his way out of the station, Bordelli tapped on the window of the guardroom.

'Mugnai, when you get a chance, go up to my office. The ladies left behind a nasty little scent as a souvenir. See if you can get rid of it.'

'All right, sir.'

★   ★   ★

Bordelli dropped in at home, deciding he couldn't go to Totò's. He wanted to eat lightly and then lie down for half an hour before going back to work. He ended up sitting at the kitchen table eating tuna and onions while Botta fussed about with his saucepans with the seriousness of an engineer.

'An extra guest'll be coming tonight, Botta, but don't be alarmed. It's only Canapini.'

'Cana? Where did you unearth him?'

'I found him at the flat of a lady friend.'

'Aha. You caught him trying to rob someone.'

'It doesn't matter.'

Botta sniggered and continued stirring the contents of a large earthenware pot with a wooden spoon, raising Dantesque clouds of smoke.

'The crazy fool! It'll be nice to see him, poor bloke. When did he get out?'

'A couple of days ago.'

'Want a few hot beans, Inspector?'

'Thanks.'

Botta poured a ladleful of steaming beans on to a plate, then started chopping parsley with a mezzaluna. In one corner of the table was a large slab of red meat beside a salad bowl filled to the brim with diced potatoes. A number of mysterious bags were lined up on the sideboard.

'What's it going to be after the Lombard soup?' Bordelli asked.

'It's a surprise, Inspector. All I can say is that it'll be a journey outside of Italy.'

'To the north or south?'

'No more questions, Inspector. Botta never talks.'

'In this heat I'm sure you'll take us south. Morocco? Tunisia?'

'This is a delicate moment, Inspector. Don't distract me.'

Bordelli finished his tuna and ate an apple without saying another word. Ennio moved nimbly back and forth between table and cooker, completely submerged in his thoughts. Seeing him so busy, Bordelli decided to get out of his way, went and lay down in bed and lit a cigarette. The blinding sunlight forced its way through the slats of the closed shutters. At that hour, two in the afternoon, the silence was almost absolute. Feeling a great sadness well up in his chest, Bordelli closed his eyes and very nearly fell asleep with the lighted cigarette in his hand. He crushed it in the ashtray and turned on to his side. He was trying to banish from his thoughts the image of Elvira brushing a blonde lock of hair away from her face, and when he finally succeeded, it was replaced by another, much older memory . . . an abandoned farmhouse at the top of a hill . . . He was on patrol with Piras Sr, climbing the slope through fallow fields. When they reached the house they stopped in the farmyard and looked around. It was spring and the insects were buzzing round the flowers. A sort of maternal warmth emanated from the hot bricks. He felt like lying down in the grass and sleeping for ever. He slung the machine gun over his shoulder and folded his hands behind his head, breathing in the scented air. Then all at once he turned round, instinctively, without knowing why, and saw the double barrel of a shotgun poke out of some bushes beside the house. He managed to grab Gavino by the arm and pull him to the ground a split second before the shot. The pellets struck the wall of the house, raising a yellowish cloud of dust. Flat on the ground, they awaited the second shot.

'Should I fire back?' asked Piras. Bordelli shook his head no. They lay there on the warm brick, carefully scanning the bushes. The double barrel was gone, but soon poked out through more shrubbery. He and Piras rolled to one side and the shot wasn't late in coming. The hail of pellets scraped the ground, cutting the grass and raising splinters of brick. At once Bordelli sprang to his feet and ran towards the shotgun, diving into the bush, where he found himself in front of an old man with a broad face, a long beard and a black peasant's cap pulled down to his eyes. The man was pointing his now empty shotgun at him, shaking the barrels to keep him at bay.

'You want my chickens, do you? Well, no chickens for you, my friend, the Germans gunned them all down, too, hee hee

hee! Ah, no chickens, no rabbits, all kaput, heeheehee! *Sprechen deutsch, ja?* Hee hee hee! Traitor rabbits, up against the wall, all of 'em, kaput!'

He goggled his eyes and burst into laughter. Bordelli heard Gavino panting behind him.

'And who is this?' asked the Sardinian. Without taking his eyes off the old man, Bordelli tapped his temple twice with his finger.

Piras came forward with a great rustling of leaves and branches.

'He may be crazy, but he was ready to make us bleed,' he said, gesturing as if to say that his cartridges were harmless, filled only with birdshot.

The old man was no longer smiling, but staring at the double barrel of the shotgun in wonder. He remained that way for a few seconds, brow wrinkled as if listening for a faraway sound. Then he set down his rifle, lowered his eyes, and sobbed three or four times, chest heaving.

'Animals!' he said, rubbing his nose and stamping his feet on the ground so hard he seemed to want to break through the earth's crust. At last he spat to one side and raised the rifle again, pointing it at Bordelli.

'No chickens, *mein general*, they're all kaput. Heeheehee! *Sprechen deutsch?* All kaput.'

Bordelli and Piras exchanged glances. They took the mad old peasant by the arm and walked back towards the field, as the man kept muttering 'kaput, kaput' without cease. Back at the infirmary they coddled him like a child. He scarfed down some American junk food and got so drunk he finally threw up. The following day they sent him along with a couple of wounded to a hospital behind the front lines. Bordelli continued to wonder whether he had done the right thing to take the old man away from his little house and not simply leave him there alone to live out his crazy life in peace.

★ ★ ★

A fly landed on his nose. He opened his eyes to look at the alarm clock. He was sure he had slept hardly at all, but in fact it was almost six o'clock. He lay in bed for a while longer, trying to revive his sluggish muscles. The stink of cigarette butts bothered him, so he covered the ashtray with a book. Stretching his legs over the hot sheets, he stared at the ceiling and turned his thoughts to Signora Pedretti-Strassen. He saw again her gnarled hands clutching at her throat, her blue-veined white feet, her sharp, slightly hooked nose, her open eyes, full of horror and almost alive, her body stiff on the great bed, alone in her large villa on the hill, high over the deserted city, surrounded by age-old trees . . . At once he felt like going back there, to breathe that air again, see that room again, look at those floors again.

He put on his shoes and poked his head into the kitchen. Botta was dicing meat, engrossed in his labours, while a white, spice-scented smoke rose up from a skillet.

'I'm going out, Ennio. I'll see you at nine.'

Botta muttered something without looking up. The inspector left him there and went out into the street, mouth still pasty with sleep. As the Volkswagen was parked in the shade, he could get in without trauma. Reaching the Lungarno, he crossed the Ponte alle Grazie and turned, as always, to look up at the church of San Miniato al Monte, his favourite. Its white façade always had the same effect, whether from up close or far away.

A few minutes later he turned up the sloping street that led to the villa. A warm, sticky wind blew in through the window. He could already see the villa's roof from afar, with the great cedar towering over it. He took the last curves with an unlit cigarette between his lips. He would smoke it later, perhaps seated on a sofa in front of some beautiful painting.

He stopped the Beetle in the usual spot and got out of the car. Crossing the street, he looked down at the city below. A maze of red roofs bristling with the churches' belfries. He felt a great urge to scream at the top of his lungs, to stop thinking about Elvira's eyes, the slap of her bare little feet on the tiled floor. He wanted to forget he was fifty-three years old, a melancholy grump with no more desire to dream, an old man fond of solitude, unable to open up to others.

Lighting the cigarette, he headed towards the villa. He entered the garden somewhat tentatively, as if violating someone's privacy. The cicadas hummed, high in the trees. All was calm. Entering the house, he went straight up to the first floor. In Rebecca's room the window had been left ajar. Bordelli opened it wide, pulled up a chair, and sat in front of it. The wind gently rustled the trees' great boughs, and soon he was asleep, chin on his chest, lulled by the cicadas.

A gust whistled through the trees, waking him up. It was almost dark outside. His cigarette had fallen to the floor and burnt down, leaving a brown streak on a floor tile. Glancing at his watch, he saw that it was almost nine o'clock.

'Shit,' he said. Dinner must be almost ready. He tried to get up out of the chair, but his legs were unsteady. Bending down to pick up the butt, he looked around for an ashtray. Spotting a wastebasket in the corner, he tossed the cigarette and missed. Rising with a sigh, he walked past the bed and noticed something moving on it. Turning round with a start, he smiled: a huge white cat was lying on one of the pillows, paws in the air and eyes half open.

'And what are you doing here?' he said.

He went up to the animal and patted it. The cat opened its eyes and meowed. Its fur was soft. Bordelli ran his hand all along its belly.

'Got to go now, pretty boy. Ciao.'

He turned to leave, but stopped in his tracks in the doorway. Perplexed, he looked back at the cat, then went downstairs and started inspecting the windows and doors. They were all tightly shut. He couldn't work out how the cat had entered. Clearly the animal hadn't been shut up indoors all this time, and it obviously wasn't dying of hunger. Why he was taxing his brain to uncover a cat's secrets, he couldn't say, but at the end of the day he was a policeman, and there was no helping the fact that strange phenomena aroused his curiosity. Thus there must be an opening somewhere. Ten past nine. His guests must already be seated at table. As he was about to leave, the cat walked past him, towards the kitchen. Bordelli followed. It headed straight towards the French door as if about to run into it, but, as though by magic, the moment its head touched the wood, a little hatch opened up and the cat disappeared outside, tail stroking the edge of the cat door. Bordelli got down on his knees for a better look. He'd never seen anything like it. The little door was hinged on top, and when at rest, it filled the opening, completely concealing it. It opened with ease from either side, like saloon doors. Brilliant. Nine fifteen. Now he had better fly. No more playing cop. The others had probably already started eating. He ran out of the villa and raced back into town, driving like a madman. When he slipped the key into his front door, it was 9.25.

'Inspector, we said nine o'clock!' said Ennio, offended. Bordelli put a hand on his shoulder.

'Sorry. Is everyone here?'

'Everyone but you. I've already served some wine.'

'Well done, Ennio.'

'Who's the guy in the doctor's smock?'

'That must be Dante. He's an inventor and mouse-tamer.'

'Mouse-tamer?'

'He calls them each by name. You ought to see it.'

Dante's voice, soaring in a baritone solo, boomed from the dining room. Botta lost interest in the mice and gestured impatiently to Bordelli.

'Now please go into the dining room, Inspector. The antipasti are on their way.'

'I can't wait.'

Going in, Bordelli saw Dante waving an empty glass in the air. He was wearing his usual work-smock with its usual stains. His white, unruly air shone in the light of the chandelier.

'. . . anyone who can grasp the world as a whole can see intolerable realities unworthy of even the simplest animal communities . . . Don't you agree, Inspector?'

'I do.'

Bordelli excused himself for arriving late, blaming some pressing matters that could not be put off. The guests all rose to shake his hand, with the exception of Diotivede, who greeted him with a nod. The inspector hurriedly made his way to the table.

'No, no, don't get up. Hello, Piras. Please remain seated, everyone. How's it going, Dr Fabiani?'

An emotional Canapini came up to him and pulled him into a corner.

'Thank you, Inspector, thank you . . . I . . . I . . .'

Bordelli put his arms round the thief's neck and shook him affectionately.

'That's enough of that, Canapini . . . And Rosa's flowers?'

Canapini sniffled and gave the saddest of smiles.

'Fine, Inspector, just fine.'

'Good. Now let's see what we can do about stuffing ourselves.'

'Thank you, Inspector, thank you.'

They went and sat down, as Dante resumed his argument.

'If you think about it, the vast majority of humanity has always worked for the benefit of a few – a gigantic mechanism creaking and churning for the amusement of a few thousand people. Something's not right. Think of a train, for example. One single engine transports thousands of people. Now reverse the mechanism: a train with a thousand engines transporting one man. Sheer folly. So one must ask oneself: how can this continue without the slightest sign of ever ending? I have never found a satisfactory answer.'

Canapini was looking at Dante with the expression of someone who doesn't quite understand the concepts but instinctively grasps the meaning of things. Dante was about to continue, but then Botta came in with two trays straight out of the *Arabian Nights*. He set them down at the centre of the table.

'Welcome to Istanbul. I can't remember the Turkish name of this dish, but I'll tell you later what's in it.' On one tray were seven dark little domes that looked as hard as cement, adorned with lettuce leaves. On the other was a quivering snow-white timbale speckled with tiny red dots and surrounded by thin slices of raw carrot. Ennio started serving.

'Naturally the ingredients are not quite the same, since you can't get them here, but the effect is the same. Be sure to pour yourselves some wine, because it's spicy.'

The dark domes turned out to be creamy, velvety, incredibly delicious and scorching with hot pepper. The timbale had a strong taste of cheese and onion and was equally piquant. The first three bottles of red were quickly dispatched. Ennio declared that Chianti was a good match for Turkish cuisine.

'It almost seems made for it,' he said with an amicable jab of the elbow at Canapini, whose sadness seemed to be slowly lifting. Dante proposed a toast to the chef, and glasses tinkled merrily. Botta blushed from the praise, raising his own glass, then removed the small plates and dashed into the kitchen to fetch the first course.

He returned with a great big pot.

'This has nothing to do with Turkey, but was requested by Dr Diotivede. *Zuppa lombarda.*'

The doctor shrugged and threw up his hands, excusing himself for the digression. Botta passed around a basket full of toasted bread and then served the soup, giving precise instructions as to the olive oil and Parmesan cheese to be added. Piras rather hesitantly sampled the transparent broth with little yellow beans floating in it, but then continued with enthusiasm after the first spoonful. Diotivede declared it perfect.

They all took second helpings, even Canapini, who held his tablespoon as if it were a screwdriver. Diotivede served himself another ladleful, then a third, slowing down the rhythm of the meal.

'Sorry, but I've been wanting this for years,' he said.

The second course took them back to Turkey: spicy beef

stew. They had no trouble emptying another four bottles. After a while, all that remained in the pot was the ring left behind by the boiled liquid. Then it was time for pudding, also Turkish, for which Botta uncorked three bottles of sweet raisin wine from Pantelleria.

'Pantelleria is more or less at the same latitude as Turkey, isn't it?' he said, gesturing horizontally with his hand. He filled their cups with an amber-coloured cream, sweet and fragrant, smelling of roses. It melted in one's mouth like gelatin, and had a thousand flavours. Nobody had ever tasted anything like it, and naturally it was all gone in a matter of minutes. The inspector proposed another toast to Botta. Then he turned towards Piras.

'Did you remember to bring those Sardinian biscuits?'

'Of course, Inspector. They're in the kitchen.' He stood up to get them, but Botta pushed him back down into his chair.

'I'll go,' he said. He returned with a paper bag that he emptied on to the table. After twenty years, Bordelli finally saw with his own two eyes what Gavino Piras had described a thousand times: little rhomboid biscuits covered with coloured sprinkles. Nobody present was familiar with them except, of course, for Ennio, who even knew how to make them.

'I learned how at Asinara. Mine are as good as any Sardinian's,' he said. And so, after their journey to Turkey, they all found themselves in Sardinia. The dinner party was getting louder and louder. When they'd finished the raisin wine, out came the grappa, three bottles of it: one white, another flavoured with rue, a third with juniper, all rigorously without labels. Bordelli pointed this out, smiling.

'That stuff's all illegal, Ennio. Where the hell did you get it?'

'From Bolla, Inspector. He sends you his regards.'

Bordelli poured himself a glass of the juniper grappa. Then the coffee arrived, and the smokers got down to business. Fabiani and Diotivede, who didn't smoke, kept refilling their glasses. Piras, hating smoke, pushed his chair back a bit, remaining nevertheless unruffled by the fools breathing smoke instead of air. Dante, who was seated beside him, lit a cigar as fat as a sausage, blowing great puffs of dense, acrid smoke between yellow teeth. Bordelli saw Piras's distress and got up and opened the other window. A gust of hot air immediately blew in, and the fog of smoke began to dissipate.

Dante began to talk about Rebecca's funeral, and all fell silent, including Fabiani, Canapini and Botta, who knew nothing about her death . . .

The basilica of Santa Croce felt bigger than ever, as it was almost empty. It was August, after all, everyone was on holiday, and hardly anyone knew that Rebecca had died. The Morozzi brothers and their wives stood motionless in front of the coffin, dressed in mourning, tiny under the gaze of Christ and the saints. Signora Maria was whimpering in a corner, nearly hidden behind the funerary monument of some illustrious poet; every so often she let out a sob that echoed throughout the church. Sitting in a central pew were three of Rebecca's lady friends. Dante knew them and greeted them from afar with a nod. All three were widows. They returned his greeting and whispered intensely among themselves, shaking their heads. There were some six or seven unknown old ladies scattered about, kneeling with hands folded, their jawbones trembling with prayer and Parkinson's. They weren't there for Rebecca, but for the mass. In the last pew was a man of about sixty, tall and rather good looking, whom Dante didn't know. Despite the heat, he wore a jacket and tie. He stared at the casket from a distance, sweating and weeping. He left just before the *Ite Missa Est*, hastily crossing himself and walking out.

'I am sure that handsome gentleman was my sister's lover,' said Dante. 'He looks like a professor, no?'

The priest was a fat, likeable little man who spoke with the accent of the Romagna. During the homily he launched into a fine speech on the serenity of the immortal soul and the resurrection of the flesh, and at that point Dante interrupted

him, approaching the altar, voice booming in the empty church.
The priest gave him a dirty look.

'*Mo ben!* This is hardly the moment, you foolish lug!' he
shouted.

Dante apologised, yelling that he was distracted and that
such things happened. Lost in his thoughts about immortality,
he had very nearly lit a cigar on the spot.

After the service, the bier was transported to the cemetery
and inserted in the appointed vault in the family chapel, a
nineteenth-century Gothic Revival structure covered with
curlicues. The stonemasons were ready with their bricks and
cement already mixed. It took them scarcely ten minutes to
finish their task. The Morozzi brothers stood stonily in front
of the chapel, looking disoriented. Signora Maria glared at them
with disgust. When the ceremony was over, Dante energetically
shook the hand of each of the brothers, which as usual felt
spongy and sweaty, and slippery as fish. Behind their oversized
black sunglasses, their wives looked saddened, heads down
and muttering.

'Poor thing.'

'What a shame!'

'Poor Auntie, to die so young.'

Hearing these comments, Dante burst out laughing, his mind
on the will. At last he lit his cigar. After kissing Signora Maria
one last time, he went home, collapsed in an armchair and,
with his first sip of grappa, burst into tears.

'But that's not very interesting,' Dante said to the dinner guests.
'Would you like to hear about the will?'

They all said yes. More grappa and cigarettes made the
rounds. Dante clutched his cigar with his teeth, to free up his
hands. He liked to draw in the air the things he described.

'All right. Imagine a beautiful room with wooden bookcases
up to the ceiling, full of thick tomes with gold-inlaid spines:
Plutarch, Herodotus, Roman law, *The Guild of Notaries*, the
History of Italy, a Bible, and then some large oriental vases, a

clock under a bell-jar, some bronze statues – a female nude, an Indian on horseback . . . Hanging from the ceiling in the middle of the room, a large, unlit chandelier with crystal pendants, a very fine Persian carpet on the floor, and an enormous desk, perfectly uncluttered . . . All this in penumbra, since the shutters are closed outside a row of three tall windows. The secretary shows us in, has us sit in the five chairs already lined up for us, and with a cold smile, she says: "Mr Balatri will be with you in a moment. He apologises for the lack of light, but he's just had an operation on his eyes." Then she leaves, heels clattering on the floor. We waited a good ten minutes without saying a word. I felt like laughing, but managed to restrain myself. Then the lawyer comes in, a tiny, quiet man who looked like he was in pain, wearing tinted glasses because of the operation. He sits down, looking us straight in the eye, and says, "My condolences." He had a funny voice, all nose, but maybe it was just me who thought it was funny, since I knew what the upshot of the whole business would be.'

Dante savoured his story between mouthfuls of smoke.

'The lawyer then opened a drawer and pulled out an envelope, which he opened with a paper knife, extracting a sheet of paper. Glancing again at all of us, to see if we were ready, he began to read: "*I, the undersigned, Rebecca Pedretti-Strassen, being of sound mind, declare that upon my death, the following shall be done according to my wishes: I bequeath all my possessions, including the villa and paintings—*" and here the lawyer paused, coughed into his hand and cleared his throat, as the nephews leaned forward in their chairs "*to the convent of the Sisters of Monte Frassineto, with the sole exception of . . .*" At this point confusion broke out: some started scraping their shoes against the floor, Giulio bit into his fingernails, drawing blood, and the lawyer politely asked for silence, so he could go on. He resumed: "*. . . with the sole exception of a small painting of a purple sky, which I leave to my brother Dante, with my best wishes for a long and happy life; a sum in the amount of three million lire, to be given to Signora Maria Dolci, with my sincerest affections; and* *four photographs, attached hereto, which I leave with all my heart to my beloved nephews, Anselmo and Giulio Morozzi, and their lovely wives, that they may keep the memory of their dear Aunt Rebecca forever alive* . . . Here are the pictures." All four reached out to take them. It was a beautiful shot of my sister standing in front of the villa. Four copies, one for each, so they wouldn't quarrel over it.'

Dante chortled and applied a match to his cigar until it caught flame. Then he knocked back a slug of grappa and took three deep puffs, filling the air with a great smelly cloud of smoke.

'There was pandemonium. My nephews were nearly in tears, the wives started shouting and pounding the desktop. Gina stood up without a word, took one step, and collapsed on the carpet. The lawyer was shocked, his hands were trembling. He summoned his secretary and told her to call an ambulance, but then Gina suddenly woke up and started punching her husband, who had come to her aid. "Stop, darling, don't hit me like that," he said. And so the lawyer dismissed the secretary with a gesture and then threw up his hands. "Please give me your attention for a moment. There is also a codicil to the will . . . Feel a little better now, signora? Come, think you can get up now?" But Gina only burst into tears and lay down flat on the carpet like a spoilt little girl, kicking her shoes off. Angela was biting her finger and moaning. The lawyer ignored them and turned back to his document; it was clear he couldn't wait for it all to be over. He raised his voice a little, so they could hear him over the whimpering, and read: "*Codicil. Dear Anselmo and Giulio, dear Gina and Angela, I anxiously await you* . . ." Ladies and gentlemen, please! One more minute of your attention . . . "*Dear Dante, please be good to Gideon, I entrust him to your care as if he were my child, since I have none* . . ." And so on and so forth. There followed some instructions as to the care of Gideon and a fond goodbye to yours truly, full of praise . . . private stuff, in short.'

Dante then lowered his eyes, perhaps thinking of that fond

goodbye, and remained that way until Bordelli asked him who Gideon was. Dante roused himself and pulled on his cigar, but it had gone out again.

'Who's Gideon? He's the cat.'

'Then I've seen him. He's a beautiful cat, big and white,' said Bordelli. Dante threw up his hands.

'I wouldn't know. I've never seen him.'

Botta chimed in that he really liked that sort of name for a cat. Then he squirmed a bit and said that he, too, had a story to tell. As nobody objected, he sat up straight in his chair.

'I'd like to say something about the Germans. It's true they did a lot of horrible things, but something happened to me which . . . well, it made me change my mind a little. Not that I think well of the Nazis or anything, but Nazis are one thing, and people are another, if you know what I mean. Maybe it's better if I get straight to the story and cut short the preamble.' He took a quick sip and went on.

'In '45 I was taken prisoner by the Germans, up in the north, along with a lot of other Italians. There were about sixty of us. They had us digging ditches and chopping wood and treated us like slaves. They gave us hardly anything to eat, and if anybody complained he got a thrashing or worse. One day the Americans bombed us, and it was like the end of the world. One bomb smashed open the wall of the room where we were imprisoned, and after hesitating for a moment, we all started running away like rabbits, every man for himself and God with us all, the bullets flying over our heads. I ran until my legs gave out, breathing hard as if the air itself was freedom. I ended up at the end of some footpath and was already feeling I'd made it, when out of the bushes comes this Nazi with a machine gun. He was as big as an ox, about six foot six, shoulders as broad as a barn, really scary. He wasn't wearing a helmet, and short blond stubble glistened on his bare head. After my run I'd practically landed on top of him, and now I was out of breath. I looked up at his big ruddy face, convinced my life was about to end. Now he's gonna cut me in two with machine-gun fire,

I thought to myself. Instead he gives me this German sort of smile and says: "Goin' home to Mamma, eh?" I couldn't manage to speak, and so I nodded "yes", and he stepped aside and let me go. I didn't wait to be asked twice. I was off like a shot, and as I was running I turned round to see what the German was doing. And there he was, waving goodbye like a friend, still smiling. The whole thing made a deep impression on me, because if that German had acted like a German, I wouldn't be here today . . . Then . . . then a few months later, another thing happened to me . . .'

Bordelli interrupted him with a smile, took his time lighting a cigarette, then pushed his glass over to Diotivede for a refill.

'My dear Botta, that's a beautiful story you just told us, very moving, but for every story you tell there's a thousand more, all different, and I'd like to tell one right now, really briefly, as long as everyone's in agreement.' He turned to look at the others and saw that there was no objection. 'All right, then, this is the story of something that happened to a friend that I met back up with right after the war, Senior Grade Lieutenant Binismaghi, and since he told it to me himself, you might think it's a happy story, but that's not really the case. When his ship was taken by the German navy, the prisoners were taken to an Italian port under German occupation and treated with the proper respect due to them under the Geneva Convention. They had comfortable cells and plenty of food, all according to regulations. Until the day, several weeks later, when the SS intervened by order of Berlin. They took all the ship's officers aside for interrogation. Lieutenant Binismaghi was led into one of the conference rooms of the town hall, which had been turned into the office of a German non-commissioned officer. And a fine office it was, bright and clean and equipped with a photo of the Führer and the Nazi flag. Behind his thin, round spectacles, the young German had a pair of blue eyes straight out of a fairy tale of Prince Charming, and he cut a rather dashing figure. He couldn't have been more than twenty years old, whereas my friend was nearly twice his age and felt a bit put out to have this young blond whippersnapper asking him questions. But these things happen in war. Naturally, he didn't answer any of the questions, but only gave his name, surname and serial number and declared his loyalty to the king of Italy. The Nazi didn't bat an eyelid and actually seemed quite unruffled. He changed the subject and started making small talk in rather good Italian. He asked Binismaghi where he was from, what his city was like, what the traditional dishes were, what the women of his region were like, and so on. And he listened very attentively, showing sympathy for this Italian officer loyal to his king. He even said some amusing things, and the two men laughed together. In the end he thanked Binismaghi for the pleasant conversation and stood up to shake his hand. He smiled, his pale blue eyes staring at Binismaghi from behind his eyeglasses. Binismaghi also smiled and turned away to leave. But he didn't make it to the door, because Prince Charming shot him in the nape of the neck from barely six feet away. My friend woke up a few hours later under the dead bodies of his comrades. The bullet had entered at the base of the skull and come out of his mouth without touching his brain. The Germans had taken him for dead and tossed him into a large pit with the rest. Since no one paid any attention to the dead, he was able to escape . . . As you see, Botta, this story also has a happy ending, but it was only due to good luck, not to any good deed by a Nazi.'

Botta raised his hands as if to defend himself from an accusation.

'But I said I wasn't saying anything good about Nazis, only that they weren't all the same,' he said. Then he wanted immediately to tell the story of the other thing that had happened to him. First, however, he served everyone a last spoonful of pudding, scraping the bottom of the tureen. Nobody refused – on the contrary – and after that last bit of Turkish cream, some of them turned to the *papassinos*.

Ennio then resumed speaking.

'A few months later, I found myself face to face with another

166

German. His uniform was in tatters, and he was unarmed. He showed me a picture of his girlfriend and seemed desperate. He told me he was a deserter and said he'd never shot anyone. He kept saying "*Italiani amici.*" He begged me to get him past the front. He wanted to go home. To Mamma, I thought. I didn't know whether to believe anything he told me, but in the end I remembered the German who had let me go and I decided I should help him. We spent the night in an abandoned barn. The front was only a few miles away, and we could hear the blasts of the heavy artillery. We lay down next to each other under a blanket, and then, in the middle of the night, it started raining mortar shells. With each explosion the German grabbed hold of my arm and squeezed and squeezed, muttering in German. The shelling lasted a long time, and the next morning my arm was covered with bruises. We got up and headed off through the fields. I helped him cross the front. And that's the story. The guy might be German, but every time I think back on it I feel I did the right thing. What do you think?'

Dante put a large hand on Botta's shoulder, crushing him into his chair.

'You did exactly the right thing. One man saves you, you save another, and he saves another. Human actions are links in a chain, whether they are good or bad. This is something you should always bear in mind: whosoever does evil not only does evil, but passes it on.'

Canapini knitted his brow and nodded solemnly. He'd had a lot to drink, and something important was simmering inside his head. Then he raised a finger and said:

'Yes, but what is good and what is bad? If a man steals to eat, is it good or bad? And if a policeman catches him in the act and instead of arresting him gives him some money, is that right or wrong?'

Canapini was clearly drunk. He actually had a happy expression on his face. Fabiani looked at him fondly.

'Good, I think, is everything that puts life above all else. Evil is everything that runs counter to this assertion.'

Canapini tried to get Bordelli's attention.

'What's an "assertion"?' he asked.

Bordelli was about to reply when Botta took the words out of his mouth. He had, in spite of everything, gone to school in his youth.

'It means statement, affirmation, declaration . . . You know, something somebody says.'

Canapini smiled and took a sip of grappa.

'So, someone who steals in order to eat is doing good,' he said, 'because he will die if he doesn't eat.'

Fabiani smiled.

'Naturally,' he said.

This made Canapini very happy. He raised his glass and toasted the psychoanalyst.

Dante was in deep meditation. A mysterious shadow had fallen over his face, as if he were hatching some new invention. Bordelli lit his umpteenth cigarette and invited Diotivede to tell a story.

'If you feel like it, of course,' he said. The doctor asked for a cigarette, even though he normally didn't smoke. Bordelli lit it for him, admiring, as usual, the old man's fitness and child-like freshness. Diotivede looked down at the millions of crumbs scattered across the tablecloth. He looked as if he were searching among hundreds of stories for the one most appropriate to the mood of the moment.

He smiled.

'This is probably a little silly, but it's something that made a lasting impression on me, I'm not sure why. It must have happened at least fifty years ago, around 1914. I was almost twenty and engaged to a beautiful girl of Greek origin. If I close my eyes I can still see her: the long, black hair, and a mole right here, next to her lip. Her name was Simonetta. We were very much in love but quarrelled a lot, especially over silly things. We both wanted to be always right. We used to quarrel everywhere, even in public. That day we were walking along, about a yard apart, hurling abuse at each other. People were giving us a wide berth and looking at us with disapproval. At one point I said something particularly nasty to her and she came at me screaming and kicking me in the shins. Then she scratched me in the face with her fingernails and drew blood, so I grabbed her by the wrists and twisted them brutally . . .' Diotivede mimed the gesture and grimaced in shame. 'At that moment, I felt someone grab my arm, and I turned round in anger, only to find an old vagrant, dirty and smelly. He looked at us with despair in his eyes, trying to say something but not managing to say it. He had the foul breath of an alcoholic. He had seized hold of our wrists and wouldn't let go, forcing us to stop hitting each other. He was staggering, and his face was covered with broken veins. I thought he might be unwell, or mad. Simonetta, too, had calmed down and was looking at the old man with a sort of disgust. He was still clutching our arms, when at a certain point he started shaking his head and saying: "No! No! *S'il vous plaît* . . . You mustn't . . . *Faut pas faire ça . . . Faut pas vous battre! Regardez-vous dans les yeux.*" I remember his face well, he had lost almost all his teeth, his cheeks were grey with the dirt of months without bathing. "*Embrassez-vous, s'il vous plaît,* whether you love each other or not, *c'est pas important, c'est pas important, embrassez-vous s'il vous plaît.*" A man in uniform walked past and told him to stop bothering us, grabbing him by the collar and pushing him away. But the old man kept yelling from far away, "*Embrassez-vous, embrassez-vous.*" I looked at Simonetta, threw myself into her arms, and she burst into tears. And there you have it. This is the first time I've ever told anyone. That old tramp didn't know us, he'd never seen us before and was probably even crazy, but he had the freedom of mind to tell us what he felt. After that day, whenever we started quarrelling, one of us would say, "*Embrassez-vous, s'il vous plaît,*" and we would both start laughing.'

Dante seemed very pleased with this story. He sucked on his cigar and ran his fingers through his hair.

'Man is a wondrous thing. I am certain even God is

sometimes surprised,' he said, and burst out laughing in his inimitable way.

Botta, who was a sentimentalist, asked Diotivede how things had turned out with the beautiful Greek girl. The doctor grinned bitterly.

'The year after the war broke out, I left for the front, and when I returned Simonetta was with somebody else. She was very beautiful.'

There was a silent pause, as if each was thinking of past loves gone wrong. Piras's eyes were bloodshot from all the alcohol, but he was full of energy and one could see he felt good. Even the smoke no longer bothered him. He pulled his chair closer to the table and rested his elbows on the tablecloth.

'Just outside my town, Bonacardo,' he began, 'there is a big grey boulder, over six foot tall, at the edge of a stream. It has a rather even hollow in the middle, forming a sort of seat that looks as if it was carved by human hands. The village elders say that long ago a woman fell in love with a man, and he with her. But they kept their love secret, because their families despised one another because of a disputed boundary. In short, the usual Romeo and Juliet sort of story. They would arrange to meet at night at the grey stone, calling it "our rock". And they would part in the morning, weary and happy. It was a great love, the kind that can last a lifetime. And that was, indeed, what they imagined for themselves, that they would live together for ever. But one day he decided to leave to join Napoleon's army, which was descending over Europe to bring the Revolution to everyone. He said he could not be happy if he didn't do this, and that love shouldn't make people selfish but give them the strength to do important things. He said that if he didn't love her, he wouldn't have the courage to leave, and that if he didn't leave, he would feel like a coward. This was the price of happiness. He dreamt of freeing the world from tyranny and promised her he would return soon, in triumph. "Wait for me at our rock," he said, "wait for me there, I'll be back soon." She wanted to cry but didn't. She held him tight

and kissed him. She wanted him to leave with an untroubled
heart. So she sat and watched his ship sail away until it vanished
over the horizon, and the very next day she went and waited for
him at the grey boulder. She leaned her back against the stone
and thought of him, his face, his kisses, of every time they had
shared their love in that place. The rock was the symbol of
their secret love. The months went by, without any news of her
beloved. She became more and more weary and desperate. She
hardly ever slept and ate only so that she would be pretty when
he returned. At night she would slip out of the house and lean
against the great rock, gazing at the stream. She would watch
the water rush past and think that time, itself, stood still.
After a year had gone by, she started to think he was dead, but
she didn't want to accept this. She couldn't. In the end she
thought that she too had to pay the price of happiness, just as
he had done. So she decided to make a vow. On her knees she
prayed before an image of the Blessed Virgin, as the little children around her made fun of her. "My dear Madonna, please
save my man. Ask me something, speak to me." The Madonna
said nothing, but the girl nevertheless believed she understood
what she needed to do. She swore she would never again quit
the place where they had loved each other, until he returned.
She would spend her life standing in front of the grey stone,
and she asked the Virgin to punish her if she was unable to
keep her vow. "If I ever step away from our rock, you must
drown me in the stream. You must kill me." But even this was
not enough. And so she convinced herself that if she ever
stepped away from the rock, her beloved would die that very
instant, felled by a ball of lead. Thus one winter's day she
headed for her rock, carrying only a blanket. A week went by.
Everyone in town thought she had gone mad, but to keep her
alive they brought her food to eat and water to drink. She
would thank them with the faintest nod of the head, and hardly
ever spoke. Fatigue clouded her vision, but she continued to
fight off sleep. She did not want to fall asleep, because she was
afraid that if she did, she would fall to the ground and lose

contact with the stone, and her beloved would die like a dog. After three weeks of this, however, she realised she could not keep it up. She had committed the sin of pride, and sooner or later she would fall to the ground and he would die. She asked to be bound to the stone, but nobody would do this for her. They all told her to go home, to stop playing the madwoman. Even her mother came, together with the priest, to try to persuade her. But she would not be moved, and to every attempt to take her away she replied that if they tried to remove her from that rock, she would throw herself into the river at once and drown. In the end, they let her be. One night she felt on the verge of collapse. Another minute and she would fall to the ground. The blood was draining from her temples. She only had time to say, "Forgive me, my love," and then she saw no more.'

Piras paused to pour himself a splash of grappa. Nobody breathed a word. Canapini was panting with curiosity, curled up in his chair like a cat. In the end, he couldn't hold back.

'And then what?' he asked. Piras took a good, deep breath.

'When she awoke, she didn't even want to open her eyes. The world no longer interested her. She extended her hand to drag herself to the river and drown, but instead of dirt she felt only air. And so she opened her eyes and saw the sky full of stars. She hadn't fallen. The rock had opened up and formed a comfortable seat, sheltered from the wind. And so she was able to wait for her man, who returned in a sorry state, but alive and in one piece. I say it's a legend, but the old folks in town tell the story as if it was true.'

'What a beautiful story,' said Canapini. Dante raised a glass and invited the guests to toast the women of the world, all of them, those who wait and those who leave.

'To women, the true salt of the earth,' he said. Seven glasses of grappa rose over their heads. To women.

The following morning Bordelli woke up with the backs of both hands massacred by mosquitoes and a name spinning round in his head. Simonetta. He too had had a Simonetta. He lay there in the dark, trying to picture her face again, but couldn't remember it. It must have been around '35. She was the only child of a Roman aristocrat. Her family had villas and estates almost everywhere. The last time he had seen her was at a dinner party with her parents, in a villa by the sea. It was a fine Fascist summer. There were many guests, almost all relatives of hers, important people. Bordelli arrived in his bathing suit, but this was taken merely as summer extravagance. Simonetta's mother absolutely wanted him to sit next to her. She was never done telling him how handsome he was and caressing his arm. Midway through the dinner she started making plans for the future husband and wife, describing to her guests the villa in which they would live, the sort of life they would lead – he would do this, she would do that, and so on. Bordelli waited for the woman to finish talking, then wiped his lips with his napkin and stood up.

'I think I have other plans,' he said. He politely said goodbye to the guests, and then left. He never saw Simonetta again. Had he married her, today he might be Count Bordelli, idle rich landowner, father of a few children, and well respected in high society. He would never have known the innocence of an old prostitute like Rosa, nor the cooking of Botta, learned while in prison, and he would never have met that old curmudgeon Diotivede. His life would have been completely different, and perhaps this very day he would have strolled through the park thinking that if he hadn't married Simonetta, he might be another man, perhaps a policeman, an inspector who dines at home with thieves who teach him how to pick locks with a hairpin, and who, when he's sad, seeks comfort from an ex-hooker with a heart of gold.

He felt the sweet taste of grappa at the back of his throat. When he moved his head, a sharp pain travelled up from the nape of his neck to the base of his nose, running over his skull like a cog. He took a deep breath and heard a whistle in his chest. He had smoked too much. His lungs burned. He vowed that he would smoke only three or four that day, five at the most, definitely not more than six. Seeing the pack of cigarettes on the nightstand, he batted it away in rage. He remained in bed, staring at the blood-swollen mosquitoes hanging from the ceiling asleep. In a little while Botta would come to wash the dishes and put the kitchen back in order. That was the agreement: Bordelli the money, Botta the labour. Spotting a mosquito within reach on the wall and feeling his skin burn, he crushed it, staining the wall red.

He heard some footsteps inside the front door.

'Is that you, Ennio?'

The steps arrived as far as the bedroom door, which opened partly. Dante's leonine head appeared.

'Good morning, Inspector. Shall we have some coffee?' he said cheerfully.

Only then did Bordelli remember that Dante had slept on the sofa.

'Go ahead, I'll be there in a minute,' he said.

'Sleep well?'

'Yes, and yourself?'

The inventor smiled majestically.

'Marvellous nightmares.'

The inspector sat up, put his feet on the floor and his hands on his hips.

'The coffee pot must be in the sink. Do you know how to use a *napoletana*?' he asked. Dante assured him he did and disappeared into the kitchen. The inspector went barefooted into the bathroom, feet slapping the hard floor much less delicately than Elvira's. Beautiful, young Elvira . . . He was unable to forget her; she returned to his thoughts at the most unexpected moments, and each time he felt older, heavier. He pissed painfully and with effort, the burning finish speaking eloquently of grappa. He rearranged his hair with his fingers and washed his face. The cold water felt good on his skin, but then the towel got snagged on his hard, short stubble. He stood there looking at himself in the mirror, hands resting on the sink, counting his wrinkles and thinking of Signora Pedretti-Strassen stiff in her bed, hands round her throat. After the pause of the night, his mind was filling again with a swirl of ideas and questions. Especially one, the usual: how did they do it? He thought of the Morozzi brothers, sweaty and hysterical, and saw their blonde, made-up wives, who had left that nauseating smell behind in the office.

How the hell had they done it? And which of the four did it? Or was it all four? Or perhaps only two? The brothers or the wives? Or maybe only one couple. Or perhaps none of them. Perhaps it was all a mistake, time to start over . . .

He thought of Dante struggling with the *napoletana* and went into the kitchen. The inventor was trying to assemble the machine upside down.

'What an odd contraption,' he said.

'Give it to me.'

'I was almost there, you know.'

Bordelli took the pieces out of Dante's hands.

'See? This goes here.'

'I'd thought of that, but it seemed too banal.'

'Not everyone has your imagination.'

'Compliment accepted. I am very vain.'

Ennio arrived, and all three went into the dining room. They took their coffee on the tablecloth of the night before, which was covered with exotic stains and crumbs. There was still a scent of spices and grappa in the air. Botta was about to open the shutters, but Bordelli raised his hand.

'Just the windows, Ennio. I'm having a little trouble with the light this morning.'

'Whatever you say.'

The temperature was rising by the minute. It was going to be another muggy, sweaty day. Dante lit one of his pestilential cigars and tossed the match into his empty espresso cup. Feeling the smoke in his nostrils, Bordelli had to make an effort not to light a cigarette.

'I've got a riddle for you,' he said to his friends. 'Interested?'

'What sort of riddle?' asked Botta, amused. Dante went and sat down in an armchair and stretched his legs across the floor, awaiting the question. The inspector downed his last drop of coffee and started toying with the empty cup.

'Pretend you want to murder someone with a powdered poison, powerful enough to kill the person who inhales it. Obviously you don't want to end up in jail, so, when the victim breathes the stuff, you have to make sure you're far from the scene of the crime. How do you do it?'

Botta scratched his head.

'Well, I'd put the poison in the soup, or in the toothpaste.'

'The poison is deadly only when inhaled.'

'Oh, right. Well, then . . . How should I know? I don't. I give up.'

Dante was contemplating, eyes half closed and lips pursed. Bordelli looked at him.

'What about you, Dante? What would an inventor do?'

'Easy. A time-release mechanism.'

'Easy to say, but to make one?'

'Oh, it wouldn't take much. You could make one at home in no time.'

Bordelli really felt like lighting up, but managed to resist the temptation.

'Give me an example,' he said.

'Easy: I take a test tube, put three dry beans in it, fill it halfway with water, take two little cork discs joined in the middle by a wire, put the first disc into the test tube halfway down, put in the powder, then insert the second disk until it seals the test tube, place the device horizontally on the lamp over the victim's bed, and go on my merry way. The dry beans will slowly swell with water, pushing out the cork. And voilà. It's done. The poison will gently flutter down towards the victim's nose.'

'And what if the police find traces of the device?'

'One need only hide it well and then come and retrieve it as quickly as possible.'

Bordelli sighed.

'That's true, but that sort of mechanism isn't so easy to hide, and, more importantly, it's not very precise.'

'In that case one would have to consider another system – I don't know, say a little pump hidden behind the switch of the nightlight, which, when you turned on the light . . . Or a mechanism of rubber bands which, after releasing the poison, would catapult the whole thing out of the window.'

The inspector shook his head.

'No, that's all too complicated and might leave visible traces. Anyone who goes so far as to plan a murder tries to leave nothing to chance.'

Botta started removing the coffee cups from the table.

'We give up, Inspector. Tell us how it's done.'

Bordelli threw up his hands and then slapped his thighs.

'If I only knew . . .' he said.

'So it's not a riddle. It's something serious.'

'Very serious, Botta. I'm trying to find out who killed Dante's sister.'

Ennio stopped short in the doorway, coffee cups in hand.

'Ah, I didn't know! . . . I'm so sorry, Mr Pedretti,' he said, slightly embarrassed. Dante smiled and waved a hand in the air by way of thanks, pulling hard on his cigar. Bordelli stood up with a sigh and went back into the bathroom to take a shower. As he was lathering up he kept ruminating on the killing; it had almost become an obsession. But they all did, sooner or later. If he hadn't become a policeman he would have found another way to obsess about things. It was in his blood. He couldn't do anything about it.

He got dressed and went to ask Dante whether he needed a lift. He found him in front of the sink with an apron on, drying the dishes as Botta washed them.

'Thanks, Inspector, but it's all right. I'll lend Ennio a hand and then have a walk.'

'Very well, then, goodbye. Ciao, Ennio, I'll leave you some-thing under the phone in the entrance.'

'Have a good day, Inspector. When you want to have another dinner party, don't be shy, just let me know.'

'It won't be long, Ennio, I promise. If I were younger I'd say the day after tomorrow.'

On his way out he left three thousand lire under the telephone. In the doorway he thought better of it, turned round and took back a thousand. As he was putting it in his wallet, he changed his mind again and put it back. Outside the flat he trotted down the stairs, remembering that he'd just been given a raise.

Mugnai greeted him with a sallow smile.

'Congratulations, Inspector Bordelli. But what should I call you now? Chief inspector, or simply inspector?'

Bordelli bit his lip.

'Whatever you like, Mugnai. Whatever sounds better to you.'

'In that case I prefer simply "inspector". "Chief inspector" is too long.'

'All right . . . Oh, listen, what about that nasty smell in my room?'

'It was face powder, Inspector. It's been taken care of,' he said in the tone of one who knew about such things.

'Thanks.'

Bordelli went into his office, sniffed the air and hurled a few insults at Mugnai. Not only was the smell of the face powder still there, but another smell had been added to it. He wondered what it might be, and then saw an empty aerosol bomb of Grey's Wax in the wastebasket. Which only made things worse. He went to open the window, hoping for a purifying wind, but the air was immobile and hot as usual. He settled in and put all the reports and transcripts of the Pedretti-Strassen murder on his desk. Every so often he looked up from his papers to reflect, but then shook his head and went on. And every so often he thought of his cousin and his mysterious lover. In the end he picked up the phone and dialled Rodrigo's number. After a few rings, someone picked up.

'Hello?' It was a woman's voice, a beautiful voice.

'Hello, I'm Rodrigo's cousin . . .'

'Then you must be the wicked policeman,' she said, laughing.

'Right.'

'Rodrigo's not here. Shall I tell him to call you back?'

'No need. I just wanted to know how he was feeling.'

'He's feeling great.'

'I'm sure he is.'

'And I'm not doing too badly myself,' she said, giggling.

'I'm so glad.'

'Me too.'

'Well, goodbye.'

'Bye-bye, policeman.'

'Bye.'

Hanging up, Bordelli tried to imagine what she might look like. She must have long blonde hair, the eyes of a wounded deer, a fine, confident gait, the kind of woman who likes to talk to herself . . . Or else she was dark and slender, with beautiful legs and tapered hands, a joyous smile and very white teeth . . . Or . . .

The ring of the telephone caught him by surprise.

'Yes?'

'Hello, my dear inspector. Do you miss your Rosina?'

'Hi, Rosa. You don't know how lucky you are to be at the beach.'

'Oh, darling, you should see how tanned I am! Whereas Valeria is peeling like a broiled pepper. She hasn't got skin like mine, you know, she's as white as a ghost . . . Oh, it's just wonderful to lie on the beach! And in the evenings we make the rounds of the nightclubs and dance all night.'

Bordelli pushed away the reports and leaned back in his chair. A phone call from Rosa was exactly what he needed. To forget everything for a few minutes and let frivolity carry him away. He listened with delight to her shrill voice in the receiver. Rosa was an adorable woman, an angel capable of opening her door to him at two in the morning and making him something to eat. Bordelli lit his first cigarette of the day and smoked it in silence, as Rosa told him a thousand things: about the people under the neighbouring umbrella on the beach, the seafood dishes the cook from Salerno had taught her, the guests at the Piccolo Eden *pensione*, the ankle sprain she'd got walking in the sand . . .

Little by little, however, the thought of the murder worked its way back into his thoughts, and Bordelli chased it away again. He absolutely needed to give his brain a rest. Rosa went on and on about her seaside adventures, giving more detail than a police report.

'. . . and about half past three that afternoon, we hired three bicycles . . . you should see how pretty the bicycles they make are these days . . . mine was white and pink. Know why I chose that one?'

'Because it was pink.'

She gave a chuckle that sounded like a sob.

'Good monkey! And so we went cycling along the promenade by the sea. I was wearing my hat because the sun was so strong . . . you know, that straw hat I like so much.'

'Right.'

'. . . and you can imagine how hungry we were after that. We went and ate at a little place by the beach: steamed mussels for starters, *spaghetti alle vongole*, and then *fritto misto*. There was a great big cat that kept prowling round my feet, a beautiful grey cat with two big yellow eyes . . . Not tabby grey, but mousy grey. I bet he never goes hungry, living in a restaurant like that. When I asked the waiter what breed he was, he said that kind are called Chartreux. You should see what a pretty face! When I come home I want to get a cat like that. And what a great big head! It filled my whole hand. I gave him two fried shrimp and the scamp devoured them, shells and all, then hopped up on my lap and started purring so loud everyone could hear him! You should see his fur, so, so soft . . . I loved just kissing his head, because he smelled like the sea . . . You know, like the song by that guy, what's his name? . . . *sapore di sale, sapore di mare* . . . C'mon, help me out, what's his name . . .?'

Bordelli turned as stiff as dried cod.

'What an imbecile!' he said.

'Come on, he's no imbecile, you're probably confusing him with someone else . . . I mean the one with the glasses . . . come on, he's famous, *sapore di saleeee* . . .'

'Sorry, Rosa, but I have to go.'

'Why, what's wrong?'

'I have to hang up, Rosa.'

'Yes, I heard you . . . How are my flowers?'

'Never been better. I'm sorry, Rosa, I really have to go. Ciao.' He hung up and sat motionless, thinking, staring through the wall. Without realising it, he lit another cigarette and set it down in the ashtray, and like an automaton lit another one immediately.

'What an imbecile,' he repeated. He picked up the phone and called his own flat.

'Ennio, it's me. Is Dante still there?'

'Yes, Inspector. We were just about to leave.'

'Put him on for me, would you?'

'Straight away . . . by the way, Inspector, thanks for the little gift. You needn't have.'

'Forget about it, Ennio, and let me talk to Dante.'

'Straight away . . . Dante, the inspector wants you.'

Dante's booming voice exploded into the receiver.

'Hello, Inspector! We've cleaned the kitchen from top to bottom. I've got an idea for a new device for washing pots and pans. As soon as it's ready I'll give it to you.'

'Sorry to bother you, Dante, but I'd like you to repeat to me everything that was written in your sister's will, including the private things, if you don't mind.'

'Over the telephone?'

'Over the telephone.'

'All right.'

Dante told Botta that this was going to take a while and then began to recite from memory Rebecca's last will and testament. At a certain point the inspector cut him off.

'That's good enough, Dante, thanks. I'll be in touch and soon . . . And thanks for washing up.'

'Aren't you going to tell us what we're waiting for?' asked Diotivede, removing his glasses and pacing back and forth in Signora Pedretti's room, hands joined behind his back. He was impatient to know why Bordelli had organised this sudden visit to the villa at 8.30 in the evening. The sun was slowly setting, colouring the sky orange. The heat was far more bearable than in the city. Piras sat in the chair in front of the secretaire, thinking, not asking any questions. The inspector glanced at his watch every minute, smoking by the window so as not to bother Piras. He had forgotten to get an ashtray and was putting out his cigarettes on the floor, under the radiator. He swore to himself that, starting tomorrow, no more than six or seven, eight at the most. As he still hadn't answered Diotivede's question, the doctor persisted.

'We've already been here half an hour. Care to tell us what we're waiting for?'

'No, Doctor, I can't, not yet.'

'Hmph!' said the doctor, and he resumed pacing about the room.

'I'm not trying to be mysterious,' said Bordelli.

'You're not?'

'I simply want to be sure I haven't made a mistake. Did you bring the microscope?'

'You asked me to, so I brought it.'

'Good.'

Bordelli kept glancing at the open door. A few minutes later he said:

'All right, it's almost time. If my hunch is correct, the killer will soon come in through that door.'

Piras shot to his feet.

'Shall we turn out the lights, Inspector?' he said in a whisper.

'No, there's no need,' said Bordelli.

Diotivede put his glasses back on and, after a moment of perplexity, he smiled.

'I think you're having us on,' he said. 'Piras, you don't know the inspector very well yet, but he's a real ball-buster.'

Bordelli put a finger to his lips, asking for silence. He looked dead serious.

'Shhh. I don't want him to get scared,' he said. He glanced at his watch. Nine on the dot. 'Now be quiet. He's going to come in and lie down on the bed.'

Diotivede shook his head.

'On the bed? What the hell are you saying?'

Following Bordelli's example, the other two started staring at the door, holding their breath, awaiting the killer. Diotivede took a hesitant step towards the door, and at that moment Gideon the cat appeared, tail pointing straight up. Seeing the three men in the room, he did an about-face, meowed twice on the landing outside, then came back into the room. He sniffed the air and started snapping his tail like a whip.

'He's nervous,' Bordelli whispered. The cat circled round a few more times, restless, then slowly calmed down and leapt on to the bed. He rolled on to his back and meowed like a kitten. At that point Diotivede looked at Bordelli, spectacles in his hand.

'Is *he* the killer?' he said.

Bordelli went over to the cat and rubbed his belly.

'He's the one all right.'

'Could you explain?' said Piras.

'Naturally, he's completely unaware of it, right, pussy?' said Bordelli, playing with the cat's paws.

Piras clenched his fists.

'The pollen!' he shouted.

'Precisely. The real killer put a good dose of the pollen between his shoulder blades, knowing that that every night at nine o'clock, Gideon came in to snuggle down with the lady.'

'The classic Trojan horse,' said Diotivede with a wry smile.

Piras punched himself in the head.

'What an idiot! Why didn't I think of that?' he said.

'It wasn't easy. It came to me purely by chance.'

'What makes you say they put the pollen between the cat's shoulder blades?'

'Because it's a spot a cat can't reach with his paws or his tongue, and therefore the pollen would have remained in his fur for a long time.'

The inspector picked Gideon up with both hands and put him upright on the bed, stroking his head so he would stay.

'Take out your microscope, Diotivede. If we're lucky, we'll still find some traces of the pollen.'

The doctor went and picked up a small sort of spatula and came towards the bed.

'Hold him still for me,' he said. He placed the instrument between Gideon's shoulder blades to take a sample, then put this between two glass slides, and set the microscope down on the secretaire. He brought his eye to the eyepiece and started turning some knobs. A minute later he raised his head.

'You were right,' he said with a sly grin. Piras also smiled. Bordelli celebrated by lighting a cigarette.

'Now it will all be much easier,' he said with satisfaction.

The pathologist, however, wasn't jumping to conclusions.

'To be honest, I still don't know what sort of pollen it is and need to examine it. But such a high concentration of pollen in a cat's fur cannot have got there by accident.'

'Well, examine it quickly and have the report sent to me. I'll bet the family jewels that it's maté pollen.'

Bordelli kept stroking the cat, as if to thank him. The doctor returned to his microscope with a kind of joy; nothing pleased him more than to scrutinise the infinitesimal movements of nature. Gideon played with Bordelli's fingers, nipping them playfully but hurting him every so often, so that the inspector jerked his hand away.

'Ouch! Easy does it, boy!'

The cat stood up, ran across the bed, slipped under the covers and started running as if chasing a mouse.

Piras stood in the far corner, thinking. He turned towards Bordelli.

'What should we do, Inspector? Interrogate all four again?'

'Absolutely. Their alibi has finally gone to the dogs. Or the cats.'

'Well, you two certainly seem pleased,' said Diotivede. 'May I ask a question?'

'By all means.'

'The lady was murdered. This we knew from the start. Now we also know how, which is a big step forward, no doubt about it. But to issue an indictment, the judge will want some proof, something beyond a speck of pollen in a cat's fur.'

Bordelli thought of Judge Ginzillo and his scrupulous ways. He was a young, arse-licking arriviste who was afraid to make mistakes and ruin his career. With him it was always a struggle.

'Don't be always such a pessimist, Doctor. We may have some luck, as we did this evening.'

The doctor raised his hands as if to say he wouldn't utter another word. He put his tools back in his bag and looked at the other two with the expression of one who wants to leave.

'All right, then, we can go,' said Bordelli. They left the cat to his games under the covers and went out. While descending the stairs, the inspector became pensive again. Diotivede took him by the arm and looked at him from behind his spectacles.

'Want some friendly advice? Sleep on it,' he said.

Bordelli smiled vacantly.

'You're right. Let's sleep on it. Piras: eight o'clock tomorrow morning, in my office.'

'Let's not waste any time, Piras. Let's try to reconstruct the whole affair in all its details, top to bottom.'

Piras was ready, fresh as a rose.

'Should you go first, Inspector, or should I?'

Bordelli had two grey bags under his eyes. He had lain awake all night, caught between the heat and the mosquitoes. He had also thought about Elvira, and Annina . . . which amounted to the same thing.

'You start, Piras . . . I'll interrupt you if I need to.'

The Sardinian began pacing about the room, as he always did when he had the floor.

'So, on the day of the crime, in the afternoon, someone, whom I'll call X for now, enters the villa with a copy of the keys, which he acquired at some earlier point. At an opportune moment, he replaces the lady's bottle of Asthmaben with an identical one filled with water, then goes out into the garden to find the cat, puts the maté pollen on his back, then leaves. At nine o'clock he makes sure he's seen at the restaurant, after which he goes dancing at a much-frequented nightspot—'

Bordelli cut in.

'You forgot the car.'

'I was about to get to that. That same afternoon, X asks to borrow Salvetti's Alfa Romeo Giulietta Sprint, saying he wants to go for a drive in the mountains the next morning, but he asks if he can have it right away, since by the time X wakes up in the morning, Salvetti will be already at the beach.'

'All right, go on.'

Piras made a circular motion with his hand.

'Let's go back to the dance club. X arrives at half past ten. It's Thursday, so X already knows that Salvetti and his wife will be there, since the Milanese couple routinely go there every Thursday night. He also knows that they will leave soon after his arrival, because they have a small son who plays until midnight with a neighbour's son. And, indeed, around midnight the friends leave. At that point, X knows that Signora Pedretti is already dead, or at least he hopes she is. He needs to go and verify this, but mostly he needs to go and switch the Asthmaben bottles again. The dance club is very crowded late into the night, and no one notices his absence. He gets into the Alfa and races into town. In a car like that, it doesn't take much more than an hour. When he gets to the villa, he sees that everything has gone according to plan. The lady is dead, the fake bottle is on the bedside table. X exchanges the medicine bottles, putting the real one in its proper place, but in his agitation he makes a mistake: he forgets to unscrew the cap. Then he drives back to the coast, slips back into the nightclub, and stays there until closing time. He gets drunk and tries to call attention to himself. The following morning, he goes on his drive through the mountains, and in the evening he returns the car to his friend, all cleaned and polished, to get rid of any eventual trace of his nocturnal excursion.'

'Good, Piras. Not one wrinkle. Now, however, try to go into a little more detail.'

Piras repeated the whole story, dwelling on the most insignificant details. X entering the villa and then hiding in a room on the ground floor, awaiting the right moment, when he won't be seen by Rebecca or Maria, putting on gloves so as not to leave any fingerprints, the real medicine bottle delicately wrapped in a handkerchief so as not to erase Signora Pedretti's fingerprints . . . The reservation for the restaurant, the dance club with the Salvettis. When he got to the part where the killer goes back for the phoney medicine bottle, Bordelli interrupted him.

'Here you should go slowly. Imagine it's you at the wheel. What do you do?'

'I get to the villa and . . . no, I don't drive all the way to the villa. I hide the car somewhere nearby and then walk. Somebody might notice the Alfa and report this to the police.'

'Good. Now let's talk about that scrape on the Alfa Romeo.'

'Do you think . . .?'

'Who knows, Piras, maybe luck's on our side. C'mon, let's go.'

Fifteen minutes later, the VW was rumbling up the hill towards Rebecca's villa. The inspector had an unlit cigarette between his lips, pulling on it every so often out of instinct and feeling disappointed at the lack of smoke.

'What do you think, Piras? Is there such a thing as the perfect crime?'

The Sardinian didn't answer. He just looked out of the car window, thinking, perhaps, of how different it was here from the Campidano plain.

About half a mile from the villa, Bordelli slowed down, and

the still-unlit cigarette went flying out of the window. He didn't feel like smoking.

'Look carefully and see if you can see a small side street, Piras.'

The Sardinian started studying the edge of the road.

'If we can find the spot where the Alfa was scratched, Inspector, the Morozzis are screwed.'

'Even if we don't, we've still got the upper hand, haven't we? We know how they did it, and they don't know that we know.'

Piras pointed to a narrow, unpaved road that led into the open countryside. They got out of the car to examine the surroundings, but found nothing. Leaving the Beetle there, they continued on foot. Farther ahead was a large, grassy clearing, but it was too close to the road. It would have made no sense to park there. A couple of hundred yards before the villa was a pebbled path that seemed made for hiding a car. They carefully studied the area but, aside from some anonymous tyre tracks, they found nothing.

'This may in fact be where they parked the car,' said Piras. 'It seems like the best place.'

'Maybe, but we haven't an iota of proof.'

The sun was high in the sky and, as usual, there wasn't a breath of wind. The inspector sat down on a large rock and pulled his shirt away from his sweaty skin. He gazed at the dark green woods that entirely covered the hill of Fiesole in the distance. It gave him a feeling of coolness. Piras continued to look for signs of the Alfa Romeo's scrape, then also gave up.

'How did you ever think of the cat, Inspector?'

'By chance, Piras. Pure chance. But I had a hunch from the moment I saw it.'

'A hunch?'

'That the murderer had used the cat. But there was still the problem of the alibi. Whoever put the pollen in Gideon's fur had to be absolutely sure of what he was doing. He couldn't leave things to chance. If Rebecca died before the appointed time, the risk was enormous. The killer's alibi hinged entirely on this, on the hour of her death. A murder so well planned could not afford to neglect so important a detail.'

'Right.'

'The killer had to be absolutely certain he could count on the cat as an unwitting accomplice. At some point I remembered Rebecca's will. If you recall, Dante broke off his story right where his sister began to talk about Gideon. So I rang Dante and asked him to tell me in minute detail everything his sister put into the will. And, bingo. In the codicil to the will, Signora Pedretti talks a great deal about Gideon. There are instructions concerning his eating habits and other matters, and she asks her brother to find a dependable person to take care of the animal. He must be certain that the person loves cats, and she concludes by saying that if he couldn't find Gideon in the garden, not to worry because he's an adult male and is always out and about. One need only wait for him to come home, because every day of the year, at nine o'clock sharp, Gideon always came up to her bedroom to see her. He never missed a day, Rebecca said. And the killer must have known this.'

Piras shook his head, twisting up his mouth.

'Disgusting,' he said.

'Poor cat. They made him a traitor.'

They resumed walking towards the villa, but there was no longer any point. There were no more side roads or clearings where the killer might have hidden the car.

'Our good luck's run out, Piras. We'll have to proceed with what we've got.'

'Ladies and gentlemen, we are now certain that Signora Rebecca Pedretti-Strassen was murdered,' said Bordelli.

Anselmo gulped, a doltish smile on his lips.

'You've already told us that, haven't you?'

'Yes, but I didn't say that it was you who did it.'

'That's rich!' said Angela.

Bordelli ignored her.

'Whether it was just one of you, or you were all in it together, I can't really say, but I suspect we'll know soon,' he said calmly.

The Morozzis squirmed in their chairs.

'That's absurd!'

'This is unbelievable . . .'

'Sheer lunacy!'

'Just one minute, ladies and gentlemen. Please calm down and allow me to finish.'

The inspector stood up, walked round his desk and moved a stack of papers from a corner so he could sit down there, right beside Gina. The sickly-sweet smell of chestnut flour brutally penetrated his nostrils. He glanced over at Piras, who was seated in front of the typewriter, frowning darkly. Then he looked at his watch.

'I'd like to give you some friendly advice. It is now four o'clock. If you confess straight away, you'll spare yourselves a lot of trouble, and perhaps – who knows? – the judge will take this into consideration. Otherwise . . .'

Angela gave a start.

'Otherwise?' she said.

Bordelli threw his hands up.

'Otherwise I'll keep all four of you here and interrogate you one at a time for as long as I see fit, perhaps until midnight, or until tomorrow morning, or even, if necessary, for three straight days. The choice is yours.'

'But we've already told you everything we know,' said Gina, trying to smile.

'We are not murderers,' said Anselmo.

Bordelli shrugged.

'As you wish. Here's the telephone. Call all the lawyers you want.'

As Anselmo was dialling, Bordelli stood up and went over to Piras. He spoke loudly so they could all hear him.

'Get a whole stack of pages ready, Piras. It looks like we'll be spending the night here.'

'That's fine with me.'

Half an hour later, Santelia, the lawyer arrived, all eighteen stone of him. He had a pair of penetrating blue eyes and the face of an insecure little boy. He stank of sweat and eau de cologne.

'Let's get one thing immediately clear, Inspector,' he said. 'Have my clients been formally charged? Because, if not—'

'It's all by the book, sir. I'm questioning suspects in the presence of their lawyer.'

'Of course, of course, what I meant was . . . well, to proceed properly, what are they suspected of?'

'Premeditated murder.'

'On what grounds?'

'On the basis of some very convincing evidence, sir. Now, if you don't mind, I'd like to begin the questioning.

'Ready, Piras?'

'Ready, Inspector.'

'Good.'

The individual interrogations began. While awaiting their turn, the other three bided their time in three separate rooms. Once the first round was over, they started all over again. Bordelli's ashtray was filling up faster than you could count the butts. Piras only sighed, resigned to breathing the foul air. He hit the keys hard, striking them with only two fingers: Q and A, Q and A . . . Same questions, same answers. One in particular.

'But we were at the coast at that time! Everybody saw us, didn't they?'

And at once the bothersome clacking of the typewriter would fill their ears. Santelia the lawyer sat as still as if he were posing for a sculpture, staring at the person being questioned. After each question he would nod, almost closing his eyes, giving the go-ahead for the answer. At one point he said the question was. irrelevant, and Bordelli retorted that he should save that objection for the trial.

'Trial? I didn't know that in Italy the innocent were put on trial,' he said.

There were two or three more irksome, pointless squabbles,

trifling matters, in fact. During one of the many interrogations of Giulio, the lawyer protested.

'It is nine o'clock, Inspector! You certainly don't want to violate the rights of your suspects, I hope! They're hungry! And I myself am ravenous!'

'You're right,' said Bordelli, and he called Mugnai and told him to bring the other suspects into his office. When they were all there, he had them sit down and sent Mugnai out for panini.

'I'd like a beer, myself,' said the lawyer. 'Actually, make that two.'

'No beer,' said Bordelli. 'Orangeade for everyone.'

Fifteen minutes later Mugnai returned with a bag full of provisions. Piras devoured his share in seconds, though the panini were dry round the edges and the prosciutto had long since turned to cardboard. Bordelli bit into his, but it was so disgusting that he shoved it into a drawer and lit up a cigarette instead. He then took to observing the Morozzis as they chewed with difficulty and in silence, and he began to feel sorry for them. For a brief moment he even doubted that they had done the deed and that money was the motive, and he wondered whether at that very moment the killer wasn't living it up somewhere, utterly indifferent to the inheritance. Then he looked at Piras's grave expression and became convinced he was on the verge of closing the case.

Gina and Angela tried to eat without smearing their lipstick. They raised their lips before sinking their teeth into the bread, incisors exposed all the way to the gums; then they closed their mouths and ruminated with lips sealed. They seemed downright batty. Still, their serenity had the look of innocence.

Although Bordelli couldn't wait to lie down in bed, by this point he had to play the part of the stubborn cop to the end. This was no time to give in. The lawyer took great big bites of his sandwich, displaying a revulsion he didn't deign to translate into words.

'They're from the bar outside. They make them in the morning, and in this heat . . .,' said Bordelli, trying to apologise for the terrible quality of the dinner. Santelia waved his hand in the air as if to sweep away this excuse, then he grabbed a bottle of orangeade by the neck.

'Have you got a bottle-opener?' he asked.

'Give it here, I'll open it for you,' said Bordelli. The lawyer handed him the bottle, and he flipped off the cap, as he always did, with his house key. Santelia watched Bordelli's operation with a sneer of pity, as if watching some street punk cut a lizard in two. While he was at it, Bordelli opened all the bottles.

'Now, let's get back to work,' he said.

The air in the room had become stifling. The window was wide open but only served to give them a glimpse of the evening's lazy progress. There wasn't the slightest puff of wind that might sweep away the foulness.

Round about ten o'clock the Morozzis began to look tired and worried. Bordelli took advantage of this fact to communicate that he knew more than he had let on. He started tossing out random statements without batting an eyelid.

'The post-mortem showed that while there was no trace of Asthmaben in your aunt's blood, it was all over her tongue. How would you explain that?'

'I'm not a doctor,' Anselmo said.

'Signora Gina, do you know what we found in Gideon's fur?'

The woman squinted and then shook her head as if she hadn't understood.

'Gideon? Who's that?' she said.

The lawyer smiled provocatively.

'Don't ask useless questions, Inspector. Get to the point.'

'That is precisely the point, sir. The maté pollen that was found in the cat's fur means that your clients' alibi isn't worth a mouse turd any more. You know what I mean?'

As the hours passed, they all grew more tired and nervous. The inspector had already filled and emptied the ashtray twice, betraying all his good intentions, and this bothered him more than a little. Piras was disgusted by all the smoke. His eyes were bloodshot, and during the pauses he stuck his head out of the window for air.

At around midnight Anselmo had a fit of rage. Irritated by one of Bordelli's questions, he shot to his feet and grabbed the edge of the desk as if he wanted to overturn it. Santelia forced him to sit back down and whispered something in his ear, squeezing his shoulder with his hand.

The clacking of the Olivetti had become unbearable to all. To Bordelli it felt as if the transcript were being typed directly on his temples. The lawyer was the only person who seemed not to suffer. Every so often he would doze off while seated, his nose emitting a buzzing sound, and each time he awoke his eyes looked smaller.

'Don't you think you're taking this too far, Inspector? This is not Nuremberg, you know,' he said.

'Sorry, but I haven't finished yet.'

'You're certainly not going to keep us here all night.'

'You can leave if you wish.'

'Lunacy!'

'Please, just let me do my job.'

The interruptions became more and more frequent and annoying. The lawyer would raise an objection and Bordelli would politely ask him not to interrupt. Around two o'clock in the morning, Bordelli's tone changed, becoming more impatient. At three, he banished the lawyer from the room and pointed his finger in Giulio's face. When alone, the younger brother seemed like a child on the verge of tears.

'You know how this is going to end up? You, Giulio, are going to pay for them all, that's how. And do you know why?'

The lawyer protested in the corridor, rattling off various articles of the penal code and yelling that he would report the matter to Judge Ginzillo. Bordelli could hear Mugnai trying to calm him down. There was a noise of chairs and then Santelia's powerful voice again.

'At least bring me a beer! I'm thirsty, dammit!'

Giulio ran a hand over his eyes, trembling and stammering

something incomprehensible. The lawyer's voice boomed outside the door again, asking for something to drink. Bordelli couldn't stand the confusion any longer and poked his head out of the door.

'For Christ's sake, Mugnai! Buy the man a case of beer and make him shut up!' He closed the door unceremoniously and turned back to Giulio. He went and stood behind him, putting his hands on Giulio's shoulders.

'I'm waiting for a phone call, Giulio. Actually, we're both waiting for this call. You and I, Giulio. Any minute now . . .' he said in a tone that made Giulio shudder.

'What . . . phone call . . .?'

'You'll know soon . . . but there's no hurry . . .'

Outside the door, calm had finally been restored. Santelia had probably decided to wait quietly for his damned beer. Bordelli turned to Piras and nodded complicitly. The Sardinian immediately got the message and asked whether he could go to the loo. Bordelli winked at him.

'All right, but be quick,' he said, pretending to be annoyed. A minute later the phone rang, and Bordelli picked up.

'Yes?'

Piras's voice sounded tinny in the receiver.

'Here I am, Inspector, calling just like you asked. Now I'll hang up and come back. If this is what you wanted, say yes.'

'Yes, of course . . . of course,' said Bordelli. Piras hung up, but the inspector carried on by himself, assuming a serious, attentive expression. Every so often he looked over at Giulio's fat, sweaty face.

'What's that? Right, yes, of course, just as I suspected. And in Salvetti's car, too? Splendid, I knew it. And what about that scrape on the Alfa? Good, good, that's what I thought. Yes, of course, thanks. Send me the reports as soon as you can. Goodbye.'

He put down the phone and then went and settled comfortably in his chair. He lit a cigarette and folded his hands behind his head.

'Good, good, good. Now we can all go to bed,' he said, smiling. Giulio, white as a sheet, moved in his chair.

'Why to bed?'

'Your fingerprints, dear Giulio. Your fingerprints on the Asthmaben bottle. Clear as a photograph.'

'Mine . . .?'

'Yours, Giulio. We also found them in Salvetti's Alfa Romeo. And that's not all.'

An enormous drop of sweat hung from Giulio's chin. Bordelli paused deliberately, blew a mouthful of smoke upwards, then turned his stare back on poor Giulio Morozzi.

'We have proof that Salvetti's car was scratched on a side street near your late aunt's villa. Do you know what this means? That my work is finished. One murder. One killer. For me, that's more than enough. Actually, it's better this way. I can close up shop and go home to bed. You, on the other hand, are screwed.'

Giulio reared back in his chair.

'I . . .? What?'

'You'll get life, dear Giulio. You know that, don't you? You'll be inside till you die, while the other three will be outside, living it up, free as birds. Of course, I'm sure they'll come see you at Christmas time and bring you delicious oranges wrapped in tinfoil. Do you like the idea?'

At that moment Piras came in and Bordelli shot him a dirty look.

'How long's it take you to have a piss? I told you to be quick.'

Piras turned his back to him to hide the fact that he was smiling, then said in a tone appropriate to their little comedy:

'Sorry, Inspector, but it wasn't only pee,' hurrying back to the typewriter.

Bordelli crushed his butt in the overflowing ashtray and rested his elbows on the desk. He pulled out a friendly smile.

'You know, Giulio, it doesn't seem right that you should pay for the others. Think about it. I want to be your friend. Tell you what: I'm going to give you one last chance. Tell me everything you know, right now, or I'll close the case exactly where it stands, and you'll go to jail while the others go free. Think it over calmly. I'll give you . . .' He removed his watch and laid it in the middle of the desk. '. . . let's say three minutes. Starting now.'

He lit another cigarette and leaned back in his chair, humming a little tune. Giulio opened his mouth to speak but nothing came out; then he looked down and began to touch himself all over, as if looking for help. He turned round to look at Piras, who returned only an impenetrable stare. A few moments later, Bordelli glanced at his watch.

'Two minutes left,' he said. Then he turned and looked at the rectangle of sky framed by the window. Among the millions of stars he hoped to see a shooting star so he could make a wish. To see Elvira again.

Giulio broke down after the second minute. He started slapping himself in the face and making strange noises with his throat, and when Bordelli checked his watch again, he burst out crying like a baby. It was a painful scene. And it was hard to understand what he said, since what came out of his mouth was a kind of wail that only later became comprehensible.

'The witch . . . was her . . . the slut . . . 's what I said . . . 's her fault . . . 's what I said . . .'

Bordelli strapped his watch back on his wrist and gestured to Piras not to start typing.

'Who are you talking about, Giulio? Her who?'

Giulio wiped his nose with his hand.

'Her . . . Gina!'

'You mean Gina, your brother's wife?'

'Yes, she did it, she organised the whole thing . . . I kept saying it wouldn't work . . . she . . . She did it.'

Bordelli stood up, dragged a chair over beside Giulio, and sat down.

'Now I'm going to ask you a question, Giulio, and I want a clear answer. Are you ready?' he said, in a tone at once severe and protective.

197

'Yes,' Giulio blubbered, drooling.

'Were you all in it together?'

Giulio couldn't bring himself to look up, keeping his eyes fixed on an inkwell.

'She did it, Inspector, she organised everything,' he said.

'Of course. But you knew about it and didn't do anything to stop her, did you?' he said.

'Yes, I mean no . . . I didn't do anything. I didn't do it.'

'All right, you didn't do it, but if you all got away with it, some of the inheritance would have gone to you, too, wouldn't it?'

Giulio said nothing and kept dribbling. Every so often a sob shook his whole body from the waist up. Bordelli brought his chair even closer to Giulio's and made a sign to Piras to resume typing. The horrible clacking began to assail their ears again.

'Did your wife and your brother know?'

'Yes, they knew, and I knew too, but it was Gina who did everything.'

'What do you mean by "everything"? Let's run through the whole thing. Who was it that switched the medicine bottles?'

Giulio started whimpering again, and sniffling.

'Gina.'

'And who put the pollen on Gideon's back?'

'Gina.'

'Good. And who went back to the villa that night to switch the medicine bottles again? Gina again?'

Giulio's face collapsed once and for all.

'No. It was my brother.'

'All right. So they did it. But you and your wife knew every-thing, isn't that right?'

'Yes, that's right.'

'One last thing. Was it you who put the nitroglycerine in Dante's bottle?'

'That was her idea, Gina's, I mean . . . I knew it wouldn't work . . . I knew it!' he said with a sob, and then he buried his fat face in his hands and started whimpering like a dog. Bordelli sighed. It was a truly nasty affair, more sordid than most.

'All right, then. Bring them all in, Piras. The lawyer, too. Let's give them the good news, and we can all go and get some sleep.'

'So, Rosa, how are things with the cat?'

It was nighttime, on the last Sunday in September. Bordelli lay comfortably on his friend's sofa in front of an open window giving on to the neighborhood rooftops. He had taken his shoes off and was sipping a thirst-quenching concoction. Rosa was deeply tanned and deeply décolletée, arms covered with clinking bracelets.

'Gideon's a darling. I couldn't live without him,' she said.

'I'm so glad you've become friends. Where is he now?'

'I leave the terrace door open for him, so he can go wandering over the rooftops. You won't believe it, but every evening at nine o'clock sharp he comes into my room to cuddle with me. He's such a dear . . . why won't you tell me where you got him?'

'I've already told you. One night he came knocking on my door and asked me to introduce him to a wonderful woman.'

Rosa looked over her shoulder at him, smiling with embarrassment and pleasure.

'You're such a liar, dear Inspector, but that's why I like you so much . . . Come on, tell me.'

'He was given to me by a friend of mine who couldn't keep him.'

'And why couldn't he keep him?'

'Because his house is full of mice.'

'Oh, you're so silly!'

'This time I'm telling the truth.'

'Of course you are.'

'I swear it's true.'

Rosa flicked his nose with her finger.

'Okay, I get it, you want it to remain a mystery.'

'No, I tell you.'

'All right, then, tell me again about the judge, it's so funny . . . What did you say to him?'

'I've told you that at least ten times; aren't you getting tired of it?'

'No, tell me again.'

Bordelli took a sip and lit up a cigarette.

'So I go in and Judge Ginzillo shows me the chair. He looks very nervous. Then he looks me in the eye and says: "Do you know that interrogating a suspect without his lawyer present is a crime?" So I say: "Then go ahead and report me."'

Here, as always, Rosa burst out laughing.

As Bordelli continued his story, flashes of the Morozzi trial came back to him. Four life sentences. Santelia had bent over backwards trying to get a reduced sentence for Giulio and Angela, waving his arms under his gown for a good half-hour, every so often bringing his fist down on the bench. But it was all for naught. The heat during the trial was unbearable, but the courtroom was nevertheless packed with people, owing perhaps to the interest the press had shown in the case. Piras even ended up getting his picture in the paper with the caption: 'Young Officer Piras, who played a decisive role in solving the murder'.

Dante had appeared in the courtroom dressed as he always was, in his oil-stained white smock. He sat in the last row, following the trial attentively, perhaps more interested in observing the people than in knowing the outcome. No one dared ask him to put out his smelly cigar. Since he was a strange person, photographers and journalists took aim at him as if he were a movie star. He simply ignored them. After the sentence was read, he had got up and left in silence.

'My good Inspector,' he had said to him over the phone a few days later, 'my mice are very worried. Please help me find some wonderful woman to care for Gideon.'

That same evening Bordelli had paid him a call, taken the cat and brought it to Rosa, who adopted it on the spot.

'Hey, are you in a daze or something?' said Rosa, waving a hand in front of his face. Bordelli snapped out of it.

'I'm sorry. Where was I?'

Rosa took the empty glass out of his hand.

'I get it. You need something strong.'

As Rosa went off in search of alcohol, Bordelli saw Elvira's face before his eyes. This was certainly nothing new. She troubled his sleep every night, in fact, walking across the hard floor in her bare feet, staring at him with her beautiful, piercing eyes.

It was an evening like so many others, Bordelli dozing on Rosa's couch, coddled like a child. He gazed at the sky through the open window, following his dreams. He had no way of knowing that only a few months later, one nasty afternoon, he would be dashing off to the park of Villa di Ventaglio after a particularly monstrous murder.

At that moment a shooting star streaked across the sky, and Bordelli became agitated. He saw his aunts' passion-flower pergola again, and Annina bent down to kiss a sad little boy goodbye.

Acknowledgements

I would like to thank my father, who fought the Nazis at the age of twenty and told me most of the war stories in this book when I was a little boy, as I listened open-mouthed and trembling with admiration and fear. I like to think that if, today, I am writing stories, it is because of his passionate and sometimes terrifying accounts. If he were alive today, I believe he would be happy to see these stories come back to life in a novel.

I thank Véronique for having invented the name of Inspector Bordelli.

I thank my cousin Francesca for having verified the scientific plausibility of the book.

And I thank Franco, at whose house I wrote this novel.

NOTES

Page 1 – 'Inspector Bordelli' – Bordelli's actual title in the Italian police bureaucracy is *commissario di pubblica sicurezza*, 'commissar of public safety'. And the position here called 'commissioner' is, in the Italian, *questore*.

Page 15 – 'zampironi' – Coils or sticks of compressed pyrethrum powder which burn slowly when lit, used chiefly against mosquitoes. They are named after their creator, Giovan Battista Zampironi. Famous for its mosquito problem in the summertime, Florence to this day abounds with *zampironi*, despite their questionable efficacy.

Page 55 – 'Doctor Morozzi' – In Italy, anyone with a university degree is considered a 'doctor.'

Page 60 – 'panzanella' – Moistened bread seasoned with oil, vinegar and herbs.

Page 60 – 'descriptions of faces reduced to pulp by sawn-off shotguns and of goat-tied bodies' – 'Goat-tied' is my translation of the term *incaprettato*, which incorporates the word for goat, *capra*, and refers to a particularly cruel method of execution used by the Mafia, where the victim, placed face down, has a rope looped round his neck and then tied to his feet, which are raised behind his back as in hog-tying. Fatigue eventually forces him to lower his feet, strangling him in the process.

Page 61 – 'his use of the plural *voi*, which in Totò had nothing to do with the Mussolini era' – During Mussolini's reign, the Fascist regime attempted to replace the seemingly archaic third-person mode of Italian formal address, the *lei*, which literally means 'she' (like the German *Sie*), with the second-person plural *voi*, considered more direct and practical, like

205

the French *vous*. For southerners like Totò, however, *voi* is traditionally one mode of formal address. At any rate, Mussolini's efforts were in vain, and after the war Italians generally dropped the use of *voi* in formal address and went back to using the *lei* with a vengeance. The southerners, for their part, still use the *voi* to this day, since to them it has no association with the Fascist regime.

Page 78 – 'also a 'doctor'' – see note, page 55

Page 94 – 'He must have spent a holiday in San Vittore' – San Vittore is Milan's oldest prison.

Page 101 – 'Celentano' – Adriano Celentano (born 1938), a popular Italian singer-songwriter.

Page 108 – 'Signor Bonaventura' – A cartoon character created in 1917, who continued to appear for several decades in the *Corriere dei Piccoli*, the children's supplement to the Milan daily *Il Corriere della Sera*.

Page 125 – '*La madonna!*' – A curse typically uttered by the Milanese and often associated with them.

Page 128 – 'an overturned *pattino*' – A *pattino* is a small, open wooden rowing boat consisting of two pontoons straddled by one or two benches, for use by holidaymakers in summer. Once quite common on Italian beaches, where they were rented by the hour, they have been slowly replaced by plastic boats, though one still sees them about.

Page 143 – 'Carlino Forzone had been a resistance fighter in the Piedmont with the *azzurri*' – A nationalist group within the Italian Resistance, formed principally of republicans, monarchists and Catholics.

Page 154 – 'Reaching the Lungarno' – The street that runs along the Arno river in Florence. There is one on both banks of the river.

Page 161 – '*Mo ben!*' – 'What is this?!' (Romagnolo dialect).

Page 174 – 'Do you know how to use a *napoletana*?' – A Neapolitan coffee pot consisting of two superimposed cylindrical elements, formerly of aluminium, and a double filter. When the water in the lower part begins to boil, one is supposed to turn the pot over to allow filtration. Seldom used north of Naples.

Page 180 – 'the song by that guy, what's his name? . . . *sapore di sale, sapore di mare*' – '*Sapore di sale*' ('Taste of the sea') was a 1963 hit song by Gino Paoli (born 1934).

Notes by Stephen Sartarelli.

If you enjoyed *Death in August*, then read on for an extract of the second Inspector Bordelli novel by Marco Vichi

Death and the Olive Grove

It's April 1964, but spring hasn't quite sprung. A grey, damp sky hangs over Florence, depressing weather that seems suited to nothing but bad news. And bad news is coming to the police station.

First, Bordelli's friend Casimiro, who insists that he's just found the body of a man in an olive grove above Fiesole. Bordelli races to the scene, but doesn't find any sign of a body.

Only a couple of days later, the body of a little girl is discovered at Villa Ventaglio: she has been strangled, and there is a horrible bite mark on her belly. Then another little girl is found murdered, with the same macabre signature.

And meanwhile Casimiro has disappeared without a trace.

The investigation marks the start of one of the darkest periods of Bordelli's life: a nightmare without end, as black as the sky above Florence.

Coming out in hardback in January 2012

HODDER &
STOUGHTON

Florence, April 1964

At nine o'clock in the evening a tiny little man no taller than a child came through the front door of the police station, out of breath. He pressed up against the window-pane of the guard's booth, yelling politely that he wanted to speak with the inspector. Mugnai, inside, told him to calm down and asked him which inspector he was referring to. The dwarf squashed a dirty hand against the glass and yelled:

'Inspector Bordelli!' as if Bordelli was the only inspector in the place.

'What if he's not here?' asked Mugnai.

'I saw his Beetle outside,' said the dwarf. In the end he was let in. Mugnai gestured to his colleague Taddei, a burly sort with bovine eyes who had recently arrived on the job. Taddei got up with effort from his chair and, with the dwarf following behind, started climbing the stairs. At the end of a long corridor on the first floor, he stopped in front of Inspector Bordelli's door.

'Wait here,' he said, glancing at the dwarf's shabby shoes, which were still smeared with mud after a cursory cleaning. Then he knocked, disappeared behind the door, and came back out a few seconds later.

'Go on in,' he said.

The little man hurriedly slipped inside and Taddei heard Bordelli say:

'Casimiro, what on earth are you doing here?' Then the door suddenly closed. Unsure, Taddei scratched his head and knocked again. He stuck his head respectfully inside.

'Need anything, Inspector?'

I

'No thanks. You can go now.'

Casimiro, repeatedly swallowing, waited silently for the ox to shut the door. He declined a cigarette from the inspector and remained standing in front of the desk.

'What's wrong, Casimiro? You seem agitated.'

'I've just seen something, Inspector, up Fiesole way . . . I was walking through a field and—'

'If you don't want to smoke, have a beer at least,' said Bordelli, pointing towards the bottom drawer of a file cabinet on the other side of the office. 'I'll have one too, please,' he added.

Casimiro dashed over and got the bottles, setting them down nervously on the desk. He was anxious to speak. Bordelli calmly opened the beers, flipping off the bottle-caps with his house keys, and passed one to Casimiro. The dwarf drank half of it in a single draught, grew a little calmer, and finally sat down. The inspector avidly took two swigs, splashing his shirt, then set the bottle down on some of the papers strewn all across his desk. Hanging on the wall behind him was a dusty photo of the President of the Republic, with a horseshoe appended from the same nail. The air in that office always smelled of rotten cardboard and mushrooms, thought Bordelli.

Casimiro was squirming in his chair. He was wearing a child's jacket that was actually too big for him. Bordelli studied the dwarf's face, which was small and narrow, as if it had been crushed in a closing door. He'd known him since the end of the war, and the little man had always had the same tragic, nervous look about him. One rarely saw him laugh. At most he might make a bad joke about his physical condition and then snigger. Bordelli in his way was fond of him and had even, on occasion, invented phoney jobs for him as an informer, so he could give him a little money without making him feel too embarrassed.

'I was passing that way by chance, Inspector . . . If I hadn't seen it with my own eyes—'

'Sorry to interrupt, Casimiro, but the second of the month was my birthday.'

2

'Happy birthday . . .'

'Is that all?'

'What do you want me to say, Inspector?'

Bordelli felt like chatting that evening, perhaps because he was very tired . . . He could only imagine what sort of rubbish Casimiro had to tell him.

'Aren't you going to ask me how old I am?' he said.

'How old are you?'

'Fifty-four, Casimiro, and I have no desire to grow old. Fifty-four, and still, when I go home, I have no one to kiss me on the lips.'

'Why don't you get a dog, Inspector?' the dwarf said in all seriousness. Bordelli smiled and slowly crushed his cigarette butt in the already full ashtray. Picking up his beer, he leaned back in his chair. The bottle had left a damp ring on a report.

'Just think, Casimiro, maybe, at this very moment, in some part of the world, the woman I have always been looking for has just been born. But if she was born today, by the time she's twenty I'll be a dotty old bed-wetter. And even if she was born forty years ago, it was probably in Algeria, Poland, or Australia . . . Fat chance of ever running into her . . . Do you ever think about such things?'

'Inspector, can I tell you about what I saw?'

'Of course, forgive me,' said Bordelli, resigned.

The dwarf set his beer down on the desk and stood up, growing agitated again.

'I was walking through a field and I almost tripped over a dead body,' he said in a single breath, for fear the inspector might interrupt him again.

'Are you sure?' asked Bordelli.

'Of course I'm sure. He was dead, Inspector. Blood was dripping out of his mouth.'

'Where was this?'

'Just past Fiesole,' Casimiro said darkly.

Bordelli stood up and, with one hand, picked up his cigarettes

3

and matches and, with the other, took his jacket from the back of his chair.

'What were you doing up there at this hour, Casimiro?'

'I was just passing through,' the dwarf said, with the eyes of a liar.

'Let's go and have a look at this corpse,' said Bordelli, walking out of the office.

'But, what about my bicycle?' the dwarf asked, trotting beside him.

'We'll load it into my car.'

Reaching the end of the Viale Volga, they turned onto the road that led up to Fiesole. Past San Domenico they began to see the city below, a great dark blot dotted with points of light. A pile of cow shit with little candles on top, thought Bordelli.

Casimiro's short legs were extended over the seat, his worn-out shoes barely reaching the edge. He was quiet. He fiddled with his good-luck charm, a little plastic skeleton barely an inch long, with two little pieces of red glass in the eye sockets. He'd been carrying it with him for years, and Bordelli had stopped ribbing him about it some time ago.

Past the piazza of Fiesole, the dwarf said to turn down the Via del Bargellino, and a few hundred yards on, he began to look around nervously.

'Stop here, Inspector,' he said suddenly, jumping to his feet on the car seat. Bordelli parked the Beetle in an unpaved clearing and got out. Casimiro hopped down, more agitated than ever.

'I'll lead the way, Inspector.' He climbed up the small, crumbling retainer wall beside the road and began to penetrate the low, dense vegetation. Bordelli followed behind him, looking around with care. High in the sky, a big bright moon cast a lugubrious glow on the countryside, but in compensation it made it easy to see. To the right was a large, untilled field with a few now withered vines and several

4

ivy-smothered trees. It seemed a shame to see a field reduced to such a state.

'Did you say you were passing this way by chance?' Bordelli asked, laughing.

'Sort of,' said the dwarf, continuing hurriedly through the brush.

'Meaning?'

'I don't have a lira in my pocket, Inspector, what am I supposed to do?'

'What do you mean?'

'Every now and then I have to go out and look for vegetables.'

'Around this time there should be some beans.'

'It's still a bit early. For the moment, there's only cabbage . . . Come, let's turn here.'

'It's probably full of toads,' Bordelli said in disgust, hoping not to step on any. The grass was tall and damp and he could already feel his shoes getting wet. It had rained all week, and every so often he stepped in a puddle of mud. It felt almost cold outside. Spring couldn't make up its mind to arrive.

'Is it much farther?'

'It's down there,' Casimiro said softly, his little feet practically running. After passing through a muddy thicket they came out into a rather well-tended olive grove. The ground was densely carpeted with a short grassy weed. After all the mud, it was a pleasure to walk on it. The light of the moon was so bright that their shadows were sharply outlined on the ground. And everything in shadow was all the darker.

'We're almost there,' the dwarf whispered, slowing his pace. Farther ahead, towering above them, was an eighteenth-century villa, a massive constuction built on a large embankment. Its garden loomed sheer over the field, supported by a high, curved wall reinforced by great buttresses covered with ivy. The stone balustrade that ran along the top of the wall was the boundary between two worlds. The shutters on the villa's windows were all closed, and no light could be seen filtering through. Casimiro stopped a few yards from the wall, in front of a gigantic olive tree, and looked around in disbelief.

'The dead man was here, Inspector. . . I swear he was here!' Bordelli threw up his hands.

'Apparently he woke up,' he said, laughing. The dwarf still couldn't believe it and kept walking round the olive tree. At a certain point he bent down to pick something up.

'Look, Inspector,' he said, holding up a bottle. Bordelli grabbed it by the neck. It was made of colourless glass and rather small, and there was still a bit of dark liquid at the bottom. It was clean, and must not have been outside for very long. He read the label: *Cognac De Maricourt*, 1913. He didn't know it. He pulled out the cork and sniffed it. It smelled like good cognac. He controlled the urge to have a sip and put the cork back in.

'The body was right here! I'm not crazy!' Casimiro insisted.

'Maybe he was only drunk.' The inspector put the bottle in his jacket pocket and, with the dwarf following behind him, approached the buttresses. They were huge and well constructed. Seen from there, the stone wall seemed even higher.

'What did this dead man look like?' Bordelli asked wearily.

'I didn't get a good look at him. . . I was walking and, suddenly, there he was in front of me, and I ran away. . . All I saw was that he had blood around his—'

'Quiet!' said Bordelli, pricking his ears. All at once they heard the sound of hurried footsteps and panting, and on the moon-whitened turf appeared the shadow of a short-haired dog running towards them. The most visible part of it was its teeth, which shone like wet marble. The inspector barely had time to pull out his Beretta and shoot the animal square in the teeth. The Doberman yelped and its feet gave out from under it, but in the momentum of its charge it rolled forward into Bordelli's legs, knocking him to the ground. It cried out again, kicking its feet in the air for a few seconds, then drew its legs in and stopped moving.

'Fuck . . .' said Bordelli.

'We're lucky you're a good shot,' said Casimiro, voice quavering slightly.

'Where the hell are you?' said Bordelli, unable to see him.

'Up here, Inspector.' Casimiro had climbed up an olive tree and was already coming down. Bordelli put his pistol away and got up. He looked around. Half his jacket was wet and his trousers spattered with blood. He cleaned himself as best he could with a handkerchief, then knelt forward to have a better look at the Doberman. Its muzzle was a bloody pulp, and it had no collar.

'You know, Casimiro, I don't like the look of this one bit,' said Bordelli, looking up, but the dwarf was no longer there. He looked around for him and saw him running through the olive trees towards the woods. He decided to let him go. He took a few steps back to get a full view of the villa. It was still dark. The gunshot apparently hadn't woken anyone up. The house was either uninhabited, he thought, or whoever lived there was a heavy sleeper. He lit a cigarette and headed towards the woods. When he reached the car, he found the dwarf sitting on the bonnet, arms folded round his legs, eyes still flashing with fear.

'What got into you, Casimiro?'

'If I'd been alone he would have torn me to pieces,' replied the dwarf, shuddering.

'Do you come this way often?' asked Bordelli, cleaning his shoes against the wall's rocks.

'Now and then,' said Casimiro, hopping down from the bonnet and looking around with a tense expression on his face.

They got into the Beetle and headed back towards town. The dwarf sat there stiff and silent, his little skeleton between his fingers. They were already at the Regresso bend when Bordelli abruptly stopped the car.

'What are you doing, Inspector?'

'I'm going back up there.'

'Why?'

'I don't know,' said Bordelli. He made a U-turn and headed back up towards Fiesole, stepping on the accelerator. The

7

Beetle's vibrations came straight up into their backbones. A short distance later he turned again onto the Via del Bargellino and parked in the same spot. He opened the car door and put one foot outside.

'You're not coming?' he asked Casimiro, seeing that he hadn't moved.

'I'd rather wait here,' the dwarf said gloomily.

'Suit yourself.' Bordelli got out of the car and, retracing the same route, rushed back to the olive grove. The moon was beginning to light up the walls of the villa, which made it look even more abandoned. He approached the buttresses, gun drawn, and saw at once that the Doberman's carcass was gone. All that remained was a bit of blood on the grass. He checked the immediate surroundings, but that carpet of compact weeds showed no footprints. He shook his head, thinking he'd acted stupidly. If he hadn't left the scene . . .

All at once he heard a sound of crunching gravel that seemed to come from the villa's garden, and he crouched instinctively behind a buttress, hiding in the shadow. He looked up, and at that moment a man's head peered out over the balustrade at the top of the wall. Bordelli was able to get a good look at him in the moonlight. The man had very white hair and a long black mark on his neck. He stood there for a few seconds, looking out at the olive grove, then disappeared.

There was deep silence. The only sound was the wind rustling the leaves of the olive trees. In the distance a dog began to bark angrily, every so often howling like a wolf. The inspector waited a few more minutes, holding his breath and looking up until the coast seemed clear. He stepped out of the shadow but hugged the wall, to avoid the risk of being seen from the villa. When he found a better-shielded path, he headed back towards the woods, turning round repeatedly to look at the house, but seeing no sign of life. He hurried back to the car and found Casimiro standing on the seat with his face against the window.

'The Doberman's gone, but I saw someone look out from the garden above,' said Bordelli, quietly closing the car door.

'That bloody dog . . .' said Casimiro with a tragic look in his eye, clutching his little skeleton.

Bordelli calmly lit a cigarette and blew the smoke against the windscreen.

'Have you any idea who lives in that house?' he asked the dwarf.

'Some foreigner who's never there.'

'How do you know?'

'Gossip.'

'Foreigner from where?'

'Dunno . . .'

'Where's the entrance to the villa?'

'Up above here, on the Bosconi road . . . Why?'

'Just curious.' The inspector started up the car, turned it round, and drove up to the top of the hill. That man with the black spot on his neck seemed familiar to him . . . He felt as if he had seen someone with a mark like that before . . . Or perhaps it was only his investigative imagination . . .

He turned on to Via Ferrucci, in the direction of the Bosconi. After rounding a few bends he stopped the Beetle in a spot where the shoulder broadened, not far from the villa's gate, which bore a plaque with indecipherable initials on it.

'You wait here,' he said to Casimiro, getting out of the car.

'Where are you going?'

'I just want to go and have a look.'

The road was feebly illuminated by a yellow streetlamp. Bordelli arrived at the gate and tried to push it open. It was locked. The garden was full of high-trunked trees and over-grown plants, which shielded the dark ground from the moonlight. Scattered everywhere were large, empty vases, terra-cotta monsters, and strange marble statues of varying size. The villa was rather far from the road and surrounded by cedars that rose well above the roof. On that side, too, the shutters were closed tight, with no visible light behind them. The inspector pulled the chain of the doorbell and heard it

9

ring solemnly inside the house. There was no reply. He rang it again, and again, then twice consecutively. In the end he saw some light filter out between the slats of one shutter. A small light came on over the stone frame of the front door, which opened at once. A human silhouette appeared on the threshold.

'Who's there?' asked a woman's voice.

'Police. Could you please open the gate for me?' The woman went back inside, and the gate opened with a click. The inspector pushed the gate open with both hands, making it creak on its rusty hinges. He entered the garden and headed down the gravel lane, through the shadows cast by the ogres and marble monsters. The woman waited for him on the threshold, wrapped in a black shawl, in front of the great door, which she had pulled to. She didn't seem dressed in night-clothes and didn't look as if she had just woken up. The inspector stopped in front of her, pulled out his police badge, and bowed slightly.

'Inspector Bordelli's the name. Sorry to disturb you at this hour of the night.'

The woman looked to be about fifty. She was tall and slender and did not look Italian. She had a hard mouth. She stood there without moving, back erect, watching Bordelli from behind her glasses.

'What can I do for you?' she asked with a strong German accent, pulling the shawl tightly around her. Her hair was all white and gathered into a perfect bun at the back of her head. Bordelli had the feeling that someone was spying on him from behind a shutter on the first floor, but he pretended not to notice.

'And you are Signora—?' he asked.

'I am Baron's housekeeper,' the woman said icily.

'And his name is . . .?'

'Baron Von Hauser.'

'And you are . . .'

'Miss Olga.'

'Is the baron at home?'

'No.'

'May I ask where he is?'

'Baron ist alvays travelink, he's not often at home.'

'Does anyone else live here?'

'No.'

'You live here alone?'

'Ja.'

'Year round?'

'I don't understand . . . Vhy all these qvestions?'

'I'm sorry, somebody called in and reported a shooting in this area.'

'I hear nothink, I go to sleep early.'

Bordelli threw his hands up and smiled.

'Well, that's all I have to ask. Sorry again for the disturbance. Good night,' he said.

'Good night,' the woman replied, poker-faced.

Bordelli gave a slight bow of respect and headed back towards the gate, but after taking a few steps he stopped and turned round to face the woman again.

'One more question, Miss Olga . . . Have you got a Doberman in this house?'

'No.'

'Do you know by any chance if any neighbors—?'

'I don't know much about dogs,' the woman interrupted him, with a note of scorn in her voice.

'All right, then. Good night,' said Bordelli, and he headed back down the dark garden path. Closing the gate behind him, he noticed that the woman was still standing in the doorway. He walked back towards the Beetle without turning round, and moments later heard the sound of the great door closing.

In the car he found Casimiro asleep. The dwarf's head had fallen to one side, and he was snoring. The moment Bordelli started up the car, the little man raised his head abruptly and rubbed his eyes.

'I wasn't asleep,' he said.

'I'll take you home.'

'Did you discover anything, Inspector?'

'No, but there's something fishy about all this,' said Bordelli, staring into space. Then he turned the car round again and headed back towards town. During one straightaway he pulled his wallet out of his jacket pocket, took out two thousand lire, and put the money in Casimiro's hand.

'You could use a little, no?' he said. The little man hesitated for a moment, as he always did, then took the money and put it in his shoe.

'Thank you, Inspector. I can't be too picky,' he said darkly.

'Cigarette?'

'No, thanks . . . If you want, I can try to find something out myself.'

'But you've already shit your pants once . . .' Bordelli said, laughing.

'I'm not afraid,' the dwarf said, slightly offended. He didn't like to be seen as a coward.

'Never mind, Casimiro, it might be dangerous,' Bordelli said in a serious tone.

'Why dangerous?'

'You never know.'

'I know what I'm doing,' said Casimiro, squeezing the little skeleton tightly in his hand.

'And what if you run into another puppy dog like the last one?'

'I'll bring a pistol this long . . .' the dwarf said, playing the tough guy. He seemed in the grips of a fit of pride.

'This isn't a cowboy movie, Casimiro . . . But I may have another little job for you in a few days,' Bordelli lied, already trying to think of something. Once he had even had the dwarf tail Diotivede, telling him the doctor was a mafioso . . .

They rode for a few moments in silence. The Beetle descended slowly towards the city. At San Domenico, Bordelli turned to pass by way of the Badia Fiesolana for no reason in particular, perhaps only because he wanted to see again the steep descent he used to take in his toy wagon, always risking a broken neck.

'Have you got any news of Botta, Casimiro?' Bordelli hadn't seen Ennio Bottarini for a good while. He wanted to arrange another dinner party at his place, with Botta at the cooker. The luckless thief actually wasn't a bad cook at all. He'd spent a number of years in jails across half of Europe and had learned recipes of the local dishes from his various cellmates.

'He must be still in Greece,' said the dwarf.

'Free or in jail?

'A few days ago I ran into a friend of his, who said Botta made a little money down there and is supposed to return soon.'

'You don't say . . .'

A few days later, a phone call came in to the station, and Bordelli set out in his VW, stepping hard on the accelerator. As usual, young Piras was with him. It was almost 7 p.m., and the sun had already set a while before.

There was a big crowd at the entrance of the Parco del Ventaglio, along with three police cars with their headlamps on. Bordelli parked the car beside the gate and got out, heart thumping in his brain. Piras walked beside him in silence. Ever since the tough, intelligent lad had joined the force, Bordelli brought him along on every investigation, and to avoid having a uniform always at his side, he'd told him to dress in civvies. He got on well with Piras, just as he had got on well with Piras's father, Gavino, during the war.

The moon was covered by a thick blanket of clouds, and the park was as dark as the sky. To their left was a grassy slope, steep and dark, and at the top of the hill shone the glow of the police's floodlights, enveloped in a crowd of people. Bordelli and Piras began to climb. The soles of their shoes slipped on the wet grass, and the cuffs of their trousers were soaked after only a few steps. They heard a siren in the distance. When they got to the top of the hill, Bordelli started clearing a path through the crowd, advancing in long strides. Piras followed right behind him, plunging into the opening before it closed again. There were already some journalists scribbling in their notebooks, as well as a few photographers. Though it was never clear how they did it, the press was always the first to arrive on the scene.

The inspector continued to elbow his way until he got to the police cordon. And suddenly he saw her: under the white light of the police lamps, the little girl looked like a bundle of rags thrown onto the grass. She lay face-up at the foot of a big tree, legs straight and arms open, like a little Christ. The inspector went up to her, with Piras following behind, and they both bent down to look at her. She must have been about eight years old. Her mouth and eyes were open wide, and she had jet-black hair tied in a braid that was coming apart. She was so white in the light she seemed unreal. And on her neck were some red marks. Her jumper was pulled up, and her belly bore the traces of a human bite. Bordelli looked at her a long time, as if to burn that image in his memory, then turned towards his Sardinian assistant. They looked at each other for a few seconds without saying anything.

Busybodies were falling over one another to get a look at the child, grimacing in horror and exhaling vapor from their mouths. A few women could be heard weeping and, further away, someone was vomiting. But what most bothered Bordelli was all the commotion of legs and shadows around the little girl's dead body. He pressed his eyes hard with his fingers. He felt very tired, though perhaps it was only disgust for what lay before him.

The sound of the siren grew closer and closer, and the inspector wondered if it was indeed coming towards the park, since at this point, he thought, the blaring sirens were useless. The girl was dead, and nobody was to touch anything before Diotivede, the police doctor, got there. Bordelli glanced at his watch. How bloody long was Diotivede going to take to get there? He took one of the uniformed policemen by the arm.

'Rinaldi, do you know if anyone saw or heard anything?'

'No, Inspector, nobody saw or heard anything.'

14

'Then please send them all away.'

'Yes, sir.'

Suddenly a man's voice was heard above the crowd:

'And what are the police doing about this?'

Bordelli stiffened and started looking for that imbecile amidst the herd of onlookers. He wanted to grab him by the collar and bash his head up against a tree trunk. What are the police doing? Come forward, jackass! What do you want the police to do? Piras saw he was upset and squeezed his elbow.

'Forget about it, Inspector,' he said.

The ambulance entered the park, turning off its siren. Bordelli and Piras stared at the ground. Five men got out of the vehicle and started climbing the grassy incline, carrying a stretcher. Bordelli scratched his head.

'What are they doing?' he said to himself. He went up to the doctor, a fat man climbing up the hill with a briefcase in his hand.

'Nobody can touch anything before the medical examiner gets here,' Bordelli said. The fat man stopped in front of him, happy for the rest.

'And who are you?' he asked.

'Chief Inspector Bordelli. Tell your men not to touch the girl.'

'I'm sorry, but we're here for a woman.'

'A woman? What woman?'

'Somebody called us about a woman who collapsed. How do you do? I'm Dr Vallini.'

The inspector shook his hand and turned round to look at the stretcher-bearers, who were walking towards a small group of people. He saw them lay a woman on to the stretcher. Then they came back, and the doctor began at once to examine the woman. He felt her pulse, looked inside her mouth, then opened her eyes and shone a light into her pupils with a small pocket torch. Bordelli got close to have a better look at her. She looked very young. Her face was pale and rested on a cushion of black hair. A beautiful girl. Her mouth was half open, and she gently

15

batted her eyelashes at regular intervals, about once per second. One of her arms slid slowly off of the stretcher, and the doctor put it back at her side.

'It's nothing serious; she's only fainted,' he said.

'Who is she?' Bordelli asked.

'The little girl's mother,' said one of the stretcher-bearers. The inspector bit his lip . . . The mother, of course. How could he not have thought of it? He leaned over her for a better look, and at once the girl opened her eyes wide, found Bordelli's face right in front of hers and stared at it as if it were something amazing. Then she raised her arms and grabbed his hand. Ten small cold fingers wrapped around his own.

'Valentina . . . Valen . . .' she whispered, staring at him with empty eyes. Dr Vallini was already preparing a shot of sedative.

'Please be brave, signora. It's better if you sleep a little now,' said the doctor, and he stuck the needle in her arm and pressed the plunger. The woman opened her mouth to speak, but it was too late. Her eyes rolled back into her head and her arms fell. The doctor gestured to the orderlies, and the group trudged off.

Bordelli pointed at the woman.

'Where are you taking her?' he asked.

'To Santa Maria Nova.'

'When could I talk to her?'

'Try phoning the hospital in two or three days, and ask for Dr Saggini.'

'All right. Thanks.'

'Goodbye, Inspector.' The doctor began his difficult descent down the slippery lawn, balancing his massive body with the help of his briefcase. Bordelli lit another cigarette and inhaled deeply. The white face of Valentina's mother, as delicate as that of her daughter, remained impressed on his mind.

The siren of the Misericordia ambulance suddenly blared and just as suddenly stopped, as if it had been turned on by mistake. The car then glided slowly and smoothly away into the darkness, motor whirring gently. Bordelli stood there watching it until it passed through the park's gate, then looked up over the roofs of the city, then down, lost in thought. Piras's voice shook him out of it.

'Inspector, can you hear me?'

Bordelli ran a hand over his eyes.

'What is it, Piras?'

'Dr Diotivede is here.'

Bordelli wasn't surprised he hadn't seen him arrive. Diotivede was as sly and silent as a beast of the forest.

'Come,' Bordelli said to Piras. They began to walk towards the doctor, whose almost phosphorescent shock of white hair was visible from a distance.

Diotivede was kneeling down over the little girl's body, his knees on a newspaper. He was studying her from very close up, touching her from time to time. His gestures were those of his profession, but he wore an offended expression on his face, as if he had just been slapped.

Bordelli and Piras stopped a few yards away so as not to disturb him. People were finally starting to leave, pushed away by the uniformed cops. The inspector smoked one cigarette after another, impatient to speak to Diotivede. A light wind was blowing, spreading a scent of dead leaves through the air. It was April, but it felt more like a nice November evening. The clouds were thinning out, and in the black sky a few stars were beginning to appear, along with a yellowish sliver of moon.

Bordelli kept an eye on the police doctor, trying to guess where he was in his examination, not daring to disturb him. He well knew that at such moments Diotivede didn't want anyone in his hair. One had no choice but to wait.

A few minutes later Diotivede had finished inspecting the corpse and, remaining on his knees, began to write in his black notebook, lips pouting like a schoolboy's. At last he rose and came towards the two policemen.

'Strangled to death. And she has a nasty bite on her belly, which probably happened after her death.'

The inspector tossed his cigarette butt far away.

'Nothing significant, in other words,' he said.

'For the moment, no. But I'll let you know after the post-mortem. You never know, something might come out of it.'

'Let's hope so,' said Bordelli, disappointed. He went up to the girl's body again and lit his umpteenth cigarette of the day. He knelt forward and looked closely at that now grey little face spattered with mud. He saw an ant walking along the sharp edges of the little girl's lips and flicked it away with a finger, very briefly touching the dead flesh. She must have been a beautiful child. She looked a little like a woman he had once loved, many years before . . . He shook his head to banish the thought. Who knows why he thought of such things at moments like these. He took a last glance at the girl, her naked little feet looking as if they'd just sprouted from the ground, and then he turned towards the others. Diotivede was clutching his brief-case tightly against his belly with both arms, ready to leave. Behind the thick lenses his eyes looked as if they were made of glass.

'I hate to say this, but this looks like the work of a maniac who may strike again,' he said.

'Unfortunately, I agree,' said Bordelli, tossing his cigarette butt to the ground.

'Unless it's a vendetta,' Piras mumbled, teeth clenched, thinking of the cruel feuds of his homeland.

'Need a lift, doctor?' the inspector asked.

'Why not?'

The inspector gestured to Rinaldi to say that the body could now be taken away. Rinaldi raised a hand, and two policemen laid a cloth down beside the little girl, picked her up and laid her down on it.

'We can go now,' Bordelli said with a sigh, heading towards the park exit without waiting to see the body being taken away. The three descended the wet, grassy slope, taking care not to lose their balance. Piras was quiet, staring into space and looking sullen. He climbed into the back seat of the VW, letting Diotivede ride in front. Bordelli started up the car and drove off, slowly, an unlit cigarette in his mouth.

'Shall I take you home, or do you want to go back to the lab?' he asked, turning on to Via Volta.

'You can take me home, thanks,' said Diotivede. He remained silent the rest of the way. They dropped him off in Via dell'Erta Canina, in front of his little house and garden. Piras came and sat down in front like a robot.

'What do you think of this murder, Piras?'

'What was that, Inspector?'

'Nothing.'

They returned to police headquarters and got down to work. Bordelli sent a few officers out to question people who lived in the neighbourhood of the Parco del Ventaglio. With a little luck they might find someone who had seen or heard something of importance, though he didn't have much hope of this. He drafted a communiqué for the television and radio to broadcast the following morning, to put the whole city on alert. And with Piras's help, he organized the shifts of plain-clothesmen for patrolling the city's parks, which were always full of mothers and children. But these were general measures that gave no assurance at all. The killer might strike again in another way and another place, as Bordelli knew well. In the meantime, however, there wasn't much more that could be done.